WIN[illegible]

CYNTHIA RACETTE

SOUL MATE PUBLISHING

New York

WINDSWEPT

Cover Design by Rae Monet, Inc.

Published in the United States of America by
Soul Mate Publishing
P.O. Box 24
Macedon, New York, 14502

ISBN: 978-1-61935-183-7
eBook ISBN: 978-1-61935-093-9

www.SoulMatePublishing.com

To my loving honey,
who never gave up on me.

To my children,
who made my life so rich growing up.

To my granddaughters, Katie and Ellie,
who have added so much humor and love.

Acknowledgements

To all who shared our joy in our own *Windswept* and to the ladies of the WNY RWA. I could not find more supportive, dedicated women. I love you all!

Chapter 1

Windswept's mainsail was up, and the jib was a clean, crisp white against the clear blue sky. Wind filled the canvas with a snap as the sails billowed. The boat immediately heeled over with the force of the wind and surged forward through the waves with barely-leashed power.

Caroline reached down to kill the engine, then stood to savor her favorite moment in sailing—the first instant with only the sound of the wind and the waves and the feel of the boat under her feet, driven solely by the power of nature. She grinned at David and he smiled back, akin in the joy of that marvelous feeling of anticipation and eagerness. They were ready, more than ready, to spend another summer season sailing up and down the bay.

Caroline handed the wheel over to David and wrapped her arms around the mast to savor the warm sun and deep blue sea. She loved *Windswept* more than she thought it was proper to love a possession. It was nearly indecent, her passion for it.

The boat had been part of the family for their entire married lives. The sailing bug had hit both of them unexpectedly after an excursion aboard a sailboat in the Caribbean. They'd decided immediately to buy the boat, and it seemed the perfect present to give each other for their wedding. It had taken every penny they had at the time, but it had been worth it. Over the years they'd spent every available minute of the summer on the boat, and it never seemed to get old.

She sighed, happier out here than anywhere else in the

world. And today, the first sailing day of a new season, was extra special. She stood by the mast for a while watching the water fly up from the bow of the boat and sweep past the side. They'd spent hours polishing her fiberglass until it glowed. The boat was aging now, gracefully, like a grand old dame.

When their fourteen-year-old daughter Lily raised her head briefly from her position sunbathing, Caroline winked at her and crept along the railing to join her. She noticed that Lily's figure in the bikini was getting almost voluptuous. In the winter, with thick sweaters and coats to hide her curves, Caroline hadn't noticed the drastic changes.

Lily scooted over to give her some room. The breeze felt great in her hair and the sun was hotter than it had been all spring. It beat down on her head and reflected off the water, making her feel over-warm in her Georgetown sweatshirt.

They stared at the white spray without speaking for a long time. Caroline nudged her daughter with her shoulder. "Long winter, huh?"

Lily had, in many ways, been raised on the boat and she could sail it with the best of them. Caroline had many fond memories of their daughter as a toddler on her father's lap, already learning about how to read the wind. There were images in her head of Lily, eight or nine years old, running along the top of the deck and leaping off onto the dock without a thought of danger. She could remember Lily as an eleven-year-old begging to be allowed to keep the helm as the wind rose higher and higher. It often reached a point that made Caroline's heart hammer with alarm as she watched the whisper-thin preteen steer through five foot waves. Lily had done it though, albeit with her father close by.

"Oh yeah," said Lily. "I'm glad I decided to go today. I can write up results tomorrow."

"You've got lots of time before the Science Fair."

"Yeah, but there's still a lot to do."

"You'll get it done."

"Sure."

"And how many days like this will we have to go out on the Chesapeake before it gets too hot? I've been chomping at the bit for weeks."

"You're telling me." Lily rolled her eyes. "You guys have been at the marina since St. Patty's Day, polishing everything. I'm just glad I got out of it this year. I mean, I love this tub and all, but I have a lot of things going on now at school with Science Club and orchestra."

Caroline let the sarcastic reference go because she knew Lily loved *Windswept*, too. Besides, she noticed the tiny grin at the corner of her daughter's lips when she said it. "It was worth it, wasn't it? Today?"

Caroline felt Lily nod against her arm. "Oh, yeah."

She put her arm around Lily and they leaned together, gazing raptly at the water as it hypnotized their senses—rushing, always rushing in a sheet of white foam past the bow.

Caroline ran her fingers through her daughter's long, silky hair as it blew away from her face in the breeze.

"Your hair is getting so pretty."

"A lot different than when it was short and curly."

"Definitely."

"Your face looks different these days too. You're going to be a gorgeous young lady."

"You're putting me on."

"No, I'm not. You're going to have to beat guys off with a stick very shortly."

"Okay, Mom. You'd better get back to the cockpit. Dad's looking impatient."

David, his white windbreaker tied around his waist in the late afternoon sun, puttered around the cockpit. His light brown hair was windblown after the spirited beat upwind. But he seemed to be trying to keep from looking at Caroline.

His distracted tinkering kept him uncharacteristically silent. Whenever she was not at the helm while they sailed, she relaxed and watched the water and the sky and the sails. David, however, performed a never-ending ritual of adjusting sails and halyards. He was a perfectionist with the details on the boat. But today it was more than that.

He was avoiding her.

"Want to put up the spinnaker?" he asked, as he placed his hands on his hips and stared up at the mast.

"It's pretty windy for it."

"Yeah, I know. I just wanted—"

"I know. Long winter."

He caught her eyes, and immediately his gaze slid away. "Yeah."

"Okay," she said with a smile, anxious to please him and make this last run home just right. "Go for it. We can handle it."

After they put up the spinnaker, their speed picked up some. It was nerve-wracking, keeping it under control. The light sail was so huge. But it was gorgeous, hundreds of square feet of blue and green nylon in a huge billow of color that undulated and swayed with each subtle change in wind direction.

"It's good to be back out on the water, isn't it?" Caroline stared skyward and enjoyed the ripple of color.

"It's fantastic." David replied, his face wistful. "Want a soda? I'm going down for a beer."

"Sure. Lily, want a soda?"

"Yes, please." Lily scrambled from her perch at the bow. She plopped down on a bench in the cockpit and put her feet up on the opposite bench.

David fetched the drinks out of a cooler below and turned to head topside. His heart stopped. It was dark in the cabin, and Caroline stood out like an angel in the sun. There was a shimmer around her body as she stood behind the wheel concentrating on controlling the spinnaker.

What in the world had he done?

Once he was back topside, he heard Lily ask her mother, "Think we'll be back by five? I told Debbie she could come over to help me with some of the data I recorded the other day. She's way better at statistics than I am."

"We should be back in time. But I think Dad has some more work to do on the boat before we head home."

"Aw, Mom, please. I've got stuff to do."

David spoke up. "You made the decision to come on this trip. We have to clean up a few things when we get back. We didn't have time to do much cleaning in the cabin or the cockpit after our new cushions arrived." He ran his hand over the fine, soft material on the settee. It was a color halfway between the blue of the sky and the green of the bay. It had cost the earth to do the entire interior of the cabin and cockpit cushions. Caroline had spent hours scouring fabric catalogues, but he was delighted with how it turned out.

Caroline turned away from admiring the new upholstery and glanced at Lily. "You know your father won't leave it until it's perfect."

"Don't I know it. He's a stickler about everything. Especially this boat."

Caroline raised an eyebrow at her daughter, letting her know she was on the verge of disrespect. "Resign yourself. If you help, we'll get home sooner." She smiled at Lily's huge teenage sigh. When they got close to their slip, David took the spinnaker down.

He took over the details of getting the outside of the boat put back together while Caroline and Lily went below to straighten up. He re-tied Caroline's granny knots into square knots, put the sail cover on and coiled the lines. When everything was clean and neat, he joined Caroline and Lily.

"Caro, I think I'll scrub some of the non-slip in the cockpit before we leave."

"Then can we go home so I can call Debbie over to work on my project?" Lily asked him.

"Yes. Then we can go home." He leaned over to peer at a smudge in the fiberglass.

"We're going to the bathhouse to clean up a little bit," Caroline said.

"I'll text Debbie that we're coming home." Lily pulled out her iPhone.

"Of course," Caroline replied with a touch of sarcasm. "She would never guess we were coming if you didn't text her. After all, it's been ten minutes since we pulled into the marina and you texted her about that, and twenty minutes since we headed into the estuary when you texted *that* to her." Lily grinned at her mother's remark.

The two climbed onto the dock and walked over to the log cabin structure that housed the toilet facilities and showers. David watched them go, Caroline with her arm around their daughter, and Lily laughing at something her mother said. He felt sick. He tossed the rag down onto the bench seat in self-disgust and capped the Soft Scrub. His stomach roiled and he couldn't stand to do any more work on the boat today, after all.

Caroline and Lily returned and he picked up the cooler. Everyone took an armload to head back to the car. Caroline stopped halfway down the pier and looked back at all thirty-five feet of their beloved sloop. "It's incredible that *Windswept* has been with us for so many years. We've always been able to come down here anytime we wanted, knowing it'd be here, waiting for us."

He swallowed past the lump in his throat and felt tears well up in his eyes. Caroline looked at him curiously, and then seemed to accept his emotion as happiness and pride. "I know, I feel the same way." She turned away from the boat. "Sometimes I wonder what I'd do now without it."

David stood alone on the dock between the rows of boats, clutching the cooler to his midriff as his girls walked away from him. He watched them go but couldn't make himself move. Fear, regret, and uncertainty kept him rooted to the weathered boards. His gaze swung toward the sleek white boat and suddenly it became a symbol of everything he had with his family.

In that moment it all crystallized, like a portrait in his head—a vision of his wife and his beautiful little girl on the deck of the boat this afternoon, laughing and happy, excited. Life as they knew it was carefree and good.

It was an illusion.

The picture vanished. David turned grimly toward the car.

Chapter 2

"Mo-om." Lily shouted from the study the next day. "Can you come take a look at this?"

"Be right there, honey. Just let me get this load in the dryer." Caroline stuffed the clothes into the machine and set the dial, then picked up the basket of dried clothes from the last load and dropped it off in the rec room on the way through.

"What's up?" Caroline asked. Lily had set up a corner of the study for her experiment and she pored over a microscope.

"Remember last month when I grew that culture and stained it so I could look at the organisms and categorize them?"

"Sure. I thought you had it all done."

"I thought so, too. I took pictures of all the stained slides and counted the numbers in the colonies so Debbie and I could do our statistics on them. Everything was fine. But now I don't know what's going on."

"How so?"

"Well, that set of cultures didn't grow very well, so I decided to grow another set to add to my first sample." Lily frowned. "Anyway, after breakfast today I smeared and stained a whole new set of slides. Some of them wouldn't even accept the stain, and the ones that did look completely different. Do you think they mutated or something?"

"Let me see." Caroline leaned over and peered in the microscope. Tiny fuchsia-colored organisms lay in dense clusters in the field of the scope, each too small to even count properly. "Do you have one of the other slides from a few weeks ago?"

"Yeah." Lily jumped up and fetched a tray of slides from David's desk.

Sliding the older slide under the holders, Caroline studied it and then compared it to the new one. "Hmm. Do you see these little round organisms from today, in with the other ones? Some of them look a lot like the other batch, but there are also some big globs of tiny little specks mixed in."

"Let me see." Lily looked through the scope. "Yeah, you're right. I was so busy looking at the other ones, I didn't notice them. What are they?"

"They look like bacteria to me."

"Bacteria? How could there be bacteria?"

"Maybe you weren't careful enough to keep the Petri dishes sterile."

"I'm always careful." Lily pouted.

Caroline rubbed her daughter's shoulder. "I know you are, sweetie. But seeding cultures requires a lot of skill. It's not hard, even for professionals, to contaminate a culture. That's why researchers always run multiples." Lily's face fell, and Caroline tugged gently at her hair. "Didn't you have a cold back then?"

Lily thought a moment. "Yeah, I did. I must have contaminated it then."

"Well, look. You know the old adage. If you're handed lemons. . . Why don't you isolate some of these new clusters and take photos of them to show how the bacteria grew and how they affected the original organisms? It can be a sidebar to your experiment."

Lily brightened. "You're right. I could. That'd be cool." With a laugh, she reached over and hugged Caroline. "Thanks, Mom."

"You're welcome."

"I don't know of any other mother who would've had the faintest clue about all this."

Caroline blushed. "Thanks. It was all those biology and biochemistry classes they made me take in college. I liked them so much I was almost ready to ditch my chemistry major and take up biology."

"Hah. You never would have done that."

"Well, no, but I was tempted once." Caroline admitted, more than willing to take up their old mother-daughter game of which was better, biology or chemistry. "Chemistry is amazing. I design the molecules I use in my job myself."

"Yeah, right." Lily smirked. "Huge chains of carbon atoms about a million miles long, twisted every which way. One looks just like the next. I don't know how you keep track of them. They're all alike."

"No, they're not. There are very subtle differences and those differences are important."

"No way."

"Yeah, way. How would you like it if the computer paper you bought for twenty-five dollars started turning yellow, three months after you bought it?"

"You'd never let that happen."

"No, I wouldn't. My beautiful designer molecules prevent it from happening."

"How?" Lily asked.

"Lots of things. Stabilizers to retard chemical breakdown, polymers to encapsulate. . ." Lily's eyes started to glaze over. "Well, you know."

"I know." She grinned at Caroline. "I wanna do cool stuff like you some day, only I wanna be a biologist instead of a chemist."

Caroline viewed all the paraphernalia cluttering the card table in the corner. "You're well on your way already."

"I guess you want me to pick that up, don't you?"

"Yes, I do. A good scientist keeps his work space clean and organized." Geez, she sounded like her mother sometimes. Her brow furrowing, she leaned over and looked harder at the clutter of slides and bottles. "Lily, you got fuchsia dye stain all over the table."

Lily grabbed a pile of stuff off the table, revealing the smear of dye. "Oh crap. Maybe I can get it out."

Caroline shook her head at her daughter. "Why do you think they call it a stain? It won't come out."

"Well, it's an old card table. . ."

"Lucky for you. But still, now it's an old card table with a purple spot in the middle. Next time, be more careful. I'm going to get some lunch. Want some?"

"No, I'll eat something later. I want to get all this done before Debbie gets here. Last night she said she'd be here by one."

Caroline returned to her laundry with a smile on her face. Saturday's sailing had put her behind in her weekend chores, but she didn't mind. Yesterday had been so wonderful. She detested housework. She was so busy at work that by the end of the week she was exhausted, and then she had to face a whole weekend of chores. It was a never-ending cycle. As she folded David's undershirt, she suddenly frowned. Now that sailing season was here again, she wanted to be freer to spend weekends on the boat, which made housework even more loathsome. Maybe a part-time housekeeper would help. Her friend Mary had one and Sue, next door, did as well. Maybe it was time for her to get one too.

She'd really looked forward to the summer season. Last year, David had been tied up in court so much, they hadn't gotten out on the water as often as usual. This year she hoped they could relax a bit more, since David's schedule had lightened after coming home from that big case in D.C. last winter. Month after dreary month that damn case had dragged on, and she'd missed David.

Sailing was good for the family and it brought them together to do something they all loved. She and David had become a well-tuned machine over the years and they both felt a closeness when they were working together on *Windswept*, that felt absent in other areas of their lives. She loved the boat, not only because she loved sailing but also for the special feeling it brought her family. Not every family was as lucky as they were to have something like *Windswept*.

Her brow puckered as she remembered how good it had felt yesterday to be working with David on the boat again. There'd been some times when he'd seemed distant, but she'd chalked them up to the stress of their first time out for the season. Plus, in the past few months they'd had a few battles. It had been nothing huge, just peculiar, odd. Maybe yesterday they were being a little. . .careful. . .with each other. But she had nothing but instinct to go on, so she was uncertain about whether she was right that something was going on with him.

She didn't know how to handle David like this. A keen analytical mind at work enabled to her manage her employees and run her projects, but at home . . . David had been the first man she'd ever been serious about and they'd fit so well together for so long without much effort. She didn't know how to resolve the situation, whatever it was, that had developed between them. With virtually no experience dealing with emotional problems, Caroline was at sea. Because David seemed to be having emotional problems of some sort.

She could see something in his eyes when he looked at her. He didn't say anything, but she could see it. All she knew was that she was afraid. Part of her fear stemmed from his reluctance to talk to her about it, and as for the rest, she wasn't sure if she wanted to know. Caroline felt like a coward not mentioning it herself, but she kept hoping whatever was bothering him would work itself out.

What if his problem was her? What if he was tired of her or wasn't in love with her anymore? What if she'd done something that had angered him? That scared her even more than the possibility something else was bothering him. Because if it was her. . .

Caroline shivered, suddenly cold.

She'd been putting off dealing with their situation, instead counting on boating season to rekindle the closeness they'd felt in past years. Could *Windswept* heal the rift between them? Was she placing too much hope on that?

In the last weeks while they cleaned and polished the boat, they'd gotten along better, even if it felt off. Still, she'd been delighted with the improvement. Then it seemed to go sour with no warning. Maybe all they needed was more time together on the boat, working shoulder to shoulder doing something they both loved.

She wandered into the kitchen where David was fixing himself a grilled cheese sandwich. "Leave the stuff out. I want to make myself one," she told him.

"What's going on with Lily and her science project?" He took a bite of his sandwich, hot off the griddle.

"Oh, just a problem with her slides. I helped her out. Don't worry about it."

"I see." He took a seat at the table to eat his lunch and pore over the Sunday paper, spread out on the surface.

She washed her hands at the sink while her sandwich browned in the pan, and then glanced outside at the clear blue sky. "It's another gorgeous day out there, isn't it?"

"Yep." He turned the page.

"I love this time of year, don't you?"

"Uh huh." He sounded distracted. "Did you see the article in today's paper about a possible second recession?"

"There are always articles about the recession these days. You know, I think the tulips are about gone now. It'll soon be time for the rhododendrons."

"If these stocks don't stop going down soon, we'll lose our nest egg," he commented.

"Maybe I should go out and get something done in the garden today. I never have time after work." She sat down with her sandwich, nibbling on the grilled cheese with a thoughtful look on her face. "That was so wonderful yesterday on the boat. I love it out there on the water. It makes you forget everything else."

"Yes, it was nice." Then, David frowned. "Futures were down this week again too."

"David, you're not listening to me."

"Yes, I am. You had a good time on the boat."

"I don't think you really know how I feel about it."

"Sure I do. You love sailing the boat. I do too."

"It's more than that. It's something we both love to do together. You've been away on business so often this winter we hardly ever got time alone. Maybe now that spring has come we'll be able to go out on the water again and spend more time together."

"I didn't have any choice about going out of town," he said defensively. "There was that Donnoli trial in D.C."

"You spent three months on it and then he plea-bargained."

"Sometimes things happen that way."

Caroline bit her lip and decided to take the plunge since they were so close to the topic. "But even when you were here, you were so tense."

"It was an important case."

"He was a punk."

"He was a punk with connections. The firm was very worried."

"I don't think that was the reason you were so tense all the time. You've had tough cases before and they never bothered you like this. What's the matter?"

"Nothing's the matter. Look, I have some work to do at the office this afternoon. I have to go."

"David, it's Sunday. There's no need for you to be in the office on a Sunday. I think we should talk about this."

"I have to go." He threw down the paper and practically ran out of the room, leaving half of his sandwich on the plate.

"David." Caroline called after him, but he was gone before she got the words out of her mouth. She sat and stared at the empty doorway, her heart beating a hundred miles an hour. She couldn't make herself move. Lily and Debbie chattered away in the den, but she sat waiting for her heart to slow down and her fear to go away before she joined them in the study.

David drove to his office but was too keyed up to work when he got there. Instead, he paced his office floor as his agitation increased. He stared out the window at the Naval Academy across Spa Creek, his hands stuffed into his jeans pockets. Each time he tried to take a deep breath, it shuddered in his chest when he drew air in.

He loved Caroline, and he'd been an imbecile. All he had to do was to recall how beautiful his wife'd looked wreathed in sun as she stood behind the wheel yesterday, to know he didn't want to lose her. It took that defining moment to show him just what he may very well have squandered.

He'd been a fool to have jeopardized what they had together. He still didn't know what had driven him to it. He remembered feeling a sense of invincibility in D.C., as if he could get away with anything because he was in a city where power ruled and money rocked. Everyone in D.C. seemed to escape unscathed with mind-blowing betrayals of every sort. The city was a separate world unto itself, and he easily saw how men betrayed family and country in an atmosphere like that. He couldn't use it as an excuse, but he also knew he'd been sucked into the same proverbial power trip everyone else rode in the capital.

But now he was here, trying to pretend to himself and everyone else that nothing ugly had happened in D.C. The stress wore at him. He couldn't face Caroline when he felt so much pressure, and it got harder every day to maintain a normal facade. He was deathly afraid a facade was all that remained. His quiet, easy-going life slipped away with the ice and snow of the nation's capital and he had absolutely no idea how to get it back. Maybe if he just continued to pretend everything was fine, it might become reality.

What was it people said? Act happy and you will become happy? Maybe if he acted normal, he could become so again. Maybe.

Then again, maybe not.

Chapter 3

Three weeks passed before they returned to the marina for another sail on *Windswept*. With spring well entrenched, the balmy, sunny day held only a light breeze. Lily was busy at Debbie's house, so David and Caroline were alone.

Caroline set the provisions for lunch down below and David got the boat ready to sail. There wasn't much conversation. There hadn't been since the scene in the kitchen earlier that month. They'd maintained a polite but distant relationship and avoided mention of the awkwardness, as if they feared what would happen if they talked about it. It was only a surface calmness though, and she could sense deep waters below the facade of David's seemingly even-tempered mask.

She let the dock lines go and jumped on board as David backed the boat out of her slip. On the water, she took the wheel as usual and held the boat into the wind while he put up the sails. They filled with wind, the breeze gently heeling the boat over as *Windswept* slowly accelerated across the rippled bay.

With only seven to eight knot breezes, she handled the wheel with ease as she steered the boat into its first long tack. She relaxed, with one hand on the wheel, while he neatened the lines and trimmed the sails again. She split her attention between their destination and watching David, as he stood looking pensively out at the water.

For a long time he didn't move a muscle. It was unusual for him to be so still. Finally he turned and glanced back at her. She caught his eye and smiled tentatively at him. He looked solemn for a moment and then sagged against the bulkhead and smiled back at her. Her smile turned into a grin and she leaned against the seat, holding the wheel with her toe to hold it steady, her arms along the rail behind her.

"It's beautiful out here today, isn't it?" she said.

"Yes. Yes, it is." David stood there with a warm smile on his face while she enjoyed the movement of the boat, then he swung around and braced his arms against both sides of the companionway as he gazed out over the bay again.

She could see the change in his demeanor as he watched the water. He looked more at ease and less tense than the last time they took *Windswept* out. This sail had been a good idea. It took some convincing to get him to go and she suspected he'd only agreed to come so as not to create another scene.

But she'd been right. This was what they needed, to spend time together doing what they both loved. There was something soothing about the water, and sailing always took her out of herself. It was a world unto itself apart from everything else in her life. It was a world they had created for themselves that belonged only to them, a place where no one else could intrude.

The next tack was another long one up the bay. She leaned against the rail and let the water and the wind work their magic on her. Soon, her mind was nearly blank, her only thought lazily adjusting the wheel to accommodate the shifts in the wind.

After a while, she asked David if he wanted to take a tack and he smiled at her. "No, you look like you're enjoying yourself. I'll get my turn another day."

They tacked again and he handled the sails while she turned the boat. "I don't know how you manage to sail this thing single-handed," she said, referring to a few times in the past he had taken the boat out alone.

He chuckled. It was well-known in the family that the bustle of getting the boat safely out on the water with all the sails up and trimmed always made her tense. When things settled down and they were sailing freely, she relaxed.

"It must be a handful when the wind is up," she added.

"I don't go out alone when the wind is more than twelve or thirteen knots. Anything below that, I can handle."

"Not me. I like to have everything organized and under control at all times."

"It's always under control." He grinned. "Just hectic for a few minutes."

"I can imagine."

"You could do it."

"Yeah, right," she snickered.

"You could. You have all the skills. Maybe not in fifteen mile-an-hour winds, but on a day like today or even a little more, you could."

"Hmph. I'm happy just to do this much. A few years ago I couldn't even steer. I was too afraid to try," she said.

"True. But you have to push the envelope."

Caroline rolled her eyes. "You push your own envelope. I'm happy with my envelope."

"It would give you more all-around confidence with the boat."

"By the end of last season I could steer the boat in stronger winds. That increased my confidence. As long as it isn't too gusty. I don't do gusty."

He snickered at her good-naturedly. "Oh, we all know you don't do gusty." He headed for the companionway stairs. "If you're happy here for a while, though, maybe I'll go below for a couple of minutes to check out some charts. One of the guys at work was talking about a new anchorage he found. I want to check it out."

"Sure. Go for it."

She gazed after him thoughtfully. If he was making plans for other trips on the bay, then maybe. . .

The breeze was steady and non-variable. After a while

she was bored with her own company and wanted some fun. She grinned to herself. David was in for a bit of a jolt.

She reached around the wheel, yanked the jib line off the winch and threw the line into the cockpit, out of the way. Then she spun the wheel through the wind and sent the boom snapping around to the other side. The boat turned on a dime, swooshing through the water with the jib whipping madly.

Below decks, David stood next to the navigation table with a pencil and a ruler, concentrating on plotting a path from their marina to the anchorage. Chesapeake Bay was notorious for its numerous shoals and charted areas of great danger for green sailors, so he had to be careful where he set down his course. Suddenly, the boat gave a lurch and he flew off his feet, banging his head on the bulkhead, charts and instruments flying. "Sonofa—"

"Heads up." he heard Caroline yell belatedly into the cabin with a laugh.

He stumbled up the companionway steps, rubbing the lump on the back of his head, then holding on to the rails on both sides as the boat slewed to port yet again. He hit the other side with his shoulder.

"What the hell are you doing, dammit?" She laughed at his consternation.

"Something you taught me."

"I—"

His words cut off as *Windswept* made another sharp swing and he lurched into the cockpit on his knees. His eyes widened as he watched Caroline swing the wheel again. "You, ah, look like you're having fun."

"I am, lots of it." She laughed again as if she was heading down the steep slope of a roller coaster. "You should probably hang on to something. We're not done."

David watched her have a ball with the sloop as he managed to seat himself. “Three-sixties?”

“Yep. Two so far.”

“How many are you planning?”

“Dunno.”

“I see.” She obviously had no idea how incredible she looked right now, with her eyes alive with joy and the wind blowing her hair across her face. He couldn’t take his eyes off her.

She glanced over at him. He had a fevered intensity in his eyes.

He took a quick look around them to make sure that they were fairly isolated on this portion of the bay.

For a few minutes more he stared at her, then, his voice shaking, he rasped, “Heave her to.”

Hell, his hands and knees and most of the rest of his body shook, too. He couldn’t breathe; his chest felt tight. It’d been so long, so very, very long. . .

“Sure,” she said, giving him an anxious glance. Did she think he was angry at her for playing around with the boat? He helped her adjust their heading until the boat was stable and stationary in the water.

Nerves stretched between them as they faced each other.

“Caro,” he whispered, and she flew into his arms with a cry. Their lips came together with a sense of urgency he hadn’t felt in forever, and he drank her in like a dying man thirsting for water. She felt wonderful in his arms.

He kissed her over and over, lost in desire as his tongue tangled with hers. Each pressed to the other, seeking the passion they craved. His hands slid under her top, moving across her skin, absorbing familiar feelings and eager responses. It wasn’t enough for him and he could tell it wasn’t enough for her, either. Fingers that knew her flesh as well as she knew herself quivered with her softness and he gave a murmur of pleasure as he reached to fondle her breasts, warmed by the sun. He flipped her top over her head and she reached for his shirt, dragging it from him.

For endless minutes they sought each other and he ran his lips over her warmed skin. He laved her breasts, suckling hungrily.

"Kiss me again, honey." Her breath caught as she gazed into his eyes. He ran his lips back up and kissed her as if she would disappear in a puff of smoke if he stopped. He pushed her onto her back on the cockpit cushion, his body covering hers ardently. As he ground his pelvis into hers, his mouth opened over her lips as if trying to fuse her into his own body. "Caro. I love you so much."

Her own body responded to his as if she'd been born for it and she lifted her hips as he slid her shorts over them. He was inside her in moments.

David moaned, "Caro, Caro. . ." He felt as if he'd come home after months of being away. His lips burrowed into her neck, his teeth scraping at her skin. They came fast, like teenagers, clutching each other desperately for endless minutes afterward.

She pulled his head up. "Oh, David. I love you so much."

He pressed his forehead against hers and started to tremble again. "I can't lose you, Caro."

"You're not going to lose me. Whatever gave you that idea?"

He stood up suddenly, shaking his head to clear it. As he pulled his clothes on, he couldn't look at her. She was so full of compassion and he so ridden with guilt.

Abruptly, he sat next to her, took a deep, shaky breath and watched her straighten her own clothes. "Sorry."

"You're sorry we made love? I'm not. It was wonderful."

He shuddered, his gaze sliding sideways. "It was more

than wonderful. I, ah. . . That's not what I meant. I meant I was sorry I fell apart a little there. Paranoia, I guess."

"There's no need to be sorry." He could tell she wanted to break the tension and not let this post-coital thing, whatever it was between them, tarnish the beauty of what they'd just experienced.

She slapped her hands on her knees and stood up. "Look, it's getting late and I'm hungry. I'm sure you are, too. We used up a lot of energy," she said with a small smile. "I think I'll go down below and fix us some lunch."

Their eyes met with an intimacy they hadn't had in a while. Then she headed down to the galley.

He stepped behind the wheel and directed *Windswept* away from the breeze until they were sailing again. "I'm going to get underway again while you do that. The sky is getting a little dark and the breeze is picking up."

"Yeah, shifting too. It was changing for the last half hour. Do you want tuna?"

"Sure, that's fine."

Caroline puttered around in the galley, enjoying the feeling of relaxation that only seemed to come to her on the boat. Caroline was hungry; a good hungry from the exercise and fresh air and the thrill of making love to David again.

Her reverie was interrupted, though, as an orange flowered scarf tucked behind some cans of soup on one of the shelves caught her eye. It was a very expensive scarf and she didn't own a scarf like that. For a brief nanosecond of innocence, she wondered how it'd gotten there.

But then a sick feeling came over her so hard, and almost doubled her over in pain. "No."

It was way too obvious. Heading up the stairs, Caroline faced David. She held up the scarf and he stiffened. She glared at him inquiringly. "Where did this come from?"

The boat lurched slightly. “I dunno, you must have left it behind after our first sail a few weeks ago.”

“No, I don’t own a scarf like this. It’s ugly. I don’t even like orange.”

“Maybe Lily?”

“God, no. Besides, I cleaned everything out at the end of the season. There was no hideous scarf like this on the boat when we left it.”

“Then I guess I couldn’t say.”

“David, this is ridiculous. I didn’t bring this scarf here. *Someone else* must have. When? When, David?”

“Oh, ah, maybe it’s Debbie’s and Matt didn’t realize it was with his stuff when we stopped to check the leak in the hatch cover last week.”

“Oh, David.” She held the label up for view. “This is a Hermes scarf. Get real. This isn’t Debbie’s scarf any more than it’s Lily’s. What are you trying to cover up?”

“Nothing!” he shouted at her.

Her heart in her throat, she faced him in the cockpit with the expensive orange Hermes scarf fluttering through her fingers in the wind. “No? Then, why are you so angry and defensive?”

“I’m not defensive.”

“Yes you are.” Suddenly her breath hitched and she said with a quiver, “Where did the scarf come from, David?”

“Oh, for God’s sake, Caroline. It’s just a scarf. Leave it alone.”

For months, she’d been trying to pretend nothing was wrong. Even when she couldn’t help but admit something was going on, she tried to ignore the situation in the hopes it would go away. But she now knew it wouldn’t go away and she would have to face it. The scarf became an ugly, ludicrous symbol of something terribly wrong in their marriage, and all at once she couldn’t stand the sight of the thing.

She flung it overboard, watching as it settled on the

water and then slowly sank as the water soaked the silk. It drifted to the rear and got caught in the wake of the boat, which pulled it under completely.

She didn't mistake the look of relief on David's face even as he stared at her as if she'd lost her mind. "Why did you throw away the scarf if it was such an expensive one?"

"A scarf that you claim you knew nothing about? Why should you care what happens to it?" She could all but smell his denial. "You think what's going on here will float away like the scarf I just threw in the water?"

"You're making too much of this, Caroline. Why destroy something pretty because you're angry? It's ridiculous to make an issue out of something like that."

"I don't think it's ridiculous at all. Actually, it's just beginning to make sense. Last weekend you were too busy to go sailing with me because you said you had to work at the office all afternoon on Saturday. But you went sailing, didn't you?"

"Don't be absurd. I told you I had to work."

"But did you *work*?"

He took a long, hard look at her set face, then swept past her without a word to drop the sails. He left them, hanging, on either side of the boom. She watched him in amazement. He *never* left them all awry.

She grabbed his arm. "What are you doing?"

"Out on the water is no place and no time to be arguing like this. We're going back."

A gust of cold wind hit her in the face and she looked up in surprise. The wind had risen alarmingly while they'd been arguing and a big storm cloud was bearing down on them. Another gust hit the slack sail and it flapped madly.

"Start the engine, Caroline."

She darted behind the wheel and turned the engine over, putting it into forward. David sat on the cabin-top and stared at her as if he were trying to decide something. She squirmed but wouldn't give him the satisfaction of showing it.

She swung the wheel and turned the boat around to head back. After a while, he faced her grimly, his hands on his hips. "We've handled situations like this on the boat lots of times before, but not in the middle of an argument. We weren't paying enough attention to the weather and the storm crept up on us. It isn't safe."

"Fine. Now it's safe. Answer my question."

"When we get back to the marina." He climbed on the cabin top, one arm around the mast again and, with the wind whipping his hair, stared out at the whitecaps that were getting bigger and bigger on the choppy water.

It started to rain and the wind gusted from the north. She was glad they'd started back when they had. David closed the hatch to protect the cabin from the rain but he didn't bother to go below to get his foul-weather gear. Nor did she.

In no time, pure stubbornness had them both soaked. Shivering, Caroline was glad of the cold and wet. It matched her inner turmoil and misery. What would David say when they got back to the marina? She almost didn't want to hear it. Wanted to pretend nothing had happened, the way she had all winter and spring. Caroline didn't want to be so certain another woman had been here aboard *Windswept* when she was not.

Gliding back into their slip, Caroline reversed the engine as he jumped off and secured the dock lines. They both settled into their routines, putting the boat to bed. The shower had stopped and David finished cleaning up topside. Caroline would rather not have bothered with cleanup, but entered the galley anyway. The cooler was on the counter, and she realized they hadn't even eaten their lunch. Even though there was nothing to do, a few minutes were wasted moving things around to avoid facing David. Finally, she went topside again.

He was making his neat, tidy Flemish coils on the dock, and suddenly it infuriated her. “How can you stand there making cute little coils like that after everything that’s happened? How can you fuss like that as if nothing is wrong?”

“I want to leave the boat shipshape,” he answered, not looking at her.

“Shipshape? What difference does it make? There are more important things going on here. We have to talk.” She reached down and dragged her fingernails through the coil of line, leaving it a heap of tangled rope.

Finally he raised his eyes, but they looked dead. “We’re not going to talk about anything here. You’re cold and wet and shivering. We’ll talk at home.”

She mimicked him. “‘We’ll talk about this after I get the sails down. We’ll talk about this after we get to the marina. We’ll talk about this after we get home.’ You don’t want to talk about this at all, do you?”

“No. I don’t.”

“Why not? Are you afraid of what I might find out?”

“I’m afraid that once we start this thing, we won’t be able to go back. We had a nice sail and some amazing lovemaking earlier today. Why don’t we leave it at that?”

“No, I refuse to. I want to know what’s going on.”

“You’ll regret it, Caroline. Leave it be.” David’s eyes didn’t look dead anymore; they looked almost threatening, but that didn’t deter her.

“I regret it already, but it’s out there now. We can’t go back.”

David glanced around the marina. “We’re drawing stares. The boats are so close together here, everyone can hear what we’re talking about. This isn’t a good place to have this conversation.”

She detested his patronizing attitude, and it only stoked the flames of her anger. “Yelling about, you mean. I don’t care. I want the truth.”

“For God’s sake, Caroline. If you insist on hashing this out now, let’s go below. At least there’s some privacy down there.”

Turning on her heel, Caroline stomped over to the companionway stairs and down into the cabin. She moved forward as far as she could in the small cabin and turned, her arms crossed protectively in front of her. He remained across the scant distance of the salon, his stance forbidding.

“I’m going to ask you one more time to let this go.” His voice shook with anger and stress. “You’re imagining things. You’re making a federal case out of a damned scarf.”

“Who brought the scarf here, David? Who do you know who can afford Hermes?” She asked him one last time, dreading his answer but still needing him to respect her enough to at least admit it.

“I did. Okay? I did.”

“Yeah, I’d figured that much out. But why were you here without me? Who was here last Saturday with you?”

David stood before her, his eyes turbulent and obviously trying to control his emotions. She could see the battle he fought with himself. She knew him so well. And all at once, any whisper of doubt she may have had dissolved and she didn’t need confirmation. Her heart banged against her ribs, her stomach turned over, and a sickening lump rose in her throat.

Swallowing past the lump, she whispered, “Who is she?” Her lips quivered.

David blanched. He swiveled away from her, running his fingers through his hair and then gripping the back of his neck so hard his knuckles turned white. Seconds went by, then minutes.

“Who is she?” Caroline repeated. “Tell me.”

"It wouldn't do either of us any good if I told you." His shoulders slumped. "Let it go."

"Then you at least admit someone was here."

"Would it do any good to deny it at this point? Yes, I took the boat out last Saturday with a friend."

"Your mistress."

"What?" He spun around. "My mistress?"

"That's what I said. How long have you been seeing her?"

"I don't have a mistress." He was getting angry now. "I have a wife."

"But you've been seeing someone, haven't you? What else would you call it?" She leaned forward. "How long?"

"Caroline. Don't do this to us."

"Don't do this to us? You're the one who's doing something to us. You're the one who obviously has a girlfriend on the side. I want to know precisely what has been going on. As your wife," she spat at him, "I think I have a right to know."

He panted, trying to control himself. "All right. Since you insist on knowing the details, sit down."

"I don't feel like sitting."

"I said, sit!" he thundered, and she sank to the settee in shock.

He sat on the other end and faced her. "Sorry. I'm a little tense. Okay, since you're so anxious to know, I'll tell you about it." His eyes squeezed closed for several seconds and, when they opened, they were wet and glistening. "I met a woman early this year when I was in D.C. for the Donnoli trial. We went out a few times whenever I was in town."

"How many times?"

"I don't know. Half a dozen."

"It was her on the boat with you last weekend?"

"Yes," he sighed. "It was her."

Caroline's fingers trembled as she covered her mouth and tried to breathe in, but she couldn't catch enough air. He had admitted it, actually admitted he had been seeing another woman. How could he have done that?

She looked up. "I don't understand. You saw her in D.C. What was she doing here?"

"She's. . .ah. . .she's moved."

"Oh, my God." Caroline's stomach fell still further and she felt suddenly ill. Gripping her stomach, she rocked back and forth. David refused to meet her eyes, his fixed on his boat shoes.

She whispered, "This woman has moved here to be with you. You're sleeping with her."

"It's not like that. I didn't ask her to move here. When she called and told me she had an apartment in Annapolis, I couldn't believe she'd actually done that. I didn't want her here. She has a formidable personality and pretty much does what she wants."

"But you didn't stop her. Did you?"

He turned whiter, if possible. "She doesn't mean anything to me. It's not serious. She's not important enough to put us through all this anguish."

Caroline's laughter rang out, distraught and hysterical. "Oh, that's a good one. Where did you get that from? A soap opera? This woman, whom you have all but admitted sleeping with, has moved her entire life over a hundred miles to be with you, and you say it isn't serious?"

"I've been trying to break it off for weeks. I told you, I don't want her here. It was a mistake. That's why it isn't important."

She stood and tried to push by him. "You're having an ongoing affair, David, and that, in my mind, is serious. Very serious."

He reached to stop her but she shoved at his shoulder, stumbling across the teak floor in her hurry to get out of the boat. On the first step, she paused and looked back at him to see him sitting on the settee with his head in his hands.

"You know what hurts almost more than the rest? That you brought her here, to *Windswept*." She saw him wince as tears leaked from between his fingers. "This is our special place David, where the two of us were the closest we've ever been, where we sailed together and laughed together and where we made love together. This was our 'thing,' David. Ours. And you brought her into it."

Reaching over to the navigation table, she snagged his car keys, which he always left there when they were out on the water. "Call your mistress for a ride."

He didn't look up.

Tears blinded her as she reached the cockpit and climbed over the lifelines onto the dock of their slip. She rushed down the center dock between the rows of boats, and stopped halfway. Slowly, she turned and looked back at *Windswept*. The image of the beautiful sloop wavered and swam as she gazed at the sleek, beloved, familiar lines.

Everything David had done was horrible, but defiling *Windswept* was the most terrible thing of all. The boat epitomized everything they had together. She didn't know if she would ever forgive him. She turned slowly and walked to the car.

Chapter 4

Caroline pulled the car into the driveway. She had no idea how the car had gotten home—there was no memory of any of the trip. The way the tears were running down her face, it was a miracle there'd been no accident and she'd made it at all. Letting herself into the kitchen with her key, it surprised her to see Lily and Debbie at the kitchen table, eating brownies.

Lily glanced up, saw Caroline's ravaged face, then jumped up and put her arms around her. "Mom. What's wrong? Oh my God, is it Dad? Did something awful happen on the boat? Is he okay? What happened, Mom?"

Caroline shuddered. She didn't want Lily to see her this way, didn't want anyone to see her this way. "Nothing's wrong with your father. At least nothing physical," she blurted out, her lips curling into a sneer.

"But what is it? You hardly ever cry. Something's happened."

Pulling away from Lily to grab a handful of tissues from the box on the counter, Caroline tried to reassure her. "Your Dad and I had. . .a. . .sort of an argument."

Debbie was watching the scene unfold with fascinated eyes and Caroline shuddered again. Lily looked back at Debbie dubiously and then went over to Caroline again. "An argument? Geez, it must have been some argument to make you cry like this."

"Yeah, it was some argument," Caroline said with a shake of her head. "Look, it has nothing to do with you. It's adult stuff. Why don't—"

"Where's Dad?" Lily looked around in confusion. "Where is he?"

"I, um, left him at the marina."

"You left him there? Just drove away?" Her voice held incredulity. "You don't leave someone stranded. How will he get home?"

"He'll find a way," Caroline retorted.

Lily glanced out the kitchen window at the sound of an engine. "It's a taxi. Dad's come home in a taxi."

"I guess he didn't take me up on my suggestion," she mumbled, turning away to escape toward the den.

"What?"

"Nothing. Tell Dad I don't particularly want to see him right now."

But David was already standing in the kitchen doorway, and he said, "I don't care if you don't want to see me. We're going to talk."

"I think we've done enough talking for a while. We've done enough everything." Her eyes flashed. "I need to be alone to think."

Lily and Debbie looked back and forth between the two adults with their mouths open in shock. David glanced at Lily. "What are you two doing here? You're supposed to be at Debbie's house."

"We needed some of my data that I left here."

"Did you get it?" he snapped.

"Yes." Her eyes looked afraid. It was patently obvious David was running on a short fuse.

"Then go back to Debbie's house and stay there until I call you."

Lily grabbed a folder off the table and slid past her father in the doorway, her eyes wide and full of fear. Debbie followed her wordlessly.

David watched them start down the driveway and then motioned to Lily to come back. "I would prefer to keep this incident within our family. Please be discreet and ask Debbie to be the same."

Behind him Caroline snickered loudly. "Yes, it would be good if someone around here was discreet, wouldn't it?"

Caroline noticed how David's fingers clenched on the doorknob as he turned toward her. Like her, his eyes were red and his face tearstained. Lily would have seen that instantly. Good God, what would she think? Then Caroline sighed inwardly. Whatever Lily thought probably wasn't as bad as the reality. What a hell of a mess. Shaking her head in disbelief, she headed for the den and plopped down on the sofa. She knew David would follow her but she didn't have enough strength left to fight him.

David sat on the side of the sofa next to her, watching her wipe at the tears that had started up again. He hated himself. He hated himself and what he had done to Caroline, to Lily, to himself—even to the woman he had slept with. And he hated himself more for what he knew he had to do next.

"Caro," he said quietly. "There is no defense for what I did. I tore our family apart and no one knows more than I do what it's going to cost us." Caroline sat very still, listening to him with her fists clenched together in her lap, her fingers trembling and her knuckles white. "I can't tell you how it happened or why it happened because I don't even know. That's one of the things I've been wrestling with the past few months. What's wrong with me, what's wrong with us, that this thing could happen with practically no warning? I didn't go to D.C. to have an affair and never intended to have one, ever."

Caroline hugged herself and sobbed, shaking her head back and forth as if to deny everything he said.

Then she lashed out at him. “Don’t blame it on being in D.C. That’s a cop-out.”

“You’re probably right, although there’s an element of being alone every night in the city.” He took a deep breath and let it out with a shudder. “Anyway, for the past couple of weeks I'd thought about leaving so I wouldn’t hurt you and Lily more than I already had. Then we had that wonderful sail together with Lily three weeks ago, and it seemed that day as if nothing had ever happened.

"And today. . .after we made love,” he looked her in the eyes, “then I wanted to stay out on the water in the worst way. Do anything it took to make it up to you. To make believe nothing had happened. I’d almost decided I could. But when Alicia—”

Caroline gasped and David kicked himself for slipping up and giving her a name to latch onto, to funnel her grief through. It would have been better for her if it was an anonymous figure.

Caroline began to cry again—great, wrenching sobs, as she pulled her knees up to rock back and forth on the cushion. Helplessly he watched her suffer. All spring he’d wondered if she suspected something was wrong. The bewilderment in her eyes every time she looked at him nearly killed him. Now she looked stunned, as if she wanted to curl up and die.

It would be best if he got this evening over with as soon as possible. She needed to be rid of him for now. He had a lot of thinking to do and she needed some time to come to grips with how he had messed up their lives.

He tried again. “When I took. . .Alicia. . .sailing,” his voice hitched, “it was awful out there without you. I felt like vomiting and couldn’t wait to get back to the marina. Alicia could see I wasn’t happy and started whining and demanding I leave you. I suspect she planted the scarf to hurt you. It sounds like something she would do. And then you and I went out today and it was nice to be together on the bay again, like last summer, and I—"

"All right, then go." she screamed at the top of her lungs as she leapt off the chair and started throwing pillows at his head. "Get out of here. We don't need you and your lies. Lily and I will be fine without you."

"I'll go up and throw a few things in a suitcase. I'll come back while you're at work to pack up the rest of my things."

Like a bad "B" movie had unfolded in front of his eyes, David heard himself say words he had heard actor husbands say to their actor wives. But this wasn't a movie. It couldn't be happening. The fact that it was real had his feet glued to the floor, afraid to make that final turn that would take him away from his family.

Her eyes overflowing with tears, Caroline didn't even see him leave the room. Some time later she heard the kitchen door open and close and she knew he was gone. Leaning against the sage green wall in the den, she laid her hot, wet face against the cool plaster and began to cry again. This time she couldn't stop. Slowly she slid into a heap on the plush green carpet.

A long time later, Caroline stirred off the rug. She got another handful of tissues and blew her nose and wiped her eyes. Then she washed her face in the bathroom. Her reflection looked horrible, as if she'd been crying for a year. She certainly felt that way.

She wandered listlessly into the bedroom, stood and stared at David's clothes hanging in the closet. There was a small gap where he'd taken his best suit and a few shirts, but everything else was still there. As if he hadn't left. As if he planned to come back.

It seemed to her, in that moment, almost as if he were

dead, lost to her. This must be what it felt like to suddenly lose a spouse to death. His departure felt as final as that.

She lay down on the bed, their bed, and looked at the king-sized pillow he liked on his side. It hurt even to look at it. It hurt to look at everything in the room that belonged to him. Even the things that were hers belonged to him as well.

Curling up on her side, she tried to think things through for the first time. What had she done wrong? Where had she gone wrong? What was there about her that had made him turn to another woman? She had no idea. There surely had to be reasons but at the moment she couldn't think very well.

Was it her work? Did she get too involved in it and leave him out of her life too much? And Lily— was she too involved with Lily as well, to the extent that she excluded him? Had she been too distant? Not loving enough? Not enough sex?

Nothing made any sense to her; it was all too new and had shocked her too deeply. She certainly hadn't been prepared for it. In the space of an afternoon she'd had a niggling sense of unease about a nebulous "something" that she thought might be wrong in her marriage. Then they'd made incredible love on *Windswept* followed by her husband's admission he'd slept with another woman. It was all too much to think about. She searched her mind for happier memories.

Caroline's thoughts naturally drifted back to times when she and David had been happy, when they had first met. They'd both been students at Georgetown, she a junior and he a first year law student. His best friend and current colleague Matt Deming, Debbie's dad, happened to be the older brother of Caroline's roommate, Michelle.

They met when they both visited Michelle at her home over Thanksgiving break. David had been there with Matt. The attraction had been instant and they'd stayed up half the night to talk. She remembered it as if it had been yesterday.

When Matt and Michelle went to bed a little while after dinner, David offered to keep Caroline company. She'd been too keyed up to sleep. She had noticed David's attention and quickly became captivated by him, attracted to his warm appeal that broadcasted his love of people and causes, his thick brown hair and handsome features. Plus, he was in that most coveted of all Georgetown majors—law school. Coeds dreamed of dating a law school man.

Thanksgiving dinner had been Michelle's latest ruse to get them to meet and it had finally come to pass. Caroline's mother had been irritated at her for not coming home for Thanksgiving, but she wasn't about to let this latest opportunity pass her by to meet the illustrious David Hartford.

He had heard a lot about her, too. He sat on the other end of the sofa facing her with his leg up on the seat and his arm along the back. Caroline's heart started to accelerate as they sat knee to knee.

He gazed into her eyes and his were warm and inviting. "Whatever will we do?" he whispered.

"I don't know, but I suspect Matt and Shelly will be disappointed if we don't do something."

"They weren't very subtle, were they?" he chuckled.

"No, they've been trying to get us together for years."

"If I'd known what I was missing, I'd have been on your doorstep in a heartbeat a long time ago." He slid forward more and wound her long hair around his forefinger. "You're looking beautiful tonight."

"You're mighty hot yourself, you know. Some nice muscles you got there," she whispered.

His eyes heated at her admission and he leaned forward. His fingers released one lock of hair in favor of sliding under the entire curtain of softness to rest on the back of her neck. He used the leverage to pull her forward to meet him and his lips touched hers with infinite gentleness.

His lips were soft and warm against hers, and Caroline felt a rush of heat and excitement. They shifted until their bodies were closer and his arms gathered her in. His lips slid more firmly across hers.

After a few minutes, he pulled back and caressed her with his eyes. "Maybe we'd better stop. I can't seduce you on my best friend's sofa."

"Why not?" Caroline said dreamily.

"Because it's not done, that's why not." His voice shook. "What if someone woke up and came down the stairs?"

"Would they be shocked to find us kissing?"

"We'd have been doing some pretty fancy kissing in a few minutes if we hadn't stopped. That might have shocked them."

"Sounds enticing. I'm game."

"Don't say something you don't mean."

"I do mean it." She leaned forward again, so close she could feel his breath on her cheek. He groaned and moved in the rest of the way. This time, his mouth came down hard on hers and he slanted his head to get a better angle. His tongue slid across her lips and her mouth opened to give him access. Their tongues tangled breathlessly for a lifetime until he broke the kiss and ran his lips down her neck.

At last, he sat back and struggled to get his breath back as she, too, panted in a haze of leftover passion. "Seriously. I think we had better cool it or we could end up in an embarrassing situation. And we just met yesterday."

"I know. I find it hard to believe I've only known you a day. It seems like I've known you forever."

"I feel the same way," he murmured, his fingers playing with a few wispy curls that framed her face at her temple. "Maybe we should just talk for awhile, though."

And they did. They talked for hours about their college studies and about life. She asked him what he liked about law and he talked on and on about his enthusiasm for law and justice. He teased her about her passion for chemistry but told her she was the most beautiful chemist he had ever met.

"And how many have you met?" she asked him with a grin.

"Couple."

"Did they both have thick black beards?"

"One of them." He laughed. "The other had a blond beard."

On and on they went, bantering back and forth, parrying and thrusting. It had been a magical night and, after it, they had spent a magical weekend with Matt and Michelle, riding the Deming's horses, and playing in the unexpected snow that fell Sunday morning.

Back at school, Caroline and David soon settled into a routine where she spent every available moment with him at his apartment near the campus. When it came time for grad school, she got accepted at Georgetown so she could still be near him as he finished up his senior year of law school. They were married a month after he received his law degree and she got her PhD in chemical engineering.

Caroline sat up on the bed and looked at the clock through the gloom that had settled into the room. It was nine-thirty. Lily would still be at Debbie's, worried sick. She had to do something, even if it was to confirm her daughter's fears.

She called the Demings and Debbie answered the phone. "Debbie, this is Mrs. Hartford. Could you tell Lily to come home, please?"

"Sure, Mrs. H. We're all done here. She'll be home in a few minutes."

"Thank you." Caroline hung up the phone and leaned

against the kitchen wall, wondering how she was going to tell Lily that her father had left them.

When Lily let herself into the kitchen a few minutes later, Caroline sat at the table, her fingers clinched together. Lily rushed over and hugged her shoulders, holding on tightly.

"Mommy, tell me everything is okay."

Caroline gripped Lily's hand on her shoulder. "Maybe you'd better sit down, sweetie."

Lily sat, looked around the room and down the hall. "Where's Daddy? Where is he?"

"He's not here, Lily," Caroline sighed.

"Where did he go? Back to the marina for something? When's he coming back?"

"I don't know where he went and I don't know when he's coming back."

"What do you mean? How can you not know? Where is he?"

Caroline could see how Lily deliberately acted obtuse in order to stave off the truth behind her father's absence. She had seen this kind of thing too many times in her friend's lives, in Debbie's in fact, not to know what had happened. Apparently, Lily would not believe it until Caroline spelled it out.

She sighed. "Something has happened between your father and me, and Dad has decided it would be best if he lived somewhere else for a while."

Lily whitened and started to cry. "I knew it. I told Debbie that was what's happening. She said it was the same way when her mom and dad split up. Tell me it isn't happening to me like it happened to Debbie. Please, Mom," she sobbed.

"Nobody has said anything about a divorce, sweetie. It's just a temporary separation until we think things over." *I hope.*

Lily jumped up from the table. "No, No. Don't even say that word. Please, tell me Daddy will be back soon."

"I don't know when Dad will be back." *I don't know if he will be back.* Caroline wouldn't say it aloud. Leave Lily with that little bit of hope. Hell, she wanted to leave herself with that same hope, and saying the words seemed like tempting fate.

Lily stood across the table, her shoulders shaking as she cried. "Why did this happen, Mom? What did you do to him?"

"Do to him?" Caroline cried in shock. "I didn't do anything to him."

"Then why did he leave?"

"I don't know why. I have no idea what I could have done to bring this on."

"Then he must have done something. Did he do something bad that caused your big fight and you kicked him out?"

Caroline sighed again. "I didn't kick your father out. He made the decision to move out. I tried to change his mind, but he thought this was best. Eventually, I did tell him maybe he should go."

"Doesn't he love us anymore?"

"Actually, I think he does still love us and that's why he's moved out."

"That's crazy. It doesn't make any sense."

"I know, sweetie. But I think he felt he'd hurt us less if he left now instead of causing us pain all the time because of what happened."

"But we hurt anyway. Doesn't he know that?"

"I think he knows."

"And you won't tell me what happened. Why? What is it?" Her face crumpled. "Oh my God, did you find out he has a mistress or something? Is that it? Is that why you didn't want to tell me?"

Caroline looked down at her fingers, clenched so hard and long they were white at the knuckles. She didn't want to confirm her daughter's fears. She didn't want to tarnish Lily's image of her father, even though he'd done what she'd suspected.

"No," Lily whispered. "That can't be true. Not Dad. I don't believe it." But Caroline sensed Lily's denials had no real substance behind them and she knew the truth in spite of her protests otherwise. Kids these days were pretty streetwise by the time they reached their teens. Lily had seen her share of sex on television and in the movies.

"Lily—" But she didn't know what else to say.

Lily looked at her and nodded tearfully. "So it's true, then. Dad has a mistress and he's left us for her."

"That's not the way it was, Lily. I really think he left because he felt he'd hurt us more if he stayed."

"It sounds like you're excusing him, Mom."

"No." She sighed. "No, I'm not excusing him. This is more painful than you can imagine and I'm really, really upset and hurt."

"How could he do this? How could he do this to us?" Lily said, in tears again.

"I don't know. I'm trying to understand what happened. It's difficult because I can hardly think straight. But I do know this isn't like the man we both love. I need to figure out a lot of things."

"I hate him. I hate what he did to us and I don't understand how you can make excuses for him. You say you're not, but you are."

Caroline rose and wrapped her arms around her daughter's thin, shaking shoulders. "Honey, please don't talk like this. Dad hasn't done anything to you. Whatever happened has happened between the two of us and has nothing to do with you. He loves you very much and he told me he wanted to stay for you."

"Then why didn't he?" she sobbed. "Why didn't he stay? Why did this have to happen?"

"I don't know, sweetie. I don't know."

A few miles away, David lay on the bed at a local motel and contemplated the disaster that had been his day. Since he hadn't had anything to eat all day, he'd stopped on the way to the motel for some take-out burgers but could only eat part of what he'd bought. His stomach had rebelled. The TV played something on Fox News but it didn't register.

All David heard was the sound of his own failure thrumming in his ears. All he thought about was the hurt he had inflicted on his family. All he could imagine was the image of his daughter's torment as she slowly became disillusioned with her father and what he'd done to her and her mother. All he could ponder was a future void of the warmth and love of his wonderful family.

He leapt off the bed and paced the confines of the room. He had done it to himself. He alone was responsible for the wreck of his family. What had he been thinking when he made that first fateful step toward unfaithfulness? And the other deliberate steps when he had continued the treachery; he must have been out of his mind. It seemed as if someone else had made all those bad moves, all those irrevocable mistakes. In the past few months he'd become a man he didn't even know.

He'd spent every day fighting those capital power brokers and banging his head against a wall of greed and the damn kid's family influence with the D.C. mob. The stress had led to him spending every night alone in some bar, drinking too much and thinking too much. Talking it out once in a while with another team member helped somewhat. But he shouldn't have let things with Alicia go further than sharing a drink and commiserating over beating their heads against the wall over the kid's Mafia father and expensive lawyers.

David glanced around the room in despair. What had he come to, that he'd wound up spending the night and God only knew how many more nights in a place like this? He had contemplated going to Alicia's place for about half a second, but then he realized he couldn't stand the thought of ever seeing her face again. Another grim task awaited him: breaking her heart, too.

He had to do something. Maybe in the morning he would call Matt into his office and talk to him. Matt hadn't done anything as despicable, but he'd been through a difficult divorce. Matt would at least understand a little of the agony of what he was going through.

Flopping down listlessly on the bed, David tried to watch a news story about unrest in the Mid-East, but couldn't rouse enough interest. It amazed him how little worldly things seemed to matter when your own survival consumed you.

Chapter 5

In her office at Chesapeake Paper on Monday morning, Caroline tried to concentrate on the images spread across her computer monitor. She manipulated three-dimensional models of organic compounds on the screen to study the resulting physical and chemical properties of new mega-molecules, or super-polymers. She used a specialized program to create the designer molecules Lily teased her about.

Instead of designing a new stabilizer for the new coating on a line of fax paper, she stared at the screen in a blue haze, unable to tear her mind away from what had happened last night. She might as well have been watching Donald Trump perform a jig on the screen for all she noticed of her polymers. Finally, she closed the program in disgust. She punched in numbers on her phone and her best friend, Mary came on the line.

"Dr. Thomas."

"Mary, it's Caroline. Have you got a few minutes to stop by my office?"

"Sure. I have to get these coating orders over to manufacturing, but I could come by after that. About fifteen minutes okay?"

"Sure, I'll be here. Thanks."

"Uh, Caro, is everything all right? You sound odd."

"I'll tell you about it when you get here."

"All right. I'll try to hurry."

Caroline waited impatiently, thumping her pencil, eraser over lead, over and over again on her desk pad. She stared at the clock, then thumped her pencil again, then checked the clock again. Twelve minutes passed before Mary came breathlessly into the room. She took one look at Caroline and closed the door.

"What on earth has happened, Caro? Did you and David wreck the boat?"

"In a manner of speaking," Caroline laughed humorlessly.

"What happened to it?"

"Nothing, nothing. The boat is fine."

"Then—"

"Mary," Caroline blurted, "I don't want to tell anyone about this but I need to talk to someone. If I tell people, it will be real, and it doesn't feel real right now." She hesitated, unable to actually get the words out.

"Hon, you can talk to me. You know that. It won't go beyond this office if you don't want it to."

"I know. I'm just getting up the courage to say the words." Caroline gulped in a breath of air and let it out shakily. "David has left me. He had an affair with another woman and now he's moved out."

Mary sat down with a thump into Caroline's guest chair, her mouth open in shock. "Tell me you're kidding."

"I wish I were kidding." Caroline's eyes filled with tears.

"Oh my God. You're serious. I can't believe this."

"Well, believe it. He's gone. He left Saturday night."

"But. . . David?" Mary shook her head. "I can't believe something like that of David. He had an affair? Are you sure?"

"Oh yes, most definitely." Caroline picked up her pencil and started playing with it again.

Mary got up and paced the small office. "This is unreal. David is the last man I would have suspected of being unfaithful. You know it for a fact?"

"He admitted it." Caroline threw down the pencil.

"He admitted it?" Mary asked, aghast. "Was it—ah—just a one-nighter?"

"Oh, no. Leave it to David to do things up right. The affair's been ongoing since winter. He met her on his trip to D.C. for that Mafia case."

"You said he admitted it. How did it come up? Did you confront him? How did you find out?"

"We had a big blow-up on Saturday. Apparently he took this Alicia woman sailing last weekend and she left something on the boat that I found when we were there Saturday."

"He took her out on *Windswept*? I find that hard to believe. That's your family thing, it's both of yours."

"Yeah, well, I guess it didn't mean that much to him."

Mary looked at Caroline's ravaged face in concern. "How are you doing?"

"Not very well."

"Maybe you should go home. You don't have to be here."

Caroline shook her head. "I can't. I can't go home. It's too empty there. I'd rather be here. I don't seem to be getting much work done, but it's better to be here than at home."

"What about Lily? How is she taking it?"

"She's devastated. She didn't want to go to school today, but I made her. I thought it was best. The girl has had a perfect attendance record for the past two years, so not wanting to go today—well, you can see how much this has upset her."

"She'll bounce back before too long. Kids are resilient."

Caroline shook her head. "I don't know. This has really thrown her. She idolizes her father."

"What are you going to do?"

"I don't know that, either. I don't know much of

anything right now. I guess all I can do is deal with one day at a time and hope it works out in the end."

"So you'd be willing to take him back after he had an affair?"

"Well, that's the sixty-four-thousand-dollar question, isn't it? Topped only by the question of whether he'd want to come back to little ole' me after a hot affair with a big D.C. lawyer."

"Oh, Caro." Mary reached for Caroline's hand. "I'm sorry this has happened to you. I wouldn't have guessed in a million years David could do something like this."

"Me neither," said Caroline, leaning back to smile wanly at Mary.

Caroline's phone rang and she excused herself and answered it, "R&D, Caroline Hartford." She listened for a minute. "I'll be right there."

"There's a problem with one of the experimental coating machines. I have to go."

"Okay. Will you be all right?"

"I don't know if I'll ever be all right again, but I'm not going to slit my wrists in the next twenty-four hours or anything."

Mary stood and gazed into Caroline's eyes for a moment as if to make sure she told the truth, nodding reluctantly before turning to leave.

Caroline was kept busy in the pilot coating facility all afternoon. It took all her attention to help the operators nail down the problem with the coater. At least there she felt in control; it was her turf. She was the expert, unlike the shaky, weak-kneed fledgling she'd felt like at home, on Sunday.

It was a good thing she had donned her lab coat and safety glasses before leaving her office, since she ended up standing on a step-stool, leaning into the big machine to adjust the tension on the rollers, cotton dust flying all over. It was messy work, but she loved it.

The light on her answering machine blinked when she got back to her office, a message from Matt Deming. She called him back in his office, at the same law firm David worked for.

"Matt? Caro," she said when his secretary put her through. "What's up?"

"Caro, I'm glad you were able to get right back to me." He hesitated. "I talked to David a little while ago and he filled me in on what happened this weekend."

Caroline was silent for several seconds. She'd wondered what was behind his call. "And you're, what, calling to go to bat for him? Make excuses for his behavior?"

"Of course not. What he did was inexcusable. I called to make sure you were all right."

"No, I'm not all right. I'm going through the motions and trying to pretend my life hasn't been turned upside down. I'm getting by purely on survival instinct at this point."

"That's to be expected for a while. I remember what it was like when Vicki and I split up. Then she decided she didn't want custody of Debbie and I had that to deal with on top of everything else. I remember what it feels like. It's not something you forget. Believe me."

"So maybe you can tell me what to do now."

"Nobody can tell you that. Like you said, you go through the motions for awhile."

"Uh," Caroline hesitated, "how is David?"

"He's not very good either, Caro. A lot of guilt, a lot of pain."

She laughed humorlessly. "Tell him to join the club."

"He regrets very much that this happened."

"What he regrets is that he got caught. I thought you weren't going to make excuses for him?"

A long sigh came over the phone. "I'm not, Caro, but David and I are good friends. I told you what he's going through because you asked."

"I'm sure it's difficult for you being friends with us both. Look, I have to go."

"Wait, Caro. I know no one can do a lot to help you through this, but I also know what it's going to be like in that house for the next few nights without David there. I'm tied up tonight, but I was wondering if you would let me and Debbie treat you and Lily to some pizza tomorrow night."

"That would be lovely, Matt. I think Lily would enjoy it."

"Good. I'll pick you up around six o'clock tomorrow."

"Thanks. See you then."

"Bye. And try not to let what's happened drag you down any more than is necessary."

"Yeah, right. Bye."

A knock sounded on her office door and Caroline groaned to herself. *What now?* Then she spoke aloud. "Come on in."

Mary poked her head in. "How are you doing, Caro? Feeling a little better?"

"Not really. I just got off the phone with Matt and he told me David looked in pretty bad shape, too."

"My heart breaks."

"Yeah, I know, but—"

"No buts, Caroline. The guy acted like a jerk. Let him stew in his own juices."

Caroline pressed her lips together and nodded. "Is that all you wanted? To see how I was?"

"Uh, no. There's something else."

"Nothing bad, I hope. I couldn't take more bad news right now."

Mary backed toward the door. "Maybe I should just go."

"No, stay. I might as well hear the bad news from you as someone else. It's more rumors about layoffs, isn't it? You know I don't listen to rumors."

Mary sat and chewed her bottom lip for a moment. “It’s more than a rumor now, Caro. Well, sort of anyway. The president’s secretary confirmed there was a meeting this morning about downsizing. Nothing official has been sent out yet, but it doesn’t look good.”

Caroline closed her eyes, trying to absorb one more shock. She knew, as well as Mary did, R&D was usually the first place a company cut. It was like cutting off your nose to cut R&D because that meant no new products coming into the pipeline. Which meant a slower recovery when the economy started to improve. It seemed senseless but it was also the way it always happened.

“Any details?”

“Nothing concrete.” Mary replied. “Word is out the cuts will be made according to project lines they do or don’t want to continue.”

“Shit, I’m screwed.” Caroline moaned.

“Don’t jump to conclusions, Caro. Your project has been doing better the past few months. That new filtering dye got rid of a lot of the defects.”

“Yeah, but it’s been in development for two years. We can’t seem to overcome the scale-up problems.”

“Don’t get into a panic. Nothing’s been announced. I just wanted you to hear it from me before someone else said something. Especially when you’re already upset by what’s happened with you and David.”

“Getting laid off would be all I need right now.”

“My project is not ironclad, either. I’ve been having problems.”

“True, but laser technology is hot right now and faxes are old hat with the texting and e-mail wireless technology jumping by quantum leaps.”

“It’s always a crapshoot trying to keep up with the latest and greatest in the marketplace these days.”

"And," Caroline said, "they're more likely to dump a project whose length of development has meant that technology has outpaced the product they're trying to replace."

"Your fax paper will be a considerable improvement on the paper now in use."

"I know, but is it worth enough in today's market to keep up the high cost of development?"

"Caro, you're going to drive yourself nuts by continuing to speculate like this. You have enough on your mind right now."

"I know." Caroline stood and paced behind her desk, dragging her fingers through her hair. "But I don't know if I could handle it if my professional life collapsed at the same time as my personal life. They're all I have."

"That's not all you have." Mary moved to Caroline's side and slid her arms around her. "And nothing has happened yet. Even if it does, they may give us time enough to wrap up projects that are close to completion. Don't give up hope."

"I'll try not to." She disentangled herself from Mary's embrace and glanced at the monitor she'd turned off. "Maybe I should get back to work. If I can find a better stabilizer for my coating, maybe it'll solve the problems they've been having keeping the solutions from breaking down in production. Then maybe I won't get canceled."

Mary backed away. "Don't work too long. You look as if you could use some rest."

"I won't. But I really should give this another go, if what you say is correct. Maybe I can get a jump on this problem and have something to fight with if I have to justify my project."

"Okay," Mary said with a smile. "Knock 'em dead."

"Or at least wound them."

A long time later Caroline looked at her watch. Six-thirty. She needed to head home and spend time with Lily.

David's Lexus SUV sat in the driveway when she got there, and her heart sank. She didn't know if she had the reserves to deal with him now. Wearily, she parked her car next to his and got out.

Once at the kitchen door, she paused with her hand on the doorknob and gazed through the window at the scene in the brightly lit room. Lily was in her father's arms, crying, and David rubbed her back, trying to soothe her. She hated to interrupt them and contemplated going back to the car to drive somewhere for a while, but David glanced up and saw her standing at the door.

His eyes locked with hers and held them for what seemed like an eternity, then dipped back down to his daughter. He murmured to her, and she pulled away from him and turned to glance over her shoulder at Caroline.

She opened the door and stood just inside the room, still unwilling to interrupt. Lily rushed over and threw herself at Caroline. "Mom, please tell him to stay. Please tell him you don't want him to go."

She glared at David over Lily's heaving shoulders. The worn out look on his face told her that he wasn't going to stay and he had probably been trying to explain to Lily. It was Caroline's dumb luck that she'd come home and caught him here before he could make his escape.

She held Lily away in order to see her face. "Honey, I think Daddy feels it would be best if he stayed away right now."

"No, I don't want him to go." Lily stomped her foot childishly.

Caroline looked beseechingly at David.

"Lily," he said quietly but firmly, "I can't stay. I wish—"

"No." With a last, desperate look between them, Lily ran past her father and up the stairs to her room, where she slammed the door.

David sank into one of the kitchen chairs, his face grim and his pallor ghastly. His elbows braced on the table, he let his head fall into his hands.

Caroline's fists clenched and unclenched as anger zipped through her body. She watched his shoulders sag as he suffered. "Not exactly the sort of scene you were picturing when you were making love to another woman, was it?"

He lifted his head and scowled at her. Then he dropped it in defeat again. "I guess I deserved that."

"And more."

"Yeah. Maybe it will make you feel better to know that I'm breaking up with her. I've been trying for some time to do that, but she's been avoiding me."

"Why? Why would you do that? I would think that now that you have a clear field. . ."

"I don't have the stomach for it," he said wearily.

"I guess the pat phrase, 'too little, too late' pretty much applies here."

"Pretty much."

"Tell me," she said. "I'm just curious. If you're not even seeing this woman anymore, why are you still going to leave again? I mean, I'm not sure I even want you back, now or ever. But why would you hurt Lily even more?"

"Because I need to know why this happened between us, why I did what I did." His expression was earnest, but Caroline didn't really care. "We can't put something broken back together again without fixing it first, Caro. This whole thing's completely out of character for me. I have to know how to fix myself before I can offer you anything beyond an apology."

She snorted. "Mary said something like that."

He winced. "You told Mary?"

"She'd probably notice eventually, anyway. Besides, you told Matt."

"Touché." He leaned tiredly back against the chair.

"We both need to know what is wrong with our marriage that made me do something so incredibly stupid."

It was Caroline's turn to wince.

"I can't move back until I'm sure that things will be different between us."

"Unless, don't you mean?"

His eyes evaded hers. "Yes, I guess that possibility must be faced. Unless I think things will be different, it would be best to stay away and spare the two of you the added pain of dealing with my doubts and self-recriminations."

"You're too kind."

He shot her a look, then got up and headed for the door.

"David." He stopped and turned back toward her. "I think it would be better if you limited your contact with Lily to phone calls for the time being. It upsets her too much to see you."

He wrestled with that for a few moments. "All right. For now."

"Have you got everything you need to take with you?"

"It's in the car."

"Good. Then you won't need to come back."

He stood silently, halfway out the door and Caroline tried to ignore the anguish in his eyes. "I won't bother you for awhile. Does that make you feel better?"

"Yes," she lied. And he left. Again.

Caroline watched the closed door for a long time before she turned and sank into the chair opposite the one David had recently vacated. She wasn't sure which had been worse—when she thought he'd left her for another woman or when she knew he'd gone because he didn't know if there was anything to come back to.

There weren't any noises coming from Lily's room upstairs, and that worried her. If only her daughter could get mad and start throwing things, maybe she could vent some of her distress. Caroline dragged herself up the stairs to check on her, and knocked on the closed door.

"Lily, honey, may I come in?"

A muffled, "Yeah" came through the door, and Caroline pushed it open. Lily lay on her back on the bed, staring at the little fluorescent stars all over the ceiling. With the drapes drawn, the room was dark enough to see their glow, under the black light Lily kept aimed toward them. Caroline lay down beside her daughter and watched the stars with her.

After a while, she held out her arms and Lily rolled into them, resting her head on Caroline's shoulder. They lay for a long time like that, taking comfort from each other. Finally, Caroline lifted her daughter's chin with her finger.

"Hungry?" she asked.

"No. I don't feel like eating."

"I know. Me neither. But we have to. We can't just curl up and die."

"Even if we want to?" Lily's eyes were luminous with unshed tears as she looked at Caroline.

"Especially if we want to. How 'bout if we grill some burgers? That's one of your favorite meals."

"I guess."

"Your enthusiasm is overwhelming."

Lily gave her a wry look. "I'll eat a hamburger. Okay?"

"Okay. Good enough."

Downstairs, Caroline defrosted some ground chuck in the microwave. While it thawed, she dragged the grill in front of the garage to preheat it.

She turned on the gas and punched the ignition button several times, but it wouldn't light. "What's wrong with this thing?" she said, frustrated. David always lit it and then came inside thirty seconds later.

"Lily, do you know how to light this grill?"

Lily popped her head out and looked at her, standing with her hands on her hips, glaring at the grill. "You just push the button. No, wait. I watched Dad out here a couple weeks ago when he was cooking those ribs and he used a match 'cause he said the flint on the ignition button was worn."

"Great." Caroline peered at the grill. "Where?"

Lily came over to examine it. "I don't know. On the side somewhere, I think."

"Wait a minute. Here's a little hole. We'll try that. Can you go get me a match?"

"Maybe I'd better get you a whole book."

Caroline threw her daughter a dirty look and said, "Fine. A book of matches."

Lily brought out the matches and watched Caroline turn the gas on, then light the match and stick it in the hole. *Whoosh*! The gas ignited with a whomp and flew up in a huge flame. Caroline and Lily jumped back in alarm.

"Wow," Caroline exclaimed. "I guess there was gas in the lines from when I punched the button over and over and it didn't light. It's lit now."

"Yes, it certainly is." Lily laughed. Caroline realized how funny she must have looked leaping back in shock from the conflagration in the grill, and laughed with her. They both looked at each other and laughed harder.

Caroline left the grill heating and returned to the kitchen to make the patties. She surreptitiously checked to see if her eyebrows were singed, but they seemed all there. Maybe charred a little.

Lily had put some French fries into the oven and now set the table. "I think there are hamburger rolls in the bread box," Caroline told her. "I'll go out and grill these."

The grill was hot by the time she got back outside, and she put the burgers on and stood back to watch them cook. The longer she watched them, the more depressed she became. This was David's territory. He always grilled the meat. It wasn't as if she couldn't do it herself, but it was family tradition for David to do it. He even had a barbecue apron with a silly saying on it.

She flipped the burgers and let them cook, then brought them inside on a clean plate. There were four of them. They would have to eat the other two for supper tomorrow to use up the leftovers.

No, wait. Matt's taking us for pizza tomorrow night. At least that'll save us from eating the stupid burgers two nights in a row.

They fixed their burgers and fries and ate in silence. After about three bites, Lily put hers down on her plate and looked at her mother. "It seems weird eating here without Dad."

"We've eaten without him plenty of times when he was working late or away on business."

"This is different."

"I know it's different. But we have to get used to it."

Lily looked down at her hamburger, her eyes infinitely sad, then she picked it up and nibbled on the edge. Caroline was terribly proud of her at that moment. It was such a small thing—a bite of burger—but there was a wealth of courage behind it. Courage to go on, in spite of how much it hurt. Caroline smiled, and Lily gave her a small smile back.

"You know what? I want some onion on mine." She jumped up and went to the refrigerator. "Want some?"

Lily wrinkled her nose at that. "No, thanks."

Caroline cut a big slice of onion, laid it on top of her burger and bit into it. It almost tasted good. After they were finished, they both cleared the table, even though Lily usually made herself scarce at clean-up time. But they needed to do these things together, these everyday chores that only the two of them were left to share.

"Want me to help you work on your science fair project?" Caroline asked.

"I'm fairly well caught up on it. I don't feel much like working on it tonight, anyway."

"The fair is in two weeks. If you're caught up, maybe you could at least show me what you've done and I can tell you if there are some ways to improve on it. Critique it for you."

"Okay, I guess I could use a good critique."

Soon they sat shoulder to shoulder in front of the computer, and Caroline read through the information Lily had written up for the essay part that went along with the exhibit. "Where did you get this stuff on bacteria? It's good."

"I found it on the Internet. I searched for it on the University of Michigan site. They have all the PhD dissertations ever written on file. Some of them are on their web site."

"Really? I didn't know that."

"All kind of things are on the Internet."

"Well, yeah, I know that, but I didn't know U of M had all the dissertations. You read through them to get this information? I'm astounded."

"Well, no, not exactly," Lily admitted, blushing. "I found a couple dissertations on the subject but they were terribly complicated. I couldn't understand them. I did manage to figure out enough of the abstracts on a couple to get the gist of what they were about. The bibliographies pointed me to some other research that was a lot easier to decipher."

"But still." She looked at her daughter and laughed. "Maybe you're smarter than you look."

"Thanks. I think."

They worked together for a while longer. Caroline finished up the paper after pointing out a few grammatical errors. "You'll need a bibliography."

"I know. That's my next step."

"Do you know how to biblio an Internet source?"

"Oh gosh, no I don't. Just books. I wonder how you'd do it. There's no publisher or date on many of them."

"I have a new reference book on technical writing in my office. I can check it for you."

"Thanks. It's kind of handy having a mother who is a scientist like I want to be."

"Yes, it must be." Caroline was not able to say what she was thinking. For how long would she have the job Lily was so proud of? And had they both cut David out with their constant little projects and esoteric conversations she thought he had no interest in? Had they made him feel like an outsider in his own family?

Lily stifled a yawn. Caroline took note of it and told her, "You ought to turn in early tonight. I bet you haven't been getting much sleep lately."

"Okay."

After Lily was in her black oversized tee shirt that read, 'I See Dark Matter,' and in bed, Caroline stopped by to tuck her in. "Mom, you haven't done this in years." Lily exclaimed.

"I know. But I thought you might need an extra hug tonight." She leaned in and gave her a big hug.

"You're right, as usual. That feels good." She looked slyly at her mother. "But was it for me or are you hugging me really for you?"

"You're too darn smart for your own good sometimes, young lady. And a little too sassy."

"But I'm right, too, aren't I?"

"Maybe."

Chapter 6

Caroline got home late the next night because a production meeting ran long and she needed to iron out some of the scale-up problems. The extra ammunition would come in handy in case they came to her to justify her project. Thus, Matt and Debbie were already there at the house when she arrived.

Everyone was in the den. Lily beat Matt at some Wii game while Debbie cheered her on. Debbie looked up when she came in and giggled, but the other two were too engrossed in their battle to notice her. She sat and waited for the game to end. Matt made some progress toward the end but he was really no match for the quick reflexes of the young. He succumbed with little more than a whimper.

He flopped down on his back on the rug and saw her behind him as he lay there. "Caro," he said. "You've got a very wicked daughter here."

"I know that, but what in particular made you realize it?"

"She's murder with that Wii game thing. Heaven help us if we ever meet up with her in a real-life battle. She's ruthless."

She laughed down at him. "Or maybe you're just a wuss."

He reared up to his full six feet and glared at her. "Hey. I resent that."

She laughed again and noticed the girls grinning at the verbal battle. "I think it's time for pizza. If we let Lily play you again, you might become too emasculated to reach for the check when it comes."

The girls ran for their coats as Matt pulled her out of her chair. They trailed out to climb into his van, the girls in the back to give them a chance to talk. He took them to the Pizza Barn which had tables on one side and video games and other amusements on the other.

Matt and Caroline sat on one side of the table and the girls on the other. Lily stared at her and Matt with an odd look on her face for a moment before Debbie distracted her with the menu. An argument ensued over mushrooms and they were forced to order one pizza with everything and one with everything but mushrooms.

The pizza tasted delicious and it felt almost like being part of a family again to be eating with Matt and Debbie, laughing and talking through a meal. She was grateful to Matt for taking them out for an evening that he knew would be difficult for them. Remembering last night's ordeal, she wished they could do this every night.

Caroline wasn't surprised when the girls gulped down a couple of slices each and then sped off to join some kids they knew over by a futuristic-looking driving simulation machine. Half of their mushroom-less pizza remained untouched. She and Matt lingered over their slices a bit longer to give the girls a chance to spend time with their friends. Even then, she only managed to eat two and a half pieces to his four, and they had some left over.

"Why don't you take them home with you," he suggested.

"We already have leftover hamburgers from last night to eat up. You take the pizza."

He nodded in understanding. "Tough cooking for two, isn't it?"

"From my one night of experience, I would say so, yes."

"What about Sunday? David said he left Saturday."

"Sunday, Lily went to visit a friend all day and we pretended nothing had happened. I think I nuked a bag of microwave popcorn for dinner."

"Ooh, nice. Nutritious."

"Actually, it isn't bad. Vegetarian meal, after all."

He laughed. "I don't think that's what the vegetarians have in mind."

"What do you and Debbie do for supper every night? Take-out? Chinese, Mickey D's, pizza, deli, BK, and then you start over again?"

"Hey, I cook." He looked affronted, then abashed. "Once in a while, anyway. Sometimes Mrs. Kelly leaves a casserole."

"Better than I thought."

"Maybe we can join forces once in a while. We're both in the same boat now, so to speak. Single parents."

Caroline was crestfallen. A single parent. How had her life come to this? She and Lily, a single-parent family? No. She and David were not divorced or anything. She couldn't let that happen. They could still get back together.

Or it could continue like this forever, too.

Her head drooped sadly. "I hadn't thought of it that way."

He covered her hand with his. "Maybe it won't come to that. Maybe David will see the error of his ways and be back in a short time."

She shook her head. "I don't think so. I know this has really thrown him. I don't think he's going to go for a quick fix."

"It's probably best he doesn't. If he comes back, you want it to be for good this time."

Caroline stared down at the edge of the placemat she had been fan-folding and systematically started to tear it into neat little strips. He was quiet for a few moments.

"I called Shelly tonight before I picked you up to fill her in on what's happened."

Caroline glanced up. "Oh, I'm sorry. I should have called your sister myself. I'll call her tomorrow and make arrangements for Lily and me to come down one weekend."

"Shelly would like that. She understood why you hadn't called," he said. "She realizes you have a lot on your mind right now." He hesitated. "She's pretty shocked. You two have always been like an ideal couple to her."

"I can understand that since she introduced us. Everyone is going to be shocked. Hell, *I* was shocked. Weren't you?"

"Yes, although I knew something was going on. I just didn't know what."

Caroline sat up straighter and abandoned her paper tearing. "You knew something had occurred and you didn't tell me?"

"Caro," he said, reaching for her hand again. She pulled it away and he sat back. "I didn't say anything because I didn't know what exactly happened. I only knew David was disturbed about something. Don't you think that if I knew he was having an affair, I would have told you?"

She stared at him, his eyes warm and brown as he leaned toward her again. "I don't know. And I don't think you can be sure, either. It would have been a tough decision for you to make, choosing between your best friend and his wife."

"True, it would have been a tough decision, but I like to believe I'd have opted for the truth. I can understand your skepticism under the circumstances, but you can rest assured I'd have tried to protect you if I'd known for sure he was stepping out on you."

Caroline reached over the table herself and gave his hand a squeeze. "Thank you, Matt."

He smiled back at her. "I don't know about you, but I

think we'd better get these kids home. It's a school night and I think they have finals coming up next week."

"I agree. Let's skedaddle."

"Good. Why don't you round them up while I take care of the bill?"

The girls didn't want to leave, of course, but Caroline dragged them away. She and Matt were waiting by the front door by the time they fetched their hoodies. The girls bickered all the way home in the car about who had done better at the driving game they'd both spent so much time playing. Lily had had one spectacular crash with her fast car while Debbie had driven more conservatively with no bad crashes but had not piled up as many points.

Matt left Debbie off at their house and then drove Caroline and Lily home. She had to wonder why he dropped Debbie off first. But when he got out and followed her into the house, she knew he must want to talk to her.

"I have homework I gotta finish," Lily said. "I'll see you later, Mom. Thanks, Mr. Deming, for dinner." And she ran up the stairs to her room.

Caroline turned to Matt. "Would you like a cup of coffee or tea?"

"Coffee would be nice. I'd prefer decaf if you have it or I'll be up all night."

"I drink it all the time. Instant okay?"

"Is there any other kind?"

"More civilized folk actually brew it by the pot." She opened a cabinet door and showed him her coffee maker. "Some of them even grind their own beans." She lifted the grinder out and held it up.

"I'm impressed."

"You should be. But tonight I'm tired, so it's instant."

She put the cups of water in the microwave and assembled the coffee, creamer, and sugar. When the microwave beeped, she mixed the coffee up and offered one. "Want to take it in the den?"

"That would be nice. After you." He gestured with his cup.

They sat side by side on the couch and chatted for a bit about their kids while they enjoyed their coffee. Then he put his cup on the end table and faced her, picking up her hand. His fingers caressed the back of hers softly and an alarm went off in her head.

"Caro, earlier when I mentioned we could get together sometimes to feed the kids—ah—I would like to do more than that for you." He blushed hotly and undid the top button of his shirt.

"How do you mean?" she asked cautiously.

"I want to help you through this thing with David. I want to be there for you. Spend time with you and Lily."

"David is your best friend. Can you do that?"

His fingers continued to soothe hers. "David is a big boy and he's made his own bed. As fond as I am of him, I know he has to go through this by himself. I'll always be there for him, but I think the best thing I can do right now is take care of his family."

"You're going to take care of us?" she asked doubtfully. "We can take care of ourselves."

"But the next few months will be a difficult time for both of you."

She started at his verbalization of her fears that this would drag on for months, and tried to pull her hand away.

He held it tighter and wouldn't let her go. "Caro, I've known you since you were eighteen years old and I've cared for you deeply all that time."

She jumped away in panic, staring at him in disbelief. "You've—you've cared for me? Deeply?"

"Caro, I've always been devoted to you. You must have known how I felt."

"No, I didn't know how you felt. You never said a word," she stuttered. "And now you think you can move in on me with my husband gone only a few days?" She leapt off the couch. "If you think that, then you've got another think coming."

He stared up at her in horror for a moment, then stood to face her. "That's what you think? You think I would make a move on you? You think I would do that to my best friend and to you right after he's left and you're feeling vulnerable?"

She backed down, literally and figuratively. "Isn't that what you meant?"

"No." He took her by the shoulders and shook her slightly. Then he looked into her eyes. "That isn't what I meant. I want to be a friend to you—a close friend. I want to help you."

Shamed, Caroline's shoulders slumped. He offered her friendship and she'd jumped all over him, accusing him of the worst. Maybe she was in danger of getting too cynical about people after what happened with David.

Matt's fingers gentled on her arms and he lifted her chin with one finger. "You're going to need someone the next few months. I want to be that someone."

He leaned down and, before she knew what he was going to do, brushed her lips with his. Then he turned and left. She touched her lips with her fingers. *Maybe my first instinct was correct.*

No, not Matt. Matt was good, reliable, always there for everyone. He wouldn't do what she accused him of. At least, he wouldn't intentionally.

Caroline went upstairs to check on Lily, and found her already in bed, reading a PD James mystery. "Hi, Mom. Mr. Deming go home already?"

"Yes," she said, sitting down on the edge of the bed. "He just left."

"He's so nice. I'm glad Debbie is staying with him

instead of her mother. Mrs. Deming was, well. . .she was kind of mean."

"You spend a lot of time at the Demings. You must have gotten to know Mr. Deming very well."

"Oh, sure. Of course, most of the time I'm over there, Mrs. Kelly is there, but I see Mr. Deming a lot, too. Like I said, he's nice."

Caroline nodded. "Yes, he is. I've known him a long time."

"You knew him even before you met Daddy, didn't you?"

"Yes, I met him at Georgetown. He helped Shelly move in when we were roommates that first year. He was a couple years older."

"And he and Daddy were roommates, right?"

"Yes. A coincidence, I guess."

"Fate. Kismet."

Caroline smiled at her daughter's romanticism. "I knew Matt for a couple of years before I met Dad and we got along great. We were good friends. But, as soon as I met your father, I knew we were meant to be together."

Tears formed in Lily's eyes. "I hope Daddy comes home soon. I miss him."

Caroline gathered Lily close. "I know, sweetie. We both do." She held her at arm's length. "But you're enough of an adult by now to know that sometimes these things don't work out." Lily started to cry again. "I'm not saying it won't. It may work out, but you just have to be prepared in case it doesn't."

"I want everything to be like it was before."

"It can never be like it was before, sweetie. Too much has happened. It might be good again someday, maybe even better than it ever was if we become a family again. But it'll never be quite like it was before. Change happens, even when we don't want it to. Sometimes it changes for the worst and sometimes it changes for the best, but it always changes. All we can do is hope and pray everything will work out."

"I'll try. I'll pray for you and Daddy to get back together."

"Pray that, whatever happens, our life in the future is better than it ever was in the past."

"It was good in the past, Mom."

"Yes. Yes, it was, honey."

Chapter 7

The next morning, in her office, Caroline called Michelle, Matt's sister. Michelle had inherited the family home in Virginia where she lived with Doug, her husband, and their two kids aged seven and eleven. She worked out of her home consulting in marketing in order to be there when the kids got home from school every day.

"Shelly, it's me, Caro," she said when Michelle answered the phone. "I wasn't sure you would be home."

"Caro, I'm so glad you called. I'm here working at my computer, dying for something to take my mind off Midland Bank."

"Mid-what?"

"One of my accounts. Bo-o-o-ring. Let me just save this and get comfortable."

Caroline heard some rustling of paper and the squeak of Michelle's ancient desk chair. "Okay, I'm back."

"Matt told me he called you and filled you in on what was happening up here. I'm sorry I didn't call you sooner."

"Hey, you've got enough on your hands. How are you doing?"

"Not great, but a little better than I was. Most of the crying and gnashing of teeth is over for the moment, I think."

"I still can't believe what Matt told me is true. David always struck me as a true-blue, all-American, loyal-husband type."

"Yeah, well, maybe this shows us appearances can be deceiving."

"How is Lily?"

"She took it hard."

"I imagine. It must be hell to go through that kind of trauma at the age of fourteen. At least she doesn't know what he did, does she?"

"She knows."

"My God, how did she find out?"

"She figured it out. Sometimes I think kids today are too smart for their own good. A little ignorance would go a long way for her right now."

"You got that right. So, Caro, when are you coming down for a visit? You need Mama Michelle's shoulder to cry on right now."

"I don't know, maybe in a few weeks when things settle down."

"No. Not good enough. How about this weekend?"

"This weekend? But—"

"Look, Caro, think about it this way. Getting away this weekend will give you and Lily a reason to get out of town for a couple of days. Give you a little distance, time to heal a bit, away from David and all the memories."

"Maybe it would be better to wait a little while."

"No, it would be better to get away *now*. You both need a distraction, some fun, something to think about other than what has happened. I think it would be good for Lily right now too, to come and romp with my kids and swim in the pool and forget about everything."

The thought, that it would be good for Lily to see her friends and have some fun again, swayed her. "You're probably right. Okay, you win. I'll talk to her and try to make the arrangements and get back to you tonight."

"Great. Then you can let me know when to expect you Friday night."

Caroline laughed. "You haven't changed. You're still bulldozing your way through everyone's lives, deciding what's right for all your family and friends."

"True," she admitted. "It's a good thing I'm always right, huh?"

"Well, your track record has been pretty good, but I wouldn't get cocky if I were you."

"Wouldn't dream of it. Call me back when you know your plans. I'll be home all evening."

"Okay. Talk to you later."

Caroline hung up the phone. The thought of spending the weekend at Michelle's family's place in Virginia made her feel better already. She spent the morning at her computer and most of the afternoon at a staff meeting. Word came down from above that project managers should compile reports about their projects to present before the directors of marketing and operations. She managed the portion of the project that dealt with scale-up to production. It was the portion that'd had the most problems in the past year. Accordingly, she had assigned some action items to others on her staff so that they could gather together their report by the end of the week.

It hadn't been all that difficult to arrange to spend the weekend away. It wasn't as if they had to consult David's court schedule or anything. Lily had spent the whole evening the previous night working on her science fair project so she could be away from it for two days. It was almost complete and ready for the science fair the following Friday night.

Caroline handed in the needed marketing progress report by noon, and left work a few hours early to pick Lily up from school mid-afternoon. Then they headed south. Lily seemed excited to be getting away on a mini-vacation, and she hadn't seen Michelle's kids in more than six months. They pulled into the beautiful country estate about suppertime and the kids and their dog ran down the porch steps to greet them.

Lily jumped out of the car and hugged Kristi and then Jimmy. Their big Irish Setter, Princess, pranced in excited circles as she leaped and barked. Caroline laughed at the mad display of affection going on, instantly glad they'd come. Score another for 'Mom' Michelle.

As she steered the brood toward the house, Michelle came out on the porch, wiping her hands on an apron. "Caro, you're here. I heard the commotion way back in the kitchen. Kids, why don't you help Lily with their luggage?"

They all tore back to the car, until Caroline stopped Lily with a yell. "Lily, take the keys." Lily turned and caught the neat throw mid-air to the delight of her friends and proceeded to open the trunk.

Michelle came down the steps and gave Caroline a warm hug. "Oh, girlfriend, I am glad to see you."

"Me, too." Caroline hugged her harder as tears gathered in her eyes.

When Caroline's emotions threatened to spill over, Michelle steered her inside. They went arm-in-arm into the big country kitchen where Michelle had dinner preparations well underway. She and Doug kept a housekeeper who came in and cleaned the huge house, and a yardman who took care of the grounds once a week, but Michelle always handled the day-to-day personal needs of the family. She was very good at it and cooked like a graduate of the Culinary Institute.

Caroline sank onto a stool in front of the island and swiped at the tears that threatened to fall. "Oh, Shelly. It feels so good to be here. I need this. I need you. I could really use one of those hours-long talks we used to have in the middle of the night."

"We can have one or as many as you need. Doug planned on helping the gardener dig out new flower beds in front of the house this weekend. He won't miss us if we spend hours talking and walking and riding. And the kids will take care of Lily. I expect 'kid stuff' is what she needs right now."

Caroline smiled a watery smile. “You’re probably right, Shelly.”

“Of course I’m right. Now, you sit right there while I finish up dinner. I have my world famous spaghetti sauce all ready and all I have to do is cook the pasta, put the rolls in the oven and toss the salad with some Italian dressing.”

The big bowl of salad sat a few feet away on the island. Caroline pulled it over to her. “I can at least do the salad while I sit here. Where’s your dressing?”

“It’s in the fridge. I’ll get it for you.” She reached into the monstrous industrial refrigerator and pulled out a jar.

Caroline looked at the jar and shook her head. “Homemade. I don’t know how you do it. The closest I ever get to homemade is Good Seasons. I figure I’m doing well to pour in oil and vinegar and water.”

Michelle smiled. “It’s not much harder than that for me to do it from scratch. The gardener keeps an herb garden in the back. He picks the herbs and I throw them in a pile and chop them up and in they go.”

“Ah, the good life,” Caroline said. “Housekeeper, gardener, pool man.”

“You can’t fool me,” Michelle said. “You wouldn’t trade that high-tech job and the house in the ‘burbs, and the boat on the bay for anything.”

“You’re right.” Then Caroline had a troubling thought. What would happen to material things like the house and the boat? She’d been so concerned with the emotional aspects of what had happened that she hadn’t given a thought to other areas of her life. She loved her house and she knew David would never jeopardize hers and Lily’s lives in their home, which would likely come to her in a settlement, but the boat. . .

She couldn’t even sail the boat alone, although David could. Of course the boat would go to him if it ever came to a legal separation or even a divorce. What good would the boat be to her if she couldn't even sail it?

All the wonderful times they'd spent on the water with *Windswept*. . .was all that at an end as well? *Windswept* was more than a boat to ride on. It was a place for them to be together, to relax and get away from the stress of both their jobs, to regain a sense of serenity, tranquility and equilibrium.

Was that turbulent sail they'd had, a week ago, the last time she'd ever experience those feelings of camaraderie on the boat with David? Would she never again have the thrill of sailing? Not if she could help it, but what could she do?

Michelle had come around the island to lay her hand on Caroline's arm. "Caro, are you all right? You look pale."

"I'm okay, I guess. Another ramification of all that has happened just hit me."

"What? What is it?"

"The boat. What's going to happen to it?" She dropped her head into her hands and groaned. "Oh God, am I crazy? My life is falling apart in front of my eyes and I'm worrying about a *boat*?"

Michelle slipped a comforting arm around Caroline's shoulders. "It's more than that to you."

"I know that. But it just seems shallow at the moment."

"It's important to you. You had a lot of happy times on it and you'd looked forward to many more. Of course you'd feel a sense of loss when that's threatened along with everything else you've lost the past week. Don't beat yourself up over something like that. You're suffering enough."

Caroline rested her head on Michelle's shoulder. "What would I do without you? What are you doing the rest of the summer?"

Michelle smiled. "Summer is wonderful here. I don't think I'd care for Annapolis in the summer. Maybe you could move here."

Caroline looked around the kitchen. "Where can I set up my organic chemistry lab?"

"Yuck." Michelle exclaimed, wrinkling her nose. "Do you think I'd allow those awful chemical smells here in my house?"

"Not all of them are bad. Some of them are quite nice."

"Anything I've ever smelled of yours is bad."

"Esters smell nice. How do you think we get lemon-fresh detergent?"

"You don't make esters and you don't make detergent."

"Well, no," Caroline admitted.

"If you came here, you'd have to work in the garage."

"Thanks just the same but I think I'll pass."

"Suit yourself," Michelle retorted as she moved to the stove. "My water is boiling away here. We'd better get a move on or the troops will be getting restless and then they'll be in here with the dog, screaming for supper."

Caroline shook the jar of Italian dressing and poured it over the salad. The fresh herbs smelled heavenly. "Remind me to bring back some of these herbs from your garden."

"Sure thing. I think he has some early peas and green beans you can have, too."

"That'd be nice, but don't forget I'm only cooking for two these days. Well, at least when your brother isn't with us."

"Is he coming over a lot?"

"No, but he did take us out for pizza mid-week." Caroline tossed the dressing into the salad. "But he says he wants to spend time with us and help us through everything."

"That's nice. I'm glad he's nearby."

"Yeah." Caroline thought about it for a moment. "I'm glad, too."

Caroline helped Michelle put supper on the table and they called the gang in to eat. The meal was a festive affair.

Michelle's kids filled them in on their activities over the past few months and regaled Lily with their plans for the weekend.

"Daddy got the pool cleaned out last week, so we can go swimming," Jimmy said. "I can dive off the diving board now."

"It's not diving you do. It's jumping." Kristi objected. "All you ever do is jump off the end of the diving board and try to make the biggest cannonball splashes."

"Is too diving," he said.

"Is not. You have to go in head first in order for it to be a dive."

"I go in head first sometimes."

"Only by accident."

"I don't mind if he does Cannonballs," Lily said, "as long as he doesn't splash us."

"But that's what he tries to do all the time, splash me." Kristi complained. "Mom, can you tell him he can't splash us?"

"Jimmy, please don't splash the girls when they're sunning themselves beside the pool. If they're in the water, I guess they're fair game."

"Mo-om. He'll get us all wet."

"You'll be wet anyway."

"But our hair—"

"Your hair will survive. If it gets out of hand, we'll deal with it then. But for now, I'm only asking him not to splash you when you're out of the pool."

Kristi pouted for a while but then became interested as Lily described her science fair project to Doug.

"I think she has a good chance of winning first in her grade," Caroline said proudly.

"That's because Lily is soooo smart," Kristi replied, her expression adoring.

"Oh, please." Lily rolled her eyes. "Mom gave me the idea. And I really had fun doing it." She looked at Michelle. "I think Debbie and Mr. Deming are going to go. Debbie has helped me a lot. I wish she could share in the prize if I get one."

"She doesn't go to your school. She goes to Catholic school," Jimmy told her in that matter-of-fact way only a kid could.

"I know but at least she can go and help me out, even if she can't compete for a prize."

"So." Doug turned to Caroline. "Done any sailing yet this year?"

Michelle threw him a glare. He looked confused, as if unsure why his question was inappropriate. He protested, "What did I say?"

"No, Shelly. It's okay." She smiled at Doug. "David and I took the boat out for the first sail of the year the beginning of May. It was a lovely day. I'd missed it during the winter."

"Are you going to get a chance to go out again, the way things are?"

"Doug." Michelle shook her head in exasperation.

"She said it was okay." He defended himself.

"It is," Caroline said. "I don't mind. I have to get all this out in the open." She noticed the kids were watching all this in fascination. "But maybe it would be better if we talked about it later."

They finished the spaghetti and Michelle let the kids take a plate of cookies into the family room to watch TV for a while. After the dishes were done, they had their own coffee and cookies in the living room.

Michelle had left the room much as it had been when Caroline visited while still in college. There were new curtains and a new sofa, but it was still homey. Michelle didn't believe in letting rooms become sterile places no one ever spent time in. Caroline agreed with her.

When Caroline entered the room, it reminded her of the first time she'd met David, when they'd stayed up half the night, talking. It had been the first time he'd kissed her.

She settled on the sofa. It wasn't the one he'd first kissed her on, but a similar style. They'd played Bridge all evening and David had kept his eyes on her mouth and eyes the entire time.

"I'm sorry about bringing up a subject that upset you over dinner," Doug said, and snapped her out of her little daydream.

"It's all right. I need to talk about it. But I can't talk about that kind of thing with Matt because he's such a close friend of David's, too." She sipped her coffee and nibbled on a sugar cookie. "I don't know what's going to happen with the house or the boat or anything else. We haven't talked about it. There hasn't really been time."

"Have you gotten a formal separation?"

She shivered. "No, I don't even want to think about the fact that it might become necessary some day."

"You need to protect yourself. Maybe you should do it now—to protect your interests and Lily's."

"I don't need to protect myself from David."

"Of course you don't want to think of him like that," Doug said kindly, "but maybe you should take legal action anyway."

Michelle leaned forward and laid her hand on Caroline's knee, with a warning look to Doug. "I don't think Caro's ready for that yet."

"Maybe not, but she shouldn't let it go too long if he doesn't come right back home."

Caroline brought a shaking hand to her mouth. "I can't. I can't do anything like that. It would be like giving up. I'm not giving up on anything yet."

"Of course you're not, Caro," Michelle assured

her. "Nobody's asking you to. This might just be a misunderstanding and he'll be home before you know it."

"All right." Doug spread his hands in a soothing gesture. "Just let me make this one point. There are things that mean a lot to both of you that will need to be talked about if he doesn't come home in the next week or two. Like the house and the cars and the boat we mentioned earlier. Who would get the boat, anyway?"

"Don't." Caroline dropped her head in her hands. With a voice barely above a whisper she said, "I hate to think of anyone *getting* the house or *getting* the boat."

"Doug." Michelle admonished.

But Doug drove on. "You both have your own car so that'll be easy and he'll probably let you keep the house, but who'll get the boat? I'll tell you who. David will get it and something you love will be lost to you forever unless you make some kind of time-share arrangement."

Caroline burst into tears. "I don't even know how to sail it by myself." She felt like a fool.

Michelle handed her a tissue. "There, Doug, are you happy now? She's crying."

"I'm only being cruel to be kind," he protested. "Caroline, you could really lose some of the things that mean the most, and I'm only using the boat as an example because it's probably your biggest asset other than the house. Once you realize this, maybe you'll be more apt to get some protection under the law. And if you need help arranging things down the line, I would like you to come to me. I think you're right in that you shouldn't go to Matt. He's too close to the situation."

"All right, fine, Doug," Michelle said. "You've made your point. Now, that will be the last time we mention David's name or the situation between David and Caroline in this house this weekend."

"That's fine with me," he agreed. Then he moved to the couch and knelt in front of Caroline, who was drying her tears with the tissue Michelle had given her. He pulled her into his arms. "We all love you, Caroline. Everything will be okay soon."

"I'm lucky to have you and Shelly." She hugged him back and offered a watery smile to Michelle.

"And Matt," Michelle said. "We'll take care of you here and Matt will take care of you at home."

Caroline was afraid she leaned too heavily on her friends already, and wasn't standing on her own two feet as she should, but she felt too upset to do anything about it for the time being. And it felt too good to let someone else shoulder some of the responsibility for the moment. She didn't have the strength for it right now. She only wanted to forget.

The next morning, the kids donned their swimsuits, while Caroline and Michelle chose horseback riding as a way to work off the huge country breakfast Michelle fixed. Caroline loved riding here through the lush green Virginia countryside at Michelle's and she'd missed that, too.

She only hoped the jostling wouldn't be too much on a full stomach. It turned out she need not have worried. Before they started on their ride, Michelle insisted on brushing down the horses, and Caroline got plenty of exercise before they even saddled up.

It was nice, though, brushing the horses' warm, soft coats and smelling their unique horsey smell. The animals stood quietly in their cross ties, enjoying the pampering and the human contact. They flicked their tails at the flies that tried to light on their short fur and nickered, shaking their heads in response to Michelle's soft words in their ears.

She and Michelle rode for a couple of hours through wildflower meadows. They walked the horses in the forest, cool glades streaked with slashes of sunshine in the darkness, pine boughs whispering over their heads as they ducked the lowest branches. They let the horses lope along country roads lined with violets and wild azaleas. They even spurred their mounts into a gallop across a farmer's pasture. It was exciting and exhilarating; she could see why Michelle talked of never leaving this place.

They circled back toward the estate, several miles from the house. Michelle led the way through a copse of trees alongside a rushing stream. Caroline's heart hammered as she recognized the spot as the one she and David stopped at years ago, the first weekend they met. It seemed a little more overgrown, but she recognized it once they got closer. . .

With Michelle and Matt galloping on ahead, intent on outracing one another, she and David had decided to make the most of a few moments alone.

They'd dismounted and tied the reins loosely to some low bushes so the horses could nibble the grass. He'd led her over to a large tree arched over the rushing stream and leaned her back against it. His hands pinned her shoulders against the tree, his eyes revealing how aroused he was to be close to her again.

"I've wanted to get you alone again all weekend," he whispered. "Shelly and Matt are sweethearts but I don't have any interest in anyone but you right now."

"I've wanted to be alone with you again, too," Caroline confessed. His hands tightened on her shoulders and he pressed his body against hers. She could feel his heart pumping rapidly. The beat matched hers.

"Then let's not waste our time talking," he rasped, pulling her toward him as his mouth covered hers. The heat and excitement were instantaneous, and Caroline felt as if she'd been thrust into the middle of a forest fire. Every thought flew from her head and she became a creature of feelings and nerve endings and heat as his body crushed hers.

They slid down the trunk and sank onto the moss-covered earth beside the stream, his weight settling on her like a warm blanket. She luxuriated in it. His rock-hard body against her own softness made her feel small and protected as his strength overwhelmed her. She could smell the intoxicatingly sharp scent of his aftershave and the earthy dampness of the moss underneath her.

Caroline's arms wound around his neck and she ran her fingers through his short, soft hair, gripping his head to increase the pressure of his mouth on hers. His lips left hers and worked their way down her throat and into the valley between her breasts.

He rose then to look at her with a question in his eyes as he started to undo a button. She weakly protested, her words unconvincing even to her own ears. "I don't—ah, Shelly and Matt could come back."

"We'll hear the horses," he said, working the button loose.

"Yeah, we'll hear them in time to straighten our clothes a little, but can we button all our buttons and zip all our zippers with fingers as shaky as mine feel right now?" She smiled tremulously at him. She wasn't refusing him, but she was nervous.

"All right," he conceded, "but I think I can manage one or two." He grinned with a devilish look in his eyes. He left the first button undone and proceeded to the next, and made the most of his limited access by sliding his tongue into her cleavage and then circling it over her breast.

He came within millimeters of her nipple and Caroline's head fell back as she relished all the delicious feelings his tongue created. She was about to beg for another few buttons but he'd returned to her lips, feasting on them, rising on his elbows to give him leverage as he crushed her mouth.

It was at that moment they heard the pounding of hooves. He barely had time to re-button her shirt and lever himself away, before Michelle and Matt rode through the opening in the trees. There was no way to catch their breath or smooth over the glaze of passion in their eyes.

Brother and sister sat leaning on their saddle horns, gazing at the spectacle of two lovers obviously interrupted in an intimate encounter.

One eyebrow rose as Michelle leaned on the pommel of her saddle. "Would you like us to leave again?"

David yelled "Yes." at the same time Caroline said, "No."

Michelle's eyes sparkled and she laughed, but Matt's eyes shot indignant bits of fire their way. He glared at David.

David's amusement at being caught was tempered by Caroline's embarrassment. They straightened their clothes under the watchful gaze of their two friends and remounted their horses to continue the ride without another word.

Caroline came back to the present with a start when she realized Michelle watched her with concern. "This is the spot where Matt and I came across you and David making out, isn't it?" she asked.

Caroline nodded.

"I'm sorry. I'd forgotten until I saw your face. Let's go on," she urged, turning away.

"No, please. I need to rest. It's been a long time since I rode a horse. I'll be fine. Let's take a break here."

Michelle hesitated. "You sure?"

"Yes, I'm sure." Caroline dismounted and tied the reins to a low tree limb nearest the stream. "It's lovely." She kept her gaze on the sparkling water, watching as it rippled over the stones and soothed her nerves. Their 'kissing tree' was at her back, but she refused to acknowledge it. Michelle came up behind her and placed her arm around her shoulders.

"I love coming here," she said. "There's something about water that calms you." She glanced sideways at Caroline. "But I guess I don't need to tell you that."

"No. I love the water. Anywhere, anytime."

"Maybe we'd better be heading back," Michelle said. "It's getting late and the kids will want lunch. I don't trust Doug with anything more complicated than peanut butter."

"Sure." Caroline turned away from the water. They mounted up and loped back to the house.

Chapter 8

That afternoon, after a lunch of grilled cheese sandwiches and chips and the requisite half hour wait afterwards, Caroline got her fill of water, in the pool with the kids. They had a marvelous time splashing and racing each other in the hot Virginia sun. They even had a cannonball contest. Much to his dismay, Jimmy lost to his mother. Doug joined them late in the afternoon for a few laps after he'd finished his gardening chores.

Michelle and Caroline lay on chaise lounges and watched him swim laps, evading the kids in their attempts to waylay him. Caroline felt blissfully lethargic and decidedly greasy as she lay slathered with sunscreen. She'd almost drifted off to sleep when she heard a car come up the driveway.

A few minutes later, kids squealed, "Uncle Matt, Uncle Matt."

She lifted her head to see him stroll over to the pool's edge.

"Well, this looks like an idyllic scene," he said with a smile, his gaze swinging over to include the ladies lying on their lounges in the sun. "Romping rugrats, gorgeous bathing beauties, and even an Olympic hopeful in the lap lane."

Michelle sat up. "Matt, you devil. You didn't tell us you were coming."

"Just decided this afternoon. I was sitting in my office on a Saturday with the sun shining outside and thinking about how beautiful it must be here. I decided to hop in the car and drive down. Sue me."

"Oh brat, you know we love to have you anytime."

He put his hand over his heart and directed his gaze to Caroline. "Be still my heart. Isn't my sister a peach?"

"You'll get no argument from me there," Caroline replied. "Where's Debbie?"

"Debbie's here. She ran into the house first to change into her suit and use the facilities."

"You look hot," Michelle commented. "You left a couple pairs of swim trunks in the guest room if you need one. Come on out and jump in."

"You read my mind. Be right back." At that moment, Debbie came running out of the house, dressed in her swimsuit, ready to join the fun.

"This is great. A party." Michelle eyed Caroline. "I hope you don't mind Matt coming down. He didn't mention David. I wonder whether he was working today, too." She stopped, realizing what she said.

"You don't have to walk on eggshells, Shelly. I'm fine. It's Saturday and if David isn't out on the boat, I'm sure he's working. He works a lot of Saturdays. Besides, it'll be fun to have Matt here. You have about ten pounds of hamburger and hot dogs and I'm sure there's plenty for two more mouths."

Michelle nodded. "Plenty. Speaking of which, I'd better go in and make the potato salad." Caroline started to jump up to help and she motioned her back down. "No, you stay put and enjoy the sun. I've had enough of it for awhile, anyway. It only takes one to make a salad."

Caroline relaxed against the chaise. "I'm not going to argue. I can't get enough of the sun."

Matt came out a few minutes later clad in a Speedo that looked pretty good on his muscular body. She knew Matt worked out at the company's gym every day at lunch. He'd once told her it was one of the only ways he could stand all the pressure at work. He jumped into the pool and swam a few laps, then he and Doug challenged the kids to a game of pool volleyball.

The kids complained about being outclassed even though there were two adults and four kids, so they made up teams of Matt and Kristi and Debbie against Doug and Lily and Jimmy. It was a ferocious game but Matt, Kristi and Debbie won. Jimmy deserted his father in the second game, for an obvious winner. Ecstatic when his new partner carried them to victory, Jimmy splashed everyone in sight.

The guys made their way around the flying water and climbed out of the pool. Matt took Michelle's lounger, and Doug nabbed the empty one next to him.

She glanced at both of them and shivered. "Ooh, I don't know if I can stand it with all this testosterone floating through the air." She put one hand over her heart and the other across her eyes in a dramatic gesture. "I may swoon." God, it felt good to laugh and joke around with her friends.

"Let me snap you out of it." Matt leaned over her and shook his wet hair over her hot, dry skin.

She screeched and leapt an inch off the lounger in surprise. She opened her eyes to find him leaning over her, water still dripping off his longish hair and laughter in his eyes. "You—you cad." she shouted at him.

"You looked hot," he replied matter-of-factly, lifting her effortlessly off the lounger and snaking toward the pool. "I think you need another dip."

Caroline cringed away from the cold wetness of his skin and suit against her sun-heated flesh. "Don't you dare. I'll never speak to you again if you throw me into that pool." She squealed, "I was almost dry."

The kids jumped up and down, chanting, "Throw her in. Throw her in."

She heard her daughter's voice rise above the rest. "Throw her in, Mr. Deming."

He stood on the apron of the pool obviously weighing the pros and cons of throwing her into the pool.

"Would I do that to you?" he whispered in her ear. Slowly he walked down the length of the pool. "But you do look hot." Before she realized what he had planned, he'd walked down the steps at the shallow end of the pool and she felt the cold water lap at her warm body.

She shrieked and recoiled and in the process almost made him throw her in, anyway. She arched her back to keep her tush out of the cold water, and flailed helplessly, laughing so hard she could barely breathe. When he reached for her wildly flying arms and legs, he couldn't find purchase, and, seconds later, they both ended up in the water in a tangle of limbs. Caroline went under, pinned by his weight as he fell on top and his legs became snagged up in hers. She came up coughing and sputtering.

"You rat. You dirty rat." she screamed. "You said you wouldn't."

"I didn't." He defended himself, dragging himself to his knees. "You jumped and made us fall."

"Oh, yeah. Right. Make it my fault." The kids laughed as they gathered around them in the water.

"Oh Mom, it was so hysterical. You should have seen your face."

At the sight of Lily, happy and carefree, Caroline regained her sense of humor and she proceeded to splash Lily and the rest of the kids as they joined the fray. Matt came to her aid and they pretty much demolished the youngsters, proving once more that adult cunning and deviousness can overcome youth and skill.

The water fight wound down, and Caroline regarded the kids. "You three look like prunes. I think you've had enough water for one day. Out of the pool."

They grumbled and yelled, "Five more minutes." But eventually they filed out of the pool and headed to the house to change. Doug decided it might be wise to head upstairs himself to keep the kids from destroying the place. He followed them inside.

Matt stood with his hands on his hips and said, “Now that you’re wet. . .”

“Thoroughly wet, thanks to you.”

“Thoroughly wet,” he agreed, “but not my fault. Anyway, why don’t we enjoy a nice quiet swim now that the troops have surrendered the battlefield?”

His smile was friendly and open as she thought about it. “Sure, why not? You’re right. I was getting too hot lying in the sun all that time.”

They swam over to the deep end and treaded water while they chatted about Michelle and Doug and the kids. She could tell he was crazy about them. He swam away from her and caught the edge of the pool. “Come on over here and rest.”

She followed him and leaned her elbows on the ledge. “It’s so nice here. So green. These hills are incredible,” she said, looking around from her ground-level vantage point.

“Yes, the view is nice,” he agreed, looking at her.

Caroline glanced back at him. “You’re not even looking at the view,” she chastised him.

“Sure I am,” he grinned. “And the view is gorgeous.”

“You’re incorrigible,” she laughed, hitting the water with the heel of her hand to splash him. He dodged her attack by pushing away from the wall and sinking into the water. He came up behind her and trapped her against the pool wall, his arms surrounding her. She swiveled to push him back but he wouldn’t budge. Her hands just slid off his chest.

Once she’d turned around, she had nowhere to hold onto and not enough negotiating room to tread water. She started to go under. Grabbing his shoulders to pull herself back up only swung her against him. She tried to push away but the buoyancy of the water kept jostling her. She finally pressed his hips with her knees to stop more intimate parts of her from making contact.

Then she groaned as she realized her actions held their own suggestion of intimacy.

Matt hung from the pool edge as if amused by the extent of her gyrations to avoid contact with him, but his eyes went dark with arousal when she finally quieted. Caroline gave him a look of consternation and quickly swung to the side of the pool, grabbing at it as if it were a lifeline on a sinking ship.

He slid closer against her and leaned forward to nuzzle her ear with his lips, whispering, “Don’t protest so much, Caro. You might find you even like it.” His hand maneuvered around her and ran up her midriff to the underside of her breast as his mouth moved to her nape.

Shocked, she reached to push him away again, but he had already slipped away and propelled himself across the pool with a powerful backstroke.

Caroline pulled herself out of the pool and sat on the side, dripping and bewildered, as she watched Matt swim back and forth with a determined stroke. Matt had told her in no uncertain terms he only intended to be a friend to her. But she’d felt his desire.

She hadn’t been intimate with anyone since she and David made love on *Windswept* over a month ago, but she sure as hell knew what an aroused male felt like.

There was no doubt about it. . .he’d been aroused. He certainly acted like someone a lot more interested in romance than friendship. She shook her head. Maybe she was being oversensitive. It had been a long time since she’d been in the dating circuit. Maybe relationships were more casual now and she just hadn’t noticed because she’d been so secure with David.

She returned her attention to Matt, certain he swam to try to work off his frustration. He was also trying to look casual. The encounter hadn't felt casual, though. Not by a long shot.

Finished with his vigorous swim, Matt climbed out of the water and grabbed his towel, snagging hers as well to drape it over her shoulders. He reached for her and slid his hands under her armpits to pull her up.

"Come on, lady. Let's go change before the gang attacks us for a game of badminton or something." He hit her backside with the towel playfully, and before she could even register a protest, walked around her to open the door for her.

In the guest room, Caroline changed into shorts and a tee shirt. After quickly towel-drying her hair, she headed downstairs to help Michelle with last-minute supper preparation. Michelle smiled gratefully at her offer of help and put her to work forming hamburgers.

"So, you and Matt have a good swim after the kids left?"

"Sure. He was right. I was overheated sitting in the sun that long. It felt good to go back in again." Caroline didn't mention the short scene at the end of the pool before they came in. Michelle would probably laugh it off as Matt being Matt, and try as she might to agree with that assessment, a niggling doubt persisted in the back of her mind she just couldn't shake.

By the time the burgers were ready for grilling, the kids had invaded the kitchen in search of food. Shooing them out of her way, Michelle handed out trays of paper plates, glasses and silverware for them to carry to the deck. She gave Kristi a message for Doug and Matt to light the grill.

Lily heard what Michelle said and burst out laughing. "Don't let Mom anywhere near the grill. She'll burn your house down."

Michelle turned to Caroline, who'd turned beet-red. "Oh, really?"

"Hey." Caroline protested. "It was only a small, ah, incident."

"The grill nearly exploded," Lily chortled gleefully.

"I wouldn't say 'exploded,' exactly."

Michelle obviously enjoyed Caroline's stammering protests. Her eyes sparkled with mirth. "And what would 'exactly' mean?" she asked.

"It was nothing." Caroline continued to protest. "I had a little trouble lighting the grill. David always did it before."

"She kept hitting the start button, but it wouldn't light because the flint was worn down," her traitorous daughter volunteered. "By the time she put a match to it like I told her to, it flared up at least three feet high with a huge 'whomp.'"

"Two feet." Caroline protested.

"Three feet," Lily repeated.

"Two. Plus, what's all this 'like I told her to' stuff?"

"Must have been quite a sight either way," Michelle said, still grinning. "It's hard for me to believe a woman who voluntarily climbs into huge pieces of machinery would have trouble with a barbecue grill."

At that point, Matt came into the kitchen. "What's this about a grill?" he asked.

"Oh, for Pete's sake." Caroline threw up her hands in disgust. "Ask them. They'll tell you everything." She stomped out the door to sit on the deck and pout. She felt silly enough about the grill incident. It made her feel like some helpless, wimpy wuss. The last thing she wanted was for everyone to know how pathetic she was without David around.

A few minutes later, Matt came over and sat opposite her with an amused smirk on his face. "If you like, I can come over and start the grill next time you want to barbecue."

He laughed when she swore at him, which only made her even more ridiculous. Sighing, she stood up to get away from his watchful eye.

When the meat was ready, they crowded the deck, gobbling up the summer picnic fare. Lily stuck to hot dogs, having had hamburgers for supper twice already, but Caroline loved hamburgers anytime, especially Doug's. His burger seasoning was a well-known secret he refused to divulge.

Matt joked with all the kids as they gathered around him like flies to honey. He even persuaded Michelle to let them make S'Mores, personally charring each marshmallow to perfection. The kids kept him at work for a long time, making one after another.

Muttering good-natured protests, he turned to the adults. "Do you guys want one? After all, I still have an arm hair or two that hasn't been singed."

Caroline nodded enthusiastically, and when Lily brought it to her she bit into the warm concoction of graham cracker, marshmallow and chocolate with relish. "Mmm. I'd forgotten how wonderful these things are," she said, licking dripping chocolate and marshmallow from her lips. Matt stood to the side, watching everyone eat, but keeping much of his attention on Caroline. Ignoring him as best she could, she took several bites, managing to smear chocolate on her chin in her nervousness. He immediately came over and reached down to wipe it off with his finger, offering it to her.

She pulled back, narrowing her eyes, a frown forming on her face. Shrugging, he lifted his finger to his own lips and licked it off, his eyes laughing but with a whisper of another kind of hunger behind the laughter. That scared her. He seemed to be overstepping the boundaries of friendship too easily and too often.

David sat in the lone chair of his motel room, pulled up to a small, round table. He picked up a tumbler of scotch and took a hefty drink, then winced as the cheap plastic rim cracked and split, nicking the corner of his mouth.

"Shit." he exclaimed, wiping at the small cut with his finger. "Well, that's a fitting end to a hell of a day," he mumbled to himself.

He'd worked all morning and then gone to see Alicia in the afternoon. He'd been avoiding it for way too long, even though she'd left messages for him everywhere. But what he had to do was obvious, and so he'd sucked it up and headed to her place.

Alicia had a small apartment in one of those tall, new buildings made of glass and steel whose design had little to do with the charming mid-century, mid-Atlantic architecture typical of Annapolis. She answered the door dressed in pink capris and a hot pink sequined top.

"Well, lover." She leaned against the doorway, thrusting out her breasts and hips. "I thought you died. Where you been hanging out?"

"Can it, Alicia. We need to talk." He swept past her into the apartment, taking care not to touch her. His gesture did not go unnoticed.

"No need to be rude, lover. You were in that bed as much as I was. I assume, since I haven't seen you lately, and you suddenly show up here, that you want to break up."

"Our affair ended months ago. Besides, if we're honest with ourselves, we never did have anything but superficial sex."

"How can you say that? Call what we had together superficial, you son of a bitch?"

"Alicia, we had nothing in common. Nothing at all."

"We had lots of discussions about the case. We talked for hours."

"That was before we started sleeping together. And we were just talking about strategy and tactics. After we got physical, we didn't do any talking at all. Beyond that, there was nothing. I want to end it."

"You're going back to her, aren't you? Sweet Caroline?" Huge tears started to fall, smearing mascara down her face.

"Actually, I'm not going back to her. Not right now, anyway."

"But you want me out of the way so you can be free to go after her. She has some sort of hold on you."

"Yes, she does. I love her." He saw her eyes flash with menace and took an imperceptible step toward the door. Sometimes Alicia had an uncontrollable temper.

"Well, I love you." she shrieked, as she picked up a coffee cup and threw it at his head. It hit the wall behind him and broke in two. "And maybe I'm not going to let you go." She grabbed a glass half full of some kind of soda and then threw it, too. The glass hit him square in the middle of his tee shirt, spilling its contents over him.

"Alicia, there's no sense in getting ugly with me. I think I should go before one of us says something unforgivable. I don't want to see you anymore and I don't want messages left at my office or on my cell."

"I don't care what you want. Don't think I'm just going to fade into the woodwork. You haven't heard the last of me. Neither has your wife. Or your daughter."

He advanced on her and his finger poked her between the eyes. "You leave my family alone. They have nothing to do with this. You and I are through because there's not anything worth salvaging. Now, I'm leaving."

She screamed profane insults at him and threw more dishes and glasses. How he'd managed to get out of there without a trip to the emergency room, he didn't know. He stood staring at her front door. Stunned, amazed he'd ever been attracted to her.

When the door cracked open again, he fled to his car, knowing there would be no reasoning with her in her present mood and certain he didn't want to try later.

Memories of the dreadful scene that afternoon sent

him back to the glass to take another swig of scotch. Where the showdown with Caroline had been gut-wrenching and wounded him to the core, it had, at least, been civil. She'd cried but she hadn't resorted to violence and profanity as Alicia had. Caroline was too classy for that kind of behavior.

David continued to sip scotch and managed to work his way through three glasses before the pain dulled enough for him to be able to stand himself. That trite, over-used phrase—*what on earth were you thinking?*—played over and over in his head. His affair with Alicia had been so uncharacteristic of him as to be laughable. The few people who knew about it were astounded he'd been capable of such deceit and betrayal.

But there was no getting around it. He had done it. Not just once, but several times. In retrospect, he recalled it as a kind of fever. He'd been worse than a sixteen-year-old kid, lusting over his first crush. He hated to blame it on middle-aged restlessness, but he accepted that element of truth. And he hated the fact he fit the standard profile of a forty-something wife cheater.

For so long, he'd been just going through the motions of his life. Easy enough to recognize and just as easy to let it slide. His life thus far had been the tedium of getting up, going to work and dealing with lowlife criminals all day, coming home and eating supper while Caroline and Lily talked about everything in the world but what interested him. Then, he'd check the news on his laptop while Lily texted her friends and kibitzed over her homework with Debbie. He'd watch a cop show on TV and go to bed. Caroline was usually already in bed with her Nook propped on her stomach. She'd kiss him good night in a friendly sort of way, but her engrossment, in whatever she was reading, often left her distracted.

Other than the times he'd sought rather routine lovemaking with Caroline, the only times he'd really felt alive this past year had been when he and Caroline sailed across the bay, speeding in the sun and wind. He experienced a kinship with her on *Windswept* he didn't in other areas of their lives, whenever they worked hand in hand to control the vast power of the big sloop.

But once the boat had been stored for the winter, a few months later the memory, of the bond they'd shared that summer, dimmed. He'd become vulnerable. And the excitement he'd been missing at home took the form of a lovely blond woman who seemed thrilled to have a torrid affair with a distinguished city lawyer.

David gulped down the last of the scotch as the edges of his consciousness blurred, enough for him to drag his body to bed in hopes of a modicum of sleep.

Chapter 9

Caroline heard the doorbell ring, but Lily streaked by her to answer it and got there first. An attractive, blonde woman stood on the stoop. Caroline peered around her daughter with a sense of dread suddenly descending on her. Instinct told her this was not the Avon lady.

Lily, friendly as always, opened the door wider. "Hi. Can I help you?"

"I hope so," the woman said with a smile that held a bit of a sneer. "My name is Alicia Williams. May I come in?"

Lily started to open the door wider but Caroline put her hand over Lily's to stay the door. "I don't think that's such a good idea."

Lily turned to her with a question in her eyes. "Why not? It's rude to leave someone standing on the porch."

The woman smiled. "You must be Lily. I've heard so much about you. You're even prettier than he said you were. Your father and I worked together in D.C. last winter when he was trying a case, you see, and we got to know each other quite well."

The truth started to dawn on Lily and she backed up, away from Alicia. Caroline put an arm over her daughter's shoulders and squeezed in a gesture of protection and love. "I think you should leave, Alicia."

"I don't think so, Mrs. Hartford. I have some things I intend to say."

"Dr. Hartford to you." Caroline's voice was chilly enough to freeze nitrogen. "You have nothing to say I want to hear." Lily looked at her with her mouth open.

"Doctor. Yes. Well, unless you want to give your neighbors fodder for backyard barbeque gossip, I think you should invite me in."

Caroline glanced outside. Across the street, old Mr. Stevens mowed his lawn and next door, Betsy weeded her garden. *Damn it.* Wordlessly, she opened the screen door to admit her adversary.

Lily's face held panic, and Caroline could hear a plea in her voice. "Mom. . ."

"It'll be okay, honey. But maybe it'd be better if you waited upstairs while the two of us. . .visit."

"No. I don't want to be shuffled away."

"Lily, I think it would be better—"

"This affects me too, Mom. Please?"

Caroline didn't want Lily hurt any more but was afraid it'd be worse if she pushed her out of the way and treated her like a child. Still, against her better judgment, she nodded.

Alicia had been casing the living room and trying to see around the corner into the den. She glanced back at Caroline when she realized the room had been silent for some moments.

"Are you done?" Caroline's voice dripped sarcasm.

"Yes. Your home is quite lovely."

"That's not why you came here, to tell me we have a nice house. Of course, I do wonder why you're here since David told me he'd broken up with you."

"Oh no," Alicia laughed. "We're still quite a hot item. He's been telling you stories."

Lily had been chewing her forefinger and her eyes were full of unshed tears. Her brave daughter tried to confront Alicia, but Caroline caught her arm and held her back. She whispered, "Shhh, sweetie."

Caroline stood proudly, even as a slight tremor showed in her voice. "No, I'm certain David was quite clear. He wouldn't tell me something like that if it weren't true."

Alicia giggled. "Right. Oh, lady. He lied to you about everything."

Lily shook Caroline's hand off and launched herself at Alicia. "You evil, filthy. . ." She grabbed at Alicia's shoulder bag and yanked, pulling the usurper with it. "Get out of our house."

"But I haven't said what I came to say." Alicia tried to pull her purse from Lily's grasp, but Lily was too strong for her. Alicia's designer stilettos afforded her no purchase and she slid on the carpet.

"I don't think this is accomplishing anything constructive. Lily's right. It's time for you to leave. Now." Caroline held the door open.

"All right. I am so out of here. But understand me. I'm going to fight for David. I love him. I can give him things you can't, *Doctor*."

Caroline and Lily both blanched. "Leave my mother alone, you. . .you. . .bitch."

"Do yourself a favor, Alicia," Caroline seethed, "go back where you came from. I'm sure in Washington you can find someone to distract you other than my husband." She placed her hand on Alicia's back, and pushed.

"Yeah. Go on. We don't want you here and my Dad doesn't either." Lily shouted.

Alicia stumbled down the porch steps with Lily right behind her. Staggering in her high heels, her ankles weak and wobbly, Alicia turned and glared. "You haven't seen the last of me. I can be your worst nightmare."

Their two neighbors, who'd been working outside, plus one of the local teens biking by, stopped and gaped at the scene. Caroline slammed the door shut and leaned her back against it, shaking like a leaf. "So much for privacy."

Lily ran to her and they clung together, crying on each other's shoulders. After a while they retreated to the sofa and sat silently, arm in arm, unsure what to say.

Finally, Caroline sat up and turned to Lily. "I want to go to the movies. We need to get out of here and stop wallowing in all this. We need some escapism. Are you game?"

Lily regarded her as if she were insane, but finally nodded. "We can go to a rom com. Dad hates those."

"Good idea. Go online and see what's playing tonight at the multiplex. I'll even buy us popcorn at those ridiculously inflated prices."

The following week, Caroline jumped every time the phone rang, anxious it would be David wanting to know what the hell had happened Sunday when Alicia barged in. There wasn't a peep from him, however, and she was at once relieved he would take Alicia's side against her, and annoyed he didn't call to reassure her Alicia had lied. She told herself she was too mature to call David and complain about the incident, but she feared she was just hiding her head in the sand.

By Friday, Lily was so nervous and excited about the science fair, she begged Caroline to take her to school to set up an hour early and then come back with Matt and Debbie at seven o'clock when it opened to the public. The girl rushed through dinner, eating about three bites. It was useless to nag her about her lack of appetite because she was too excited to eat.

Aside from the Alicia incident, Caroline was upset she hadn't heard from David about the science fair and whether he planned to attend it. He knew the fair was important to his daughter, and she trembled with anger on Lily's behalf. She'd refused to remind him. If it was important enough to him, he'd have phoned and then shown up at the school. On time.

She knew he hadn't called Lily, since her daughter would have made a scene with him about Alicia bursting into their home. Caroline hadn't spoken about it; she was afraid to upset Lily. After Sunday's debacle, Caroline just couldn't handle the stress if she and Lily started fighting. They had to hang together. The whole horrid situation was painful and emotionally complex and getting worse by the day.

Caroline had just finished brushing her hair when she heard the doorbell ring. She grabbed her purse off the living room sofa and opened the door to Matt and an excited Debbie. The two of them looked like a breath of fresh air after what she'd been though on Sunday.

Closing the door behind her, she followed them out to his van. He drove the two miles to the school while Debbie kept up a running commentary about all the fascinating things she and Lily had done to prepare their final table display.

At the school, they followed the crowds to the gym and located Lily next to the first row of displays. She was obviously in her glory, explaining a set of slides she had sitting beneath a microscope to a family with two small, grade-school age children. Her display looked very nice and Caroline took the opportunity to study the booth further.

A backdrop made of three big, heavy-duty poster boards taped together, contained diagrams of the cultures she had grown. The diagrams looked very professional, thanks to Matt's computer. He'd let them use his Excel and Photoshop.

On the tabletop, two microscopes showcased some of her slides, labeled in the order she'd grown them. Another set of slides were mounted on cardboard and individually labeled. They'd included a sheet of calculations with statistical information on the population growths of her cultures. The requisite, ten-page paper accompanied their project.

Caroline felt very proud of how it'd turned out. Lily had spent a lot of time on it and had become extremely interested in the topic. She'd even hinted she might want to become a cell biologist, someday. Of course, Caroline knew Lily would become interested in many more topics before she made a final decision on what she wanted to do with her life. Caroline, herself, hadn't had a clue what her own future might hold, until she stepped into her first chemistry class in high school.

The family left and Caroline stepped up to Lily's booth. Matt stood next to her and Debbie joined Lily in front of the table.

"I am so jealous, Lil," Debbie said.

Lily hugged her friend. "You've helped me so much. I wish you could be here with me when the judges come by." She looked up at Matt as he gazed proudly at his daughter. "Mr. Deming, do you know what a computer genius Debbie is? Look at these diagrams we made. And she helped me write a program to do my statistics for the cultures 'cause we didn't have any statistics programs at home."

"Wow," Matt exclaimed. "I'm impressed. But where did you even learn about the statistics you needed?"

"Oh, Mom taught us all about it. And she brought us a book from work that had some stuff in it. But we didn't have any software to do it and it would have taken us forever to do it by hand."

"Ah, but didn't it take you a long time to write the program?" he asked.

Lily looked doubtful for a moment. Then she brightened. "But we learned something. We learned how to write the program, plus we learned the statistics. See?"

Matt nodded at her youthful logic. "Yes, you're right. It was better that way."

Just then Lily let out a small squeal. "They're coming. They're coming."

"What? Who's coming?" Caroline asked, looking around in a small panic and thinking maybe David would've shown up with his mistress.

"The judges are starting down at the end of my row. You have to go. I have to get ready." She paced back and forth, waving her hands in the air in distress.

"Okay, we'll go." Caroline backed off and Matt pulled Debbie away from the table. "We'll be over there," she said, but Lily was too worried about the judges to pay her any attention. "Just over. . .uh, there." Caroline's voice trailed off and she frowned in the direction of the judges. *They'd better be nice to my little girl.*

Matt led her and Debbie to some of the other displays in the rear of the gym. "She'll be fine, Mom. Come on. Let's look at some of this other stuff."

He pulled at the back of her short sleeved cotton sweater, but she backed away slowly, trying to keep an eye on Lily. "I don't want to go too far. I want to be able to see how the judges react."

Matt rolled his eyes, but left her alone. It took forever for the judges to check every display in the row and, by the time they reached Lily, Caroline was a nervous wreck.

Matt put his hand on the back of her neck, gently massaging out the knots, and then leaned forward to whisper in her ear. "Relax. You're probably more nervous than she is."

"I know. I can't help it. I wish David could have been here."

Matt pulled his hand away and said grimly, "He's not."

"I know," Caroline said miserably. She threw a short glance in Matt's direction. "Did he mention anything about the science fair when you saw him at the office this week?"

"No."

Caroline's stomach clenched as she watched the judges, a man and two women, step up to Lily's table. They made notations on their clipboards after they asked Lily questions. They each peered into the microscopes and one of the women pointed to the diagrams on the backdrop. Lily spoke for a few minutes about them, indicating different diagrams in the sequence as she talked. They nodded and shook her hand, thanking her for taking part in the fair. After a few final notations, they moved on.

Caroline rushed back to Lily's table. "How did it go?" she asked.

"They seemed to be impressed. They asked me lots of questions and I knew all the answers."

"So you think you did well?"

"Yeah. They really liked the thing about discovering the bacteria in my culture after I had a cold. I have no idea how everyone else will do, but I think I did well."

Caroline reached over the table and gave Lily a quick hug. "That's all I care about, honey. That you know you did well and are proud of yourself. I don't care if you win, as long as you tried your best and are happy with your accomplishments."

Caroline took note of a group waiting to view Lily's display, and she gave her daughter one last squeeze. "You have a lot of people who want to see your stuff. After all, this is what you worked for all this time. Enjoy yourself. We'll be around looking at some of the other displays."

"Bye, Mom. Thanks."

As a couple approached and started talking to Lily, Caroline smiled, then turned and bumped straight into Matt. He put his arms out to steady her and her smile faded. "Damn David for missing this."

"She has you here and she has Debbie and me," he said.

"That's no substitute for her father." Caroline rubbed at her temples.

Matt paled. "Right."

"Oh, Matt, I'm sorry. I didn't mean it that way."

"Yes, you did. And you're right. I'm no substitute for David where Lily's concerned."

She grabbed his arm. “Come on. Let’s forget David and case the competition.”

They left Debbie hanging around Lily’s table, and visited the other booths. Caroline kept an eye on Lily from time to time and was proud of the way she interacted with the people who visited her booth.

Around eight-thirty, a murmur went through the gym that the judges were ready to announce the winners. Caroline rushed back to Lily’s table. They stood, hands clasped together tightly, waiting.

The judges announced the seventh grade winners first and then Lily’s eighth grade. They did the honorable mentions, and then third and second place. When they hadn’t announced Lily’s name for any of the other prizes, Caroline didn’t know whether to be happy or anxious. It either meant she'd won first or nothing at all. Then they finally announced first. “And the first prize for eighth grade goes to Lily Hartford.”

The crowd clapped and Lily hugged Caroline while Debbie screeched. Lily looked more excited than she had ever seen her as her glowing daughter went forward to get her trophy. The judges shook her hand and told her that her exhibit was very nice. Lily brought back her trophy and gave it a good looking over, fingering her name on the plaque.

Meanwhile, the judges awarded the prizes to the ninth graders amidst a cacophony of cheers and claps. Lily was still admiring her trophy when they announced, “And now the Grand Prize, for the highest score for the entire middle school goes to Lily Hartford.”

Lily’s eyes widened and she clapped a hand over her mouth. Debbie jumped up and down and the crowd in the gym cheered enthusiastically. She set down her first prize and accepted the grand trophy.

When they handed her the microphone to say something, she looked terrified, but eventually her youthful ebullience took over. “I want to thank my mom for giving me the idea for this project and for helping me whenever I got stuck. And I want to thank my best friend, Debbie Deming, for helping me with the computer diagrams and tons of other stuff.”

Appearing unsure about how to end her speech, she laughed nervously and said, “Well, thanks everybody.” She lugged the big trophy back to her table and set it down next to the smaller prize. From that point on she was deluged with people wanting to see her display and talk about what she had done, so Matt and Caroline watched from a distance. Lily’s generosity, for including Debbie and thanking her for all of her help, made Caroline proud. Her daughter wasn't trying to take all the credit.

After a while the furor died down and Caroline moved back to Lily’s side. Matt stood beside her, his hand across her shoulders companionably. Lily was higher than a kite from all the attention and talked nonstop about her experiences that evening.

Suddenly, she stopped in mid-sentence and looked over Caroline’s shoulder. “Dad! Oh, Dad, you came.”

Caroline shivered and turned to face her husband. Matt dropped his arm from her shoulders.

David, his suit rumpled and his top shirt button undone, approached the table, a little unsure of his reception.

“I’m so glad you came. I thought you’d forgotten.” Lily bounded over to give him a big hug. He sighed and closed his eyes, breathing in Lily's essence. He kissed her on the cheek over and over, hugging her slender body tightly. He never wanted to have to let her go.

When he’d entered the gym, he’d seen Matt’s arm around Caroline and the way he’d dropped it suddenly when Lily noticed him. He knew Matt and Caroline were close friends, but was it really necessary for him to be standing there with his arm around her? And why hadn't Matt mentioned he was going to attend the science fair with his family in any of the numerous conversations they'd had at the office in the past week?

"I'm sorry I'm late. I got held up with a client who got arrested. I meant to be here sooner."

"The science fair is almost over and I thought you weren't going to come. But you did." She excitedly grabbed hold of the sleeve of his suit. "Dad, Dad, you missed it. You missed it. I won. Look at my trophies."

David took in the two trophies sitting on the table and his face broke into a grin. "Oh, Lily, that's wonderful." He leaned down to read the inscriptions on the plaques. "You won first prize for eighth grade and you won the Grand Prize?" He looked at his daughter.

"Yes, isn't that great? I won the Grand Prize for the highest score of the whole school."

"You even beat ninth graders?" he asked, impressed.

"I beat everybody." she exclaimed.

"Well, that deserves another big hug." He lifted her up in the air to swing her around as he hugged her ferociously. "And, I think it deserves a trip for ice cream."

"Oh, that would be fantastic. I'm so hungry." Lily's eyes showed a second of doubt. "We can all go together, can't we, Daddy?"

"Of course we can. I invited everyone." David looked back at Caroline and Matt, standing there, watching. He raised his eyebrow. "Everybody up for some ice cream? My treat."

"That would be very nice, David," said Caroline. She turned to Matt. "Join us?"

Matt hesitated, and David could see he was unsure if he should accompany them. But when Debbie started tugging on his arm and complaining she was hungry too, he shrugged. "Sure. We'll follow you. Peppermint Pam's?"

Caroline nodded. "We'll be there in about fifteen minutes. We have to help Lily take down her display and pack it in the car."

"All right. See you there." He turned and put his arm around Debbie, leading her out of the gym.

David watched him cross the room, jealous of the intimacy he'd spotted between Matt and his wife and daughter. It had been an interesting little tableau he'd walked in on unexpectedly. He didn't like his best friend's arm around them, laughing and nonchalantly chattering with the two of them. *What the hell is going on?*

"David." Caroline said, sharply. "Can you get the other end of this?" She held one side of the tri-fold backdrop and was waiting for him to help her fold it while Lily packed up her slides. He took the backdrop from her, put it under his arm, and grabbed some of the other things on the table.

"I'm going to take a load to the SUV." He turned to Caroline. "Did you bring your car?"

"No, I—ah—I came with Matt and Debbie."

"I see."

He was in a black mood when he carried the load out to the car. Was Matt trying to be a good friend to Caroline or was there more to it? His male instincts told him the latter.

When he came back, Caroline and Lily had everything else packed up. Lily called good-bye to everyone they passed. Nearly everyone congratulated her again on her win. Lily popped into the back seat and Caroline buckled herself into the passenger side. In a sobering moment, he mourned everything he'd caused them to lose. It was his fault and he knew it. He suffered for it.

It seemed such a simple thing, all being together like a family in the car again, but David found himself a little choked up by the time they reached the ice cream parlor. He almost didn't want to get out of the car, but Lily and Caroline were already climbing out and heading for the front door of the restaurant.

Once inside the cheerful red and white striped ice cream palace, they readily found Matt and Debbie, impossible to miss with Debbie wildly gesticulating from a corner booth. Lily slid in next to Debbie and he and Caroline took the bench seat opposite the other three.

Matt reached across Debbie and punched Lily playfully on the arm. “Congratulations again. Did you have room in the back seat for that huge trophy?”

Lily giggled. “Yeah, we managed to squeeze it in.”

Debbie and Lily immediately launched a debate about the relative merits of Triple Fudge Super Sundaes versus Banana Split Ultras. Caroline interrupted them. “You need to eat some real food first,” she reminded Lily.

“But I want ice cream,” she objected.

“You can have ice cream after you have something solid to eat.”

“For Pete’s sake, Caroline,” David retorted. “It’s a celebration. Let her have ice cream.”

“She didn’t have any dinner,” she said, her jaw clenched tightly.

“So? Let her have ice cream for dinner for once. It won’t kill her.” He narrowed his eyes and Caroline glared back.

Lily looked alarmed at the two of them arguing. She put her hand up and said, “What if I have some fries while I wait for my sundae? Would that be okay, Mom?”

Caroline relented. “Of course. That would be fine. But I expect you to order the biggest ice cream sundae they make here.”

“Okay,” Lily said, smiling.

David leaned back in the booth, also more than a little relieved that a serious argument had been averted. He'd felt so guilty for nearly missing Lily’s big night and for not being there for her the last few weeks, he had been ready to go to battle for her. But he hadn't stopped to think, in the heat of the argument, that a small squabble in front of Lily might hurt her more than it helped her. *What an ass I am, sometimes.*

When the waitress came back, Lily ordered the fries and asked that they come before the ice cream. Debbie decided she wanted an order of them, too. They all ordered their ice cream, and Caroline ordered her usual M&M sundae.

Lily laughed. "Mom, you always get that."

"So? I like them."

"Why don't you try something else now and then?"

"Because I like M&M sundaes and this is the only place in town where they make them this good. That's why."

Matt picked up his water glass. "Hey, stop bickering, you two. We're here to honor an incredible new scientific mind looming on the horizon." He raised his glass further. "Here's to Lily, Grand Prize winner of the Annapolis Middle School Science Fair."

"To Lily." They all clinked their glasses together while Lily blushed furiously. David fumed silently and glared at the way Matt casually took over the toast that should have been his privilege.

He turned to Caroline. "What have you two been up to? Anything exciting?"

"Lily and I went down to Shelly's last weekend."

"Yeah. Lily texted me Saturday night and said you were there. That's great. How are she and Doug and the kids?"

"They're doing good. The place looks better than ever and the grass there is greener than anywhere else in the world, I think."

"We went swimming," added Lily.

Debbie added. "And me and Daddy and Kristi beat Lily and Doug and Jimmy in pool volleyball." The French fries arrived and she immediately picked one up and popped it into her mouth.

"You and your dad were there?" David asked Debbie. He glanced at Matt, who met his gaze with a steady one of his own. Funny, how his best friend hadn't told him about spending the weekend with his family.

"Yeah, we drove down on Saturday," Debbie told him around a mouthful of fries. "I was going to go to the movies but Dad came home and we decided we were going to go to Aunt Shelly's. We had a lot of fun. We ate hamburgers and hot dogs and Daddy made us S'Mores over the fire."

"Sounds like you all had a fantastic time," David said, knowing he should be grateful to Matt for keeping his family together but unable to stem the tide of jealousy toward his friend, who seemed to be taking over his role in Caroline and Lily's lives.

The sundaes came then and Lily and Debbie's were enormous. Caroline shook her head. "You girls will never eat all that."

"Betcha we will," Lily snickered.

"Betcha we will." Debbie grinned.

"I'll believe it when I see it," Caroline teased. Sure enough, though, each girl determinedly ate through the entire colossal mass of ice cream, hot fudge, marshmallow and pieces of brownie. David watched in amazement. Matt teased them and told them they'd burst if they ate another bite. David eyes never strayed from his daughter. He needed to drink in the look of her, to memorize her face.

Later, David surveyed the carnage of the empty sundae dishes and smiled. Lily and Debbie rehashed the evening's events, but Lily was clearly feeling the effects of too much excitement. Caroline grabbed for the bill, but David beat her to it. While he took it to the counter, he saw Matt give Lily one more hug before leaving.

David ushered Caroline and Lily toward his car and

they piled into it. He drove to their house and stopped in the driveway. Lily jumped out, but Caroline hesitated, looking at David. "Can you come in for a few minutes after we unload the display stuff?"

He could see by the look in her eyes she wasn't happy, and figured he knew why. He'd been far less than gracious earlier. But what a shock it was, to walk into the gym and see them all standing there together.

Relieved to be invited inside on any pretext, he replied, "I'd like that."

He needed to see Caroline tonight, but it felt odd having her invite him into his own house. He drank in the atmosphere as soon as he stepped inside. It had always been an intimate haven to him, full of comfortable, overstuffed furniture, clever knick-knacks that each meant something to him and his family. He missed it. The motel was more than a poor substitute; it was pathetic.

Lily looked at them uncertainly, but seemed to realize they wanted to be alone. David wished her goodnight, and she headed upstairs as he wandered into the den. He sank into the soft, brown leather sofa and let out a ragged breath. It'd been a difficult evening at the police station trying to arrange bail for his client, and he'd almost missed Lily's science fair altogether.

He relaxed against the warm leather and looked around the room. It had always been his favorite. His eyes lit upon a seascape he and Caroline had found in St. Michael's across Chesapeake Bay, many summers ago. It was a lovely painting, but what made it so special was he and Caroline had both fallen in love with it at the same time.

And he was fond of the ship's lantern on the desk. Caroline had given it to him for Christmas three years ago. He was still thinking those warm thoughts when Caroline swept into the den and impaled him with a hot look as she stood glaring at him.

He sat up abruptly. “What’s the matter?”

“What’s the matter?” she repeated in amazement. “How can you ask that?”

“Because obviously I don’t know what the matter is.”

“Do you mean to tell me Alicia didn’t call you about the incident here?”

“Alicia?” He tried unsuccessfully to shift gears. It seemed he’d been terribly mistaken about the reason Caro had invited him in. And the reason was going to be far worse than he’d feared.

“You told me it was all over between you and Alicia. David, we don’t stand a chance of getting through this if you’re still seeing her.” She stood in front of him with one hand on her hip and the other pointed to the front door. “Because if you are still seeing her, just turn right around and go back out the door and don’t ever come back. Ever.”

“Wait a minute,” he said, rising to his feet. “What the hell are you talking about? I did break up with her. Twice. The first time, on the phone, didn’t take, so I went over to her place and laid down the law. Whatever gave you the idea I hadn’t broken things off?”

“She told me herself, when she was here Sunday night.” Her lips trembled.

“What are you talking about? She came here? You’re not serious.”

“Yes, she pushed her way in and gave us some song and dance about how she was in love with you and was ‘going for you.’ We actually had to push her bodily out the door.”

David felt his stomach drop. “We? Don’t tell me Lily was here,” he pleaded. “Don’t tell me that.”

“Oh, yes. Lily actually opened the door. Neither of us knew who she was at first and, when she introduced herself, I tried to get Lily to go upstairs but she wouldn’t have any part of it. Anyway, after about two minutes we threw her out.”

David hesitated, but it needed to be said. "Alicia can be very vindictive, Caroline. After I called her to tell her we were over, she kept calling and calling and leaving messages at my office and texts on my phone. Even though I ignored every one of them, she refused to believe I wasn't interested anymore. She even followed me a few times. I caught her behind me but I was with colleagues going to lunch, and I couldn't confront her. God knows how many times she's followed me and I didn't notice her."

David could see a tiny glimmer of doubt in Caroline's eyes. He had to convince her Alicia was lying to stir up more trouble and doubts. "When I finally decided I had to go over there to get her to stop stalking me, she went completely ballistic and started throwing things. She's nuts."

Caroline had her hand over her mouth, no doubt realizing how close she and Lily had come to an explosive situation that might easily have turned violent. "Why didn't you tell us any of this, David? Lily. . ." She started to cry.

He took her in his arms. "I'm so sorry. I put both of you in danger. If I'd had any inkling. . ."

He pulled away and faced her, his fists clenched. Then, knees shaking, he sank back onto the sofa and dragged his fingers through his hair. "I suppose you want me to go now. Hell, I'd want me to go."

"No, I don't want you to go. Not yet, anyway. I want to talk about tonight."

David sighed and wearily leaned his head against the back of the sofa. "What about tonight?" he said to the ceiling.

"You can honestly sit there and tell me you're completely oblivious of the tension you caused with all of us tonight when you so belatedly decided to join us for Lily's big moment? You popped in at the last minute and played the hero with her. You deny the suspicious glances? The innuendoes?"

David sighed. "I looked forward all week to seeing Lily

at her science fair tonight and to seeing you again. You want to spoil it by fighting over a few unintentional remarks and glances?"

Caroline stood with her hands on her hips. "I didn't spoil anything, David. You spoiled it the minute you walked into the room tonight."

"Yeah, well, I figured that out pretty soon after I got there. Let's just say I was surprised to see my best friend with his arm around my wife." He threw his hands up in the air. "And for God's sake, will you sit down? You look like an avenging angel looming over me like that."

She sat and turned to face him. "Better?" she said snidely.

"Much."

She took a deep breath. "The first thing I want you to know is that you didn't interrupt anything."

"Oh, and Matt has not been camping out on our doorstep ever since I left, is that right? He didn't spend the weekend with you at his sister's? He didn't take you to the science fair when I should have been the one to do that?"

"You weren't there. And Matt has just been standing by us as a friend."

"That's not the way it looks from here."

"You're imagining things. And you're a fine one to talk. I don't think you have any right to judge me after what you did with that other woman."

David paled. "Okay. I deserved that."

"That, and more."

"I just spent ten minutes telling you how I broke up with Alicia."

"Bully for you."

He drew a shaky breath. "I thought you would be pleased."

"I thought I would be, too. Strange that it doesn't seem to matter, now that you tell me."

He glanced at her, uncertain what she really meant. "When you first found out what happened, I got the impression you didn't want me to leave. Are you telling me you don't still feel that way?"

"I don't know." Caroline sighed. "I know I feel like a fool for even wanting you back. I must have been crazy for thinking it didn't matter what you had done as long as you came back to me. But over the past few weeks, I've seen it does matter. I don't know why I reacted like that at first. Maybe I just felt numb and panic-stricken at the thought of losing you. Maybe now I'm truly starting to realize the ramifications of what you did, of your betrayal of me and of our vows, our home and family. And suddenly it matters. It matters a lot."

David felt so dizzy he was practically seeing stars. Was she telling him she wanted a divorce? "I know it matters. Believe me, I do. And I am more sorry than I can ever make you understand that it happened." His eyes were glued to his white knuckles, clenched together between his knees. He couldn't look at her, couldn't face the hurt and pain in her eyes.

"So, what are *you* saying? That you want to come back, now that I'm not sure I want you to?"

"No," he said forcefully. Caroline gasped, and his head jerked up in alarm. Her eyes were wide and watery and he could clearly see the hurt. The last thing he wanted to do was to hurt Caroline more, but he had to be honest with her if there was any hope of saving their marriage.

He spoke softly. "I'm sorry if that hurts you even more. I don't think I'm ready to come home. I'm still working through various degrees of self-disgust over what I found I'm capable of. If I hate myself this much, how can I expect you to do anything but hate me as well?"

"Well, now I don't want you back and you don't want to come back. What's to disagree about?" Her voice dripped acid. She picked up the pillow on the sofa and hugged it to her chest.

David slumped forward, his head in his hands. He sat like that for a long time, not saying anything.

Finally, Caroline spoke again. "There's something else I wanted to talk to you about."

He turned slowly toward her in disbelief and then he laughed humorlessly. "There's more? I don't know if I can take more."

Caroline took a deep breath, gripping the pillow as if her life depended on it. "It's something about tonight. I want to talk to you about how you treated Matt. He's been there for me when you have not. Lily heard every snarl in your voice. I don't care whether you like it or not, but you need to control yourself when Lily is around. She has enough to worry about with us being separated."

David winced. Up until now neither of them had actually said the word 'separated,' and it seemed official. "I won't have you making things worse than they already are for her," Caroline added.

"I had no intention of hurting Lily and I'm sorry if I did tonight."

"You should be. If you have a problem with Matt and his friendship with me and Lily, please keep it to yourself when she's around."

"Fine. Although I have to tell you I *do* have a problem with it. Matt looked like anything but a friend tonight. If I didn't know better I'd think he's wanted you for himself all these years."

"That's ridiculous. He told me himself he just wanted to be a good friend to us, to be there for us."

"And do you think he would tell you otherwise if he was planning on making a move on you?" As he replayed the night in his head he was even more certain Matt wasn't being entirely altruistic.

"So what if he does? Maybe I would enjoy it."

David gasped. "I don't think you could do it." He knew she was just being defensive, but the thought of Matt with her made him nauseous.

"Why not? You did. And you're not here," Caroline pointed out. "He is."

David leaned back against the sofa tiredly. "Caroline, don't do something you'll regret just to get even or to spite me."

"I'm not planning on it. But maybe, just maybe, I'll find his company is preferable to no company."

He closed his eyes. It was only through sheer force of will he hadn't started crying himself. "I guess I can't stop you at this point."

"No, you can't."

David opened his eyes and looked at everything in this room that meant so much to him, that stood for his family and his home. It was slipping away. Things between him and Caroline were worse than ever after this disastrous evening.

"David?" He turned toward Caroline and saw tears streaming down her face. He swiped at his own eyes angrily. He deserved this. He deserved everything he got.

"What?" He was afraid of what she might say at this point. She could very well end the whole thing.

"I think we should go to a marriage counselor if we expect to make any real headway toward picking up the pieces of our marriage. All we're doing is working at cross purposes."

"I guess I could do that. Let me know who and when." Bone weary, he'd have agreed to anything to get her off his back for five minutes.

"I also wanted to tell you I'm planning to go to the marina tomorrow. It's been a difficult week here and at work and I just need to get away for a bit. It's the one place where

I can always relax. I'm hoping to convince Lily to come along."

"You can't sail *Windswept* alone," he said, puzzled.

"I know, but I can bring a picnic and do some of the teak or something. Just drink in the atmosphere, I suppose–watch the water, this year's crop of ducklings. But, ah, I thought I should give you fair warning in case you were thinking about using the boat tomorrow."

"You mean was I planning to take it out?"

"I need some time, David. I don't think it would be good if—"

"Relax, Caroline," he cut in. "I won't be there. I have to spend the day at the office tomorrow. This client who was arrested. . .I have to do some work on things for him. I may go up on Sunday."

"Okay." Relief shone on her face.

David looked at her for another long moment and then rose from the sofa. She started to get up too, but he motioned her down. "Don't bother. I know my way out. I'm going say good-night to Lily again and then I'll be off."

He didn't have to go upstairs to say good-night to Lily because he found her hunched on the floor outside the family room. Her face pink and puffy, she'd been sobbing quietly.

"Oh, Lily." David scooped her off the floor. Caroline rushed out, too. David held Lily against him protectively as the floodgates opened and she cried her heart out against his white shirt.

"Bring her in here," Caroline said.

David moved back to the leather sofa and sank back down with his daughter in his arms. She buried her face against his shirtfront. "Honey?" he asked. "Were you listening at the door?"

Lily nodded against his shirt, crying harder. David looked at Caroline. What Lily had heard must have devastated her. Caroline's eyes filled with concern for her daughter but there was an element of something else there, too. Accusation?

David's heart sank and he wondered if anything would ever be all right again with his family. He held Lily tighter against his chest and rested his face against her hair.

"Shh, honey. It's okay." He tried to soothe her.

She looked up at him, tears streaming down her face. "How can you say it's okay? It's not."

"We'll make it okay somehow, Lily."

"But you said you didn't want to come home."

"Uh, no. Not yet anyway," he admitted. "But Mommy and I are going to work very hard on getting through this thing in order to be a family again."

She leapt off his lap and confronted him with critical accusation on her young face. "You're going to work hard? How can you guys work hard to get back together if you're not even here? What I don't get though, is why you didn't want to work hard at being my father instead of sleeping with that other woman. She's a despicable person. Why did you want to be with her and not with us? What's wrong with you?" she cried.

David met Caroline's eyes again. It seemed this incident had made Lily grow up much too fast. They never would have heard her make a remark like that a few months ago. It cut David to the core to have his daughter say things like that to him. He knew it was just her anger talking, but it made him feel like the lowest, meanest person on earth.

"And you, Mom," Lily accused, whipping around to face her mother. "You could have forgiven him and let him come back. It's your fault too we're not a family. What did you do to make Dad not love us anymore?"

Caroline started, her face turning ashen. "Lily, I know you're hurting, and I'm sorry. There are adult things going on here you don't understand. Your father and I have to settle this between the two of us."

"No, I count, too. I've lost my Dad."

"We know you count," David said. "I think about you all the time and I know your mom is doing the best she can."

"No, you don't," she reproached him. "Or you'd move back home. If you really loved me, you'd move back here with Mom and me."

She started crying again, and David closed his eyes, so weary he thought he might collapse. After a moment he looked at Lily. "I would if I could, honey. Believe me, I would." His eyes begged her to understand.

"I don't believe you. I'll never believe you again."

Lily turned and ran out of the room, and the heavy thud of footsteps pounded up the stairs. Her door slammed shut and both he and Caroline cringed. Caroline fell into the arm chair and they both sat still for long, long moments.

It wouldn't do any good for either of them to try comforting Lily right now. She was too upset. Later, after she'd had a chance to cool down, maybe Caro could try to talk to her. It was painfully obvious she didn't want to hear a word he had to say.

David chewed his knuckle, his stomach churning and his mind shell-shocked. Finally, he couldn't stand it anymore and he got up to leave. He moved to the bottom of the stairs, staring at the landing in anguish. He didn't want to leave things like this.

"Don't." Caroline spoke behind him. "Give her time."

He turned away from the stairs, then pushed past her and nearly ran out the door. His hands shook on the steering wheel as he started the car.

He hoped there was some scotch left in the bottle in his room.

Caroline heard his car door slam as she sank onto the bottom step. She leaned her forehead on her clenched hands and waited for the trembling to stop. She had to be calm before she talked to Lily. She envied David his ability to drive away and leave the mess that was their lives behind him. The speed with which her life fell apart continued to astound her. What also amazed her was how far they'd fallen in such a short time. They were shouting. They weren't communicating. They couldn't even look at each other without accusations surfacing. They couldn't share a family triumph without hurt and bitterness marring the event. How could it all have unraveled so badly in such a short time?

Maybe it would do Lily good to get away at the marina tomorrow. She hoped she could talk her into it. At that moment, Caroline would do just about anything to re-forge the bond between them.

Chapter 10

Of course, Lily didn't want to go up to the marina. In typical teenage fashion, she wanted to spend the day with Debbie and some of their friends at the mall. Caroline agreed she could go with her friends. At least when she was around them one area of her life still felt normal. With all the upheaval teens faced even in a perfect world, Caroline knew their situation must be tearing Lily apart.

Her friend Mandy picked her up at ten. Mandy's mother told Caroline the girls could come to her house for pizza after the shopping trip. Caroline wouldn't have to worry about hurrying back home later.

Caroline eyed the heavy canvas bag she was packing to take up to the boat. She didn't want to go by herself. She couldn't stand the thought of spending the day alone with her thoughts.

The phone rang and it was Matt. "We've been deserted," he said in greeting.

Her fingers curled around the phone. It was good to hear his laughing, happy voice. "I know. I've been packing for the boat and thinking I didn't want to go alone. Want to come along with me?"

"Thought you'd never ask. When do you want me to pick you up?"

"Half an hour? If you're going, I should fix something better than peanut butter and jelly. We might as well plan on having dinner up there."

"Why don't we just stop for subs on the way?"

"Good idea. I'll pack up some snacks."

"Twenty minutes?"

"Whatever," she said, laughing and hanging up on him.

She was standing on the porch with the cooler and the bag of food when Matt arrived.

"Man, you weren't kidding when you said you'd be ready to go."

"I see no reason to waste more of this beautiful day." Caroline slid into the passenger seat.

The sun shone with a warm breeze off the bay when they stepped out of the van and headed toward *Windswept*. Caroline paused to look at her for a few seconds before boarding. Damn, she looked good, solid and powerful and dependable, unlike anything else in her life right now. When everything changed with dizzying speed, *Windswept* was timeless. She stepped onto the boat and jumped into the cockpit. Matt jumped in beside her and set his small bag of goodies on the seat.

Their friends and slip-mates, Bob and Kathy, were on their thirty foot boat next to *Windswept*. Kathy leaned over the lifelines of her boat to shout, "Hello."

"Kathy, hi. I haven't seen you yet this season," Caroline said, delighted to see her. She waved to Bob, who was taking off the sail cover in obvious preparation for going out on the water.

"We've only been here one weekend so far," Kathy explained. "And you weren't here that weekend." She and Bob were retired and did most of their sailing during the week when there was less traffic on the water. "We came today because we couldn't resist this fine weather. Where's David?"

"Uh, David had to work today, and my neighbor, Matt, said he'd come with me."

"Hi, Matt." Kathy waved gaily. "Are you a sailor?"

"Not hardly," he replied chuckling. "I've gone out with

David and Caro a few times but all I did was pull the ropes they told me to."

"Lines," corrected Caroline. "Ropes on board a boat are called lines."

"See?" he snorted again, holding his arms out in surrender. "Caught red-handed being a landlubber."

"You going out?" Kathy asked Caroline.

"I, uh, I don't think I would feel comfortable taking the boat out without David," Caroline said.

"It's going to be beautiful out there today. It's five or six miles per hour here in the marina." Kathy pointed to their digital meter readout. "It'll probably be ten or twelve out on the bay. Perfect."

"I know," Caroline said wistfully. "You guys have a good time, though. See you later."

Bob climbed back down into the cockpit and started the engine. Kathy waved as the boat started to slide backwards.

Caroline watched them go slowly along the line of boats toward the entrance of the marina and head out to the bay, wishing she could be out there. But at least she was here and it felt good just to be at the marina. A kind of peacefulness had settled over her as soon as she stepped onto the dock.

She pulled the keys out of her pocket and unlocked the padlock on the hatch cover so they could stash their bags. In the cabin, she opened portholes to air the boat out; it was always a little stuffy after being closed up. She dug a novel out of her bag and turned to Matt. "It's so beautiful outside, I think I'll just go up and laze around and read for awhile. Did you bring anything?"

"No, I didn't think to."

Pulling a couple of business magazines out of her own bag, Caroline handed them to Matt. "Want to read these?"

"Sure. I've been meaning to pick this one up at the grocery store," he said, looking at the one on top. "It has a big summary of the last five years' performances of the top one hundred mutual funds."

"Sounds fascinating."

"Top twenty-five Blue Chips too," he grinned.

"Be still my heart." She laid her hand over her chest. She handed him a tube of sunscreen. "Better put some of this on if you don't want to look like a tomato tomorrow."

"Good idea." He took it from her and squeezed some into his hand. Caroline applied her own sunscreen, then collected her sunglasses and returned to the cockpit. Figuring they might as well get comfortable, she pulled out a couple of boat cushions to set on the cockpit seats.

With a long, satisfied sigh, she sank onto the cushion with her back against the boat and looked over the water, her book temporarily forgotten in her lap. "Oh, I love it here," she told Matt as he settled opposite her. "There's something about the atmosphere—the boats, the fishermen, the water, people laughing and having a good time with their families."

Boaters were different, and yet in so many ways the same. It fascinated Caroline.

She watched a big cruiser move slowly out of its slip. Two women, long past the time they looked good in bikinis but still wearing them, prowled the deck. Power boaters often invited bunches of friends, and anchored in shallow spots tied together with other power boats to swim and barbeque.

A few minutes later, a couple of runabouts, loaded down with fishing gear, motored by. A smaller day sailor put-putted along. Crammed with teenagers clad in life jackets, they laughed delightedly at the prospect of an exciting ride. She waved at them.

Matt's eyes met hers across the room. "Are you sure you can't sail this thing? You look like you're dying to be out there."

"I don't know." Caroline wrinkled her nose. "David

said he was sure I could do it with no problem, but I don't feel comfortable trying it alone."

"What am I? Chopped liver?"

"No." She giggled. "But you don't know enough about sailing to be much help."

He immediately adopted an indignant attitude, and Caroline wasn't sure whether to take him seriously or not.

She opted to tread lightly just in case she'd hurt his feelings. "I mean, you could help with the lines and all, but if something went wrong you wouldn't know what to do."

"I'll pretend my feelings aren't hurt," he retorted.

"Seriously. This is twelve thousand pounds of boat. When it gets going, it takes a lot to stop it. And it will do whatever it wants to if you don't know how to do the right thing. Besides, it's always windier out on the bay by at least five knots than it is here in the marina where we're protected a little."

He held up his hands. "I'm convinced. I don't think I would like to jeopardize several thousand dollars of David's money by breaking his boat."

"I'd worry more about breaking your neck."

"You do have a point there."

They both relaxed and took in the scenery for a few minutes more and then retreated to their separate reading material. Caroline fetched them both a fruit drink after a while and they continued to read. Or, at least Matt read. Caroline couldn't settle down to read her book. She kept wishing she trusted herself enough to try going out for a sail. Then she had an idea.

"Matt, let's go out on the water."

He looked up, startled. "What? After you just convinced me we would be crazy to try it ourselves?"

"Not with the sails up."

He raised his eyebrows and looked up at the big mast looming over his head. "Isn't this a sailboat?"

"Yes, of course. But we don't have to put the sails up, silly. We have a motor. We use it to get out on the water and some days we use it to motor around to find a place to anchor out and swim. We could just go out on the water and motor around a little, like a motorboat."

"You feel confident enough to do that?"

"Well, I've never actually done that all by myself either and, to tell you the truth, I've never even backed it out of the slip, but I'm sure I could. I back it when we anchor."

Matt's eyebrow rose still further. "And that qualifies you?"

"I can do it. I know I can." Caroline knew nothing of the kind and, truth to tell, she was terrified, but she wanted to try it. What was insurance for, anyway?

He shook his head doubtfully, but then he relented. "It's your boat, Caro."

"Great, let's go." Caroline snatched the magazine out of his hands and threw it into the cabin with her book. She took two life preservers out of the storage area under the seat and fished around for the keys in her pocket. "Maybe we ought to wear these, just in case."

He gave her a wry look. "This is getting better and better."

With shaking hands, she turned the key and pushed the start button to let the engine warm up. It turned over immediately. She circled the boat with Matt and explained what he needed to do with the dock lines. Then, with a check all around her, a deep breath, and a wink from Matt, she put the engine into reverse.

"Ready?" she asked him as he held the last wrap on the deck cleat that held the boat against the dock.

"Ready," he called back.

Caroline gradually backed the boat up until they had enough steerage to turn. She turned the big wheel like she backed the car, and the thirty-five feet of boat swung in an arc into the small channel between rows of other boats.

Her heart in her throat, she gradually eased forward in the water. She had a short moment of panic when a returning boat appeared in front of her, forcing her to maneuver around it before proceeding out into the inlet that led to Chesapeake Bay.

There were boats everywhere. People had come out of the woodwork on this fine Saturday to take advantage of the balmy weather to sail or cruise. The bay was a madhouse.

After successfully dodging the plethora of water traffic coming into the inlet, Caroline then needed to start dodging lobster pots in the outer portion of the channel. The vast edifice of the Annapolis Naval Academy lay off to their left. She decided to go north since the bay seemed less busy up there. Most of the sailboats went south, where the wind took them. She watched a few that had been in front of them turn into the wind to put up their sails. *Someday, that'll be me*.

Out on the open water, she glanced up the mast at the anemometer cups going full tilt and then at the wind gauge on the bulkhead. Fourteen miles per hour. She'd been right about the wind being stronger out here in the bay.

She looked over and saw Matt leaning against the hatch with his arms crossed and a big grin on his face. "You're enjoying yourself, aren't you?"

He was right. The marina made her relax every time she was there. The breeze caressed her skin and the knots in the back of her neck eased. In fact, she felt great.

She grinned back at him. "Yeah."

"Shall I hoist the fenders and coil the lines, Captain?"

"Aye, aye, Mate. I want this boat shipshape or else I'll hang ye from the yard-arm at dusk." She tried for a serious expression but just couldn't do it. She grinned again.

He looked around. "Where's the yard-arm?"

"I have no idea," she admitted, giggling with glee. "But I'll find something, don't ye worry. Get to work."

"Aye, aye Captain." He saluted.

Caroline headed toward the far shore and made a big circle around the top of the bay, staying only far enough off shore to have sufficient water under the boat for the big keel to safely clear the bottom. Great blue herons stood in the shallows with scores of terns and sea gulls. A family of ducks swam by, momma duck in front and seven tiny baby tails wiggling along after her like lemmings.

After a while they came abreast of the Naval Academy, from the other side. Caroline weaved her way through the parade of boats again and headed down the bay along the western shore. Checking her watch, she reluctantly decided they should turn back. They had been out a couple of hours and it was growing late. She'd accomplished a lot, but she was tired after her long stint at the wheel. She didn't know if she dared turn the helm over to Matt. The boat turned in a big arc as she spun the wheel to starboard.

By this time, dozens of boats that had probably gone out in the morning were heading back in, and the traffic was even denser heading in than it had been earlier. Annapolis was a sailboat mecca, and they were certainly out in full force today, but Caroline handled the boat comfortably with this leg of the trip. She usually piloted *Windswept* back to her slip while David took down the sails.

She told Matt what he needed to do when they docked, and then steered the sloop into the marina and down the line of boats again to bring her home. Halfway in to their slip, she pulled the gear lever into reverse and revved the engine up to bring the boat to a stop inches from the end of the slip.

Matt jumped onto the dock to throw the loop of the aft dock line over the cleat and then ran forward to hold the bow of the boat as he tossed Caroline the other lines.

He looked at her as she straightened, and grinned. “I’m impressed. What a landing.”

She beamed back at him. “I did it.” She did a little happy dance. She leaned out over the pulpit and gave him a big hug. “I didn’t sail the boat but at least I took it out for a ride.”

She tightened and wrapped the deck lines around the cleat on the dock. They stepped off the boat briefly to use the restrooms. After they returned to the boat, they headed below for their subs.

Some quilts she’d brought from home to keep on the boat for chilly nights, were folded on the counter where she’d left them. She carried them forward to store below the vee berth. She shoved them into the locker, and when she straightened to close it, she saw a bright splash of color on one edge of the new vee berth cushion.

God, don't let it be another scarf or hankie or sunglasses case. She climbed on the cushion to see what the spot of color was, and her stomach fell like a rock. Orange nail polish. What was it with this woman and orange? Yuck. The owner of the scarf had spilled or. . .

Who was she kidding? She'd dumped a large amount of orange nail polish on the newly upholstered cushion.

The cushions were not yet a month old and this woman had maliciously destroyed the most expensive one. She'd struck where she knew it would obviously hurt most. Nail polish was one thing that would never come out. Ever.

Caroline seethed. She nearly trembled with anger and humiliation, as if this woman had beaten her by throwing indelible nail polish all over an obviously new cover. She flipped the vee-shaped cushion over so it couldn't be seen as easily. Maybe she could hide it and not tell anyone.

It took a good ten minutes of pacing the cabin before she was calm enough to bring their dinner up to the cockpit to enjoy with Matt. Her stomach churned with the first few bites but she exercised hard-won self-control and managed to tolerate the second half of her sub. She wouldn't let this ruin the remainder of her day.

Eventually, she managed to enjoy their marine picnic. Everything tasted great after they'd enjoyed being out on the water, and they made short work of the brownies Caroline brought for dessert. As she brewed coffee on the propane stove, her eyes kept flitting to the vee berth cushion. Even though she couldn't see the stain anymore, she knew it was there. It grated on her nerves.

Later, relaxing on the settee in the cabin, Caroline tried to put it behind her and, with a new attitude, looked around her at the interior. If she shut out the image of orange nail polish, it felt like a haven, like a warm little home floating in the marina.

"This is nice, sitting down here, enjoying some quiet moments with you," Matt said, sipping his coffee.

"I can never decide which I like best, being up in the cockpit watching the boats and the ducks, or down here in my own private sanctuary, away from the world." The weather had cooled as the day turned into the evening. She twirled the warm cup in her hands, greedily absorbing the heat.

They finished their coffee and dessert and Matt placed their dishes in the tiny sink before returning to the settee and sitting close to Caroline. He picked up her hand and ran his fingers softly over her knuckles. Caroline shivered at his touch, trying not to recoil away.

Matt was important to her and after all he'd done for them, she didn't want to offend him, but neither did she want to lead him on. She regarded him warily.

"Caro, do you remember a couple of weeks ago when I told you I only wanted to be a friend to you?"

"Yes," she said cautiously.

"I have to tell you something about that night," he hedged.

"What?"

"That night. . .well, I lied."

Caroline flinched, remembering what he'd said to her. She tried to pull her hand away, but he entwined his fingers with hers and held on.

"I knew it." she spat out. "I told you that night you were making a move on me but you denied it. What the hell is going on, Matt?"

"Caro, Caro." He tried to placate her. "I didn't lie to you on purpose. That night I meant what I said when I was saying it. I tried to be just a friend to you."

She hesitated, her brows knitted together. She wasn't sure whether to trust him or not. "I don't understand. When we've been together these last few weeks," she paused, and tried to ignore his heart in his eyes, "I've been with you, watching you, letting you touch me. I've realized we can't pretend to be just friends. I thought we could. But maybe I was wrong."

David was right last night. She'd believed Matt when he'd told her she was mistaken about his intentions. But, looking back, she had to admit she'd seen the signs. His attentions had been more lover-like than friendly. She'd ignored all that because she'd needed a friend.

In spite of what she told David last night, she wasn't at all sure she wanted Matt as a suitor. The scene with David the night before had made her want to defy him and turn to Matt, but now, with him so close and his intentions becoming clear, her confusion grew.

Matt brought their entwined fingers to his lips and gently kissed them. "Let me tell you a story, Caroline." He watched for a few seconds before he spoke quietly. "Once upon a time, there was a young law student who went to Georgetown University."

She smiled in spite of herself and he returned it, his voice lowering. "This young man's little sister joined the university when he began his second year of law school. She moved into the dorm and the young man discovered she had a lovely young roommate. The young man wanted to get closer to the lovely roommate, so he spent more time with his sister and found himself falling in love with the lovely roommate."

Caroline's eyes widened and she again tried to pull her hand away, but he held it firm and caressed it with his lips. "The young man was very, very shy and figured if he became good friends with the lovely roommate she would look kindly upon him and realize his love for her."

She softened as his voice stroked her senses nearly as much as his lips stroked her skin.

"Unfortunately, the sister began to get ideas about her lovely roommate and the young man's best friend. The sister thought they would make an ideal couple and began to plot ways to get them together. The young man foiled several of the plots in a desperate attempt to keep the two apart."

Caroline started. She'd had no idea Matt actually orchestrated some of the failures that had kept her and David from meeting for nearly a year. She was also flattered and a little thrilled he'd gone to such lengths.

"Why didn't you say something?" she couldn't help asking.

Matt answered her question in an indirect manner. "The young man acted much more reticently than his flashy friend. His friend, for instance, went on to practice high-powered criminal law while the young man was content with civil law. The young man knew his best friend would sweep the lovely roommate off her feet, but was unable to prevent the meeting from finally taking place, one Thanksgiving. As expected, the best friend and the lovely roommate fell madly in love and the young man's heart was broken. Eventually he married and had a pretty little girl but the marriage was doomed to failure because the young man was still in love with the lovely roommate."

Caroline's mouth fell open. She'd been the one to break up his marriage? Had he really carried a torch for her all these years?

"Then, one day many years later, the best friend broke the lovely roommate's heart by betraying her. The young man, now a little older, couldn't resist taking the opportunity to make a much-belated, but heartfelt bid for the lovely roommate's heart."

There was a buzzing in her ears and, entranced, she could not take her eyes from his as he leaned forward. Leaning forward, he whispered, "I've waited for over fifteen years, Caroline. All that time, I haven't known the wonder of your kiss, the softness of your skin, or the beauty of making love to you. I've needed you and wanted you. It felt like a fruitless fantasy. I've waited long enough. Make my fantasy come true. Let me kiss you, my Caroline."

His lips settled on hers gently, as if afraid to frighten her away. Slowly, they explored hers, warm and increasingly urgent. His fingers released hers to pull her close and they sank down to the settee cushion.

As his lips moved over hers, she responded in a haze of surrealism. He bewildered her with his ardor after his story had mesmerized her mind. Her addled brain kept trying to reconcile this warm, impassioned man with the friend he had been for fifteen years. But he felt good and it seemed natural to be kissing him.

She was still mulling the shift in his status from friend to lover when he rose over her and his lips became more insistent. They hardened on hers, became more eager and heated. She gasped when his fingers slid under her tee shirt as he pushed her back against the cushions. All at once it scared her. It scared the hell out of her.

She broke away from him, panting from the breathlessness of their kiss, and looked into his eyes in a desperate attempt to see some sanity there.

"Oh, Caroline, the thousands of times I imagined this moment in my dreams, it never came close to the reality. You are the most lovely, the most incredible, the most wonderful woman in the world." His mouth swooped down on hers again and against her better judgment she got caught up in his passion once more.

He trailed his lips over her neck and nuzzled her sensitive skin. Suddenly he stopped, propping his head up on one elbow to gaze down at her lovingly. "Let's take a breath."

He helped her sit up and framed her face with his hands, running the pad of his thumb across her swollen lips. She shook her head, her senses coming back to her bit by bit. "I hope you're not upset this happened. I know I'm not. I waited a lifetime for it."

Caroline ran her fingers through her hair to straighten some of the tangles he'd made with his fingers. "You told me the other day you've been interested in me for a long time. You weren't kidding."

"I tried to put it gently. I didn't want to scare you away."

Caroline gasped. "What about now?" She jumped from the settee and paced to the sink to fiddle with the dirty dishes. Anything to give herself some room to breathe. She loved Matt's friendship, but she couldn't bring herself to just give up on David and let him go. She still loved her husband deeply, in spite of what happened between them. Too much remained unresolved between her and David. Getting into a relationship with Matt was the last thing she needed. Or wanted.

Matt came up behind her and closed in on her again, reaching to brush the strands of hair off her neck. "I love you, Caro."

She dropped the glass she held. He tucked the lock behind her ear. "I'm not ashamed of it. I love you now and I've always loved you." Caroline heard him as if she stood in the bottom of a huge ocean. He sounded far away and strange.

She opened the cabinet beneath the sink and pulled out a bottle of dish detergent. "I have to get these washed up before we go pick up the girls." She filled the sink with hot water and soap, grabbed the dishcloth and started washing the glass she'd dropped a moment ago, concentrating as if her life depended on it.

Her grip on reality was slipping, and she had to do something sane or she'd lose it completely.

With a sigh, Matt turned away and packed their things. She braced her hands on the edge of the sink and bowed her head. She had no idea how to react to Matt's confession. He'd blindsided her with it.

She certainly wasn't ready for anything serious with him, which it seemed he wanted. She still hurt from her tumultuous clashes with David, yet felt far from ready to concede defeat, even though she'd told him last night she wasn't sure she wanted him back. But there were two decades of history there and she had loved him almost from the first moment she saw him. History like that couldn't be tossed aside, as much as Matt wanted her to.

Caroline looked at his back as he stuffed his sweatshirt into a bag. He was quite a man. But, then, so was David. They both were. Caroline shivered. What would she do? David didn't want her at the moment, and she guessed that simplified things. Matt couldn't get hurt, though. He had been hurt enough over these past years with his tumultuous marriage and divorce. It would take a lot of care to be sure his feelings didn't get hurt too badly.

A lot of care.

Chapter 11

The next afternoon, David stepped out of his SUV at the marina and strode down the pier. He couldn't wait to get out on the water. His nerves were shot after two long, difficult days, tenser than he'd ever been in his life. The water and the wind and the activity of controlling the boat would settle him down and relax him. It always did.

He reached *Windswept*'s slip and was about to step over the lifelines onto the boat when he noticed the dock lines. They were wrapped haphazardly around the cleat. He knelt down and fingered the line, certain he'd left them coiled. He always left them that way. In fact, he remembered Caroline screaming at him that last day they'd been here because he had taken the time to do it when she'd wanted to have it out with him over Alicia.

Someone untied the dock lines since he'd been here. Caroline must have taken the boat out. He chuckled to himself in amazement. Caroline took the boat out—all by herself. "I'll be damned." He jumped into the cockpit. Throwing his gear onto the seat, he climbed on the cabin top to undo the sail cover and checked the knots in the sail ties.

Square knots. If Caroline had put the sails up and then retied the sail ties afterwards, the knots would have been granny knots. Huh.

Kathy came out of the cabin of their boat and called to him. "Hi, David. Caroline with you? She was here yesterday but she said you were busy."

"Uh, no. I'm here alone. Caroline couldn't come today. Did she take the boat out yesterday?"

"Gosh, I don't know. She said that she and her friend were just going to relax and she didn't think she would go out, but she might have changed her mind. They were gone when we got back in."

"Friend? I thought she was coming down with Lily."

"Lily wasn't here," Kathy said. "I haven't seen her since last year. I'll bet she's grown over the winter."

David had a feeling he wasn't going to like the answer to this question, but he had to ask it. "Was Caroline here with a girlfriend of hers?"

"Why no," Kathy answered, looking bewildered. "Your neighbor, Matt, was here with her. He seems like a nice man."

Reeling, David grabbed hold of one of the shrouds and tried to appear nonchalant. He couldn't believe she had come down here with Matt the day after they'd argued and she'd thrown Matt in his face.

"Yeah, Matt's a great guy. Well, you two have a fantastic day. I can't wait to go out there. Looks like a good, brisk wind."

Actually, it gusted and seemed pretty windy, stronger than he'd ever sailed in single-handedly. But he welcomed the challenge. He only hoped he didn't kill himself.

He felt Kathy's concerned gaze on him as he puttered around, preparing to shove off. She watched him with a troubled expression on her face. After all, Caroline had sailed without him, and today he arrived without her. He hadn't known she had brought another man. He didn't know whether to tell her about his troubles with Caroline, or bail and get out on the water.

He pulled on his foul weather gear and started the engine to let it warm up while he shoved off. Bob climbed off his boat and came over.

"Want a hand shoving off?"

"Thanks. That'd be great."

Bob untied the dock lines and held the boat. David

reversed and started to slide out of the slip. Bob waved him off and Kathy came up from below and waved, too. "Have a nice sail," she yelled.

David waved back and headed out to sea. When he got out in the bay and checked the meter, he realized the wind was blowing a lot harder than he'd thought out on the open bay. He almost decided to turn back, but, feeling reckless, stubbornly kept going.

He headed the boat into the wind and engaged the autopilot so he could go forward and put up the sails. He let out a little bit of the jib, figuring he wouldn't need much. After checking the adjustment on everything, he shut off the engine.

David's hands were full all day with the waves crashing up over the bow. The gusts were variable and strong. The boat heeled over lustily, plowing through the waves. Even so, beating into the wind became an adventure. For the most part the only trouble he had sailing alone was when he tacked the boat, but the autopilot helped. Handling the boat in these conditions gave him a feeling of control that was missing from his life lately. He felt a keen sense of accomplishment every time he successfully tacked the boat. On a starboard tack it hit the waves head-on. When the water crashed over the bow it sent sheets of spray into the cockpit, drenching him from head to toe. Every time it happened, David laughed and yelled in delight at the fierceness of the elements that matched the fierceness in his soul.

Turning the boat around to head back was a humbling experience. He tried to get everything ready, but not surprisingly the boat heeled wildly, forcing David to let the line go entirely. Luckily, when the boat returned upright, he could pull it in properly. Once he guided the boat toward the marina she fairly flew, swishing her way through the waves with the wind at the back, pushing the boat along like a toy.

David was exhausted when he finally returned to the

marina several hours later. But it was a good kind of tired, and he felt more relaxed than he had been for a month. Though his muscles quivered with the release of physical tension, his mind was at ease and he felt happy, at least for the moment. Thankfully, Bob and Kathy were still out on the water. He'd seen their boat across the bay as he'd come back. He was thankful for small favors; he didn't have to talk to anyone or make explanations. Eventually he'd have to tell everyone he and Caroline were separated, but not yet. Not yet.

The entire boat was in disarray. His hands were full just controlling the boat, he'd no time to stash anything properly. It took him a while to put everything away. He puttered for some time and then, reluctantly, left to head for his barren motel room.

Caroline's phone was ringing when she returned from a production meeting on Monday morning.

"R&D, Hartford."

"Caroline? It's me."

Caroline stiffened at the sound of David's voice. "Hi," she said cautiously.

"Hi. I was at the marina yesterday."

"Yes, you said you might go up."

"Yeah. Kathy said you were there Saturday." He paused for a beat. "With Matt."

"Oh, David. Please don't start," she begged.

"I wasn't going to. Honest. I was just wondering something."

"What?"

"Did you take the boat out?"

Caroline didn't answer for a moment. What was he getting at? Did she leave something awry when she left? It had never even occurred to her she might've done something to damage the boat.

"Caro? You still there?"

"Yeah, I'm still here. Why are you asking if I took the boat out?"

"No real reason. I noticed someone wrapped the dock lines around the cleats and I knew I hadn't left them that way. I figured you must have taken the boat out. I wondered, that's all."

"Yes, I did," she answered in a defensive tone. "Did I do something to it?"

"Do something to it? Oh. . .no. No, no, that's not it at all. The boat's fine. Merely satisfying my curiosity, I guess. So you took it out by yourself. That's great."

"What?" she asked, not sure she heard him right.

"I said, that's great. I'm glad you were able to take it out all by yourself. I think it's wonderful."

"Uh, thanks. I wasn't really completely by myself. Matt was there."

"Sure, I know. But he doesn't know anything about boats. He probably wasn't much help."

"No, not really. He enjoyed it, though."

"Did you put the sails up?"

"No, I didn't dare. I felt it was enough for one day to just drive the boat out by myself."

"Of course it was. That's marvelous. You'd never even backed the boat out of the slip, had you?"

"No, I hadn't."

"Were you nervous?"

"Of course. I was a nervous wreck. Matt just stood there on the deck, probably figuring I had everything under control and knew what to do. I was a basket case, though."

"But you did it."

"Yes." Did she hear a note of pride in his voice? She must have imagined it. He was angry at her. But he didn't sound angry.

"Where did you go?" he asked.

"Around. I took it up past the bridge and then down the west side of the bay. So, you were there yesterday. Did you go out?"

"Yes. For about four hours."

"Wasn't it pretty windy on the bay yesterday? It was windy here."

"Yeah, and I almost turned back, but I decided to go for it."

"Wow, it must have been quite a handful alone."

"It was rather exciting," he admitted.

"I bet," she said wistfully.

He hesitated. "I'd have done better with you there."

The lump in her throat prevented her from responding, and her chest hurt. He had to ask her again if she was still there.

She didn't dare let him know how much it bothered her not being there to share his day with him. "I'm here," she finally managed to say. "It's not my fault we weren't together yesterday, David."

"No." She could hear his regret over the phone. "I know all this has been my doing. I'm not likely to forget it."

"Is there anything else, David? I have to get going here," she said, pushing some papers around the desk.

"Ok, I'll let you go. I just wanted to make sure you knew I was proud of you for doing that. It's a big step for you."

The lump, still in her throat, felt larger. "Thanks," she croaked.

"Oh, and Caroline. Next time put the sails up."

"I—I can't."

"Yes, you can."

He hung up and she was left staring at the phone. She slowly returned it to its cradle and sat gazing into space. He'd called to tell her he was proud of her. She tried to swallow. He was proud she'd taken the boat out without him, even though she hadn't even put the sails up. Question was, would he still have been proud of her when she lay stretched out along the settee, being kissed passionately by his best friend?

David stared at his phone after he broke the connection. Sailing solo yesterday had been a real challenge, but there was no doubt in his mind he would rather have gone with Caroline. They were a team. He wondered if she thought along the same lines.

Probably not. She'd reminded him he was the one who broke up their team when he told her he'd missed her.

He heard a noise and looked up to see Matt standing inside the doorway with his hands in his pockets. David groaned. Not really in the mood to stir things up with his good ole' friend Matt. "What is it?" he growled.

"I think we should talk about Caroline. Do you want to break for lunch so we can have a talk?"

"I don't think it's such a hot idea for us to have lunch together right now."

"Why not? We do it all the time."

"Not lately. I think it would hurt my digestion if I ate lunch with you today."

"Bad weekend?" Matt sneered.

David glared at him. "Why don't you say what you really want to say, right here, and get it over with?"

"Are you sure you want to do it here in your office?"

"Just close the door. It's probably better to talk this out in private."

"Maybe you're right." Matt closed and locked the door. David's eyebrow went up at the audacity, but it might be a good idea to have it locked in case his secretary tried to open the door at an inopportune moment.

"You don't have a gun in your pocket, do you?" he said, only half joking.

"No. Not this time. Maybe later." Matt took the chair opposite David's. "I spent the day at the marina with Caroline on Saturday."

"I know."

"You knew?" Matt said in surprise. "Who told you?"

"Kathy."

"Right," Matt said, nodding. "The gal in the boat next to yours. Nice lady."

"Yes, she is. What's this about, Matt?"

"I'm getting to it. Like I said, I went to the marina with Caroline. We had a great time. She took the boat out."

"I know."

"You knew that too? Wow, you're practically a one-man detective agency."

"I figured it out first by myself." He explained about the Flemish coils. "But then Caroline confirmed it a few minutes ago when I talked to her."

"You talked to Caroline?" Matt appeared obviously disconcerted the conversation wasn't going the way he wanted it to.

"Yes, I did." David was rapidly losing what little patience he'd had when Matt came into his office. "Something else you wanted to say?"

Matt shifted in his chair. "Well, anyway, we went out on the water and took a ride for a couple hours. It was a beautiful day."

David waited, wondering what he was getting at.

"And then, after we got back, we had dinner."

Was there a point to this? David was wondering.

"And then I kissed her."

That got his attention. "You what?" he thundered, bolting out of his chair.

"She seemed to like it. We went at it for quite some time." Matt plowed on.

David couldn't believe his ears. It was surreal, hearing

his best friend calmly telling him, right here in his own office, that he had kissed his wife. He was furious.

"I'm telling you this because I want you to know, up front, that I'm going to go after Caroline." Matt's eyes hardened and he didn't look unsure anymore.

"You're 'going after her?'" David's voice echoed his incredulity. "What the hell does that even mean, Matt?"

"Sixteen years ago, I yielded to you because Caroline fell in love with you right from the first and I wanted her to be happy. But she's not happy with you now, David, so I'm planning to make her happy myself."

"Sixteen years ago? And what do you mean, you yielded to me? You've nursed feelings for her all this time? I can't believe this." David strode around his desk and turned back to face Matt. "You have a lot of nerve—"

He grabbed Matt by the lapels of his expensive suit and thought seriously about hitting him.

"Yeah, I have nerve," Matt retorted, leaping to his feet, nose to nose with David. "I have the nerve I should have had a long time ago."

They backed away from each other until they stood a few feet apart, measuring each other up. Each knew the other as well as he knew himself. But nothing like this had ever come up between them.

"Why are you telling me this?" David crossed his arms over his chest. "Why not just go about your business, seducing my wife behind my back?"

"Because I want to be fair."

"You think it's fair for you to be making plans to take *my* place in *my* home, in *my* bed with *my* wife?"

"You're separated from her."

"Not legally."

"I can take care of that," Matt replied, raising his eyebrows.

David's anger had been escalating as the conversation

went on. Suddenly, he snapped and charged Matt with an uppercut that landed on his cheekbone, sending Matt flying backward against the door.

"You leave yourself out of our affairs," David shouted at Matt, who seemed to be trying to keep himself from sliding to the floor. David was shaking and visibly trying to control himself. It wasn't the time or the place to deal with this, but he was too furious to really care what anyone heard or thought.

"I have been doing, and will continue to do, whatever is best for Caroline." Matt rose, his palm covering his rapidly swelling cheek.

"If you sleep with her, I'll kill you."

"If that's what she wants, I'm not going to refuse her."

"I think you should go before I do something more than leave a mark on your face," David snapped, trying to keep his voice down. "Now get the hell out of my office."

Gingerly, Matt felt the cut on his swollen cheek, glared at David for a few moments, then silently left.

There goes a beautiful friendship. David swiveled and stared out his window. He needed to calm down, but he was ready to spit nails. He still couldn't believe Matt had the nerve to come in here and say those things to him. He also couldn't believe he'd actually hit him. Never in a million years had he imagined something like this could happen.

Strangely, he believed Matt intended to remain honest about his intentions toward Caroline. Matt was that kind of guy, which was one of the reasons he'd been David's best friend. They'd known each other for more than twenty years. He idly wondered how many other friendships had been lost down the years for the love of a beautiful woman.

Something else he couldn't help running through his head was whether Matt actually stood a chance with Caroline. He said they had kissed for a long time. Had he exaggerated?

The thought of Caroline and Matt in a long, steamy clinch made his skin crawl. He couldn't let it happen.

Maybe he should just return to Caroline right now. To hell with all his self-doubts and soul-searching. He couldn't afford such luxuries if it meant Matt might steal her from under his nose while he vacillated. But she'd said she didn't want him back. She might want him even less after having a warm and fuzzy evening with Matt.

On the other hand, maybe she'd be better off with Matt.

What the hell did he do with his flask of bourbon? He fished it out of the bottom drawer and took a couple of quick gulps out of the bottle, growing angrier and angrier with each slug.

"Shit," he cursed, picking up his paperweight and flinging it. It hit the far wall with a thud and left a hole the size of a baseball in the sheetrock.

How was he going to explain *that* to his partners?

Caroline looked at the phone for the hundredth time, trying to find a reason to call David back. "Oh. I meant to tell him the date and time of our first meeting with the marriage counselor." She called him right back but had to leave a message with his secretary, who said he'd just left for court.

Caroline's phone rang again and she just stared at it for a minute. She still reeled from her conversation with David. If it concerned work, though, she couldn't afford to ignore it.

"Caroline? Matt."

"Matt?" she asked, still distracted from David's phone call. "Matt," she repeated more surely. "What can I do for you?"

"It's not what you can do for me, it's what I can do for you."

"And that is?" She couldn't help the note of impatience in her voice, but Matt didn't seem to notice.

"Wednesday is the last day of school for the girls, right?"

"Yes."

"Have you and Lily made any plans to celebrate her first day of freedom for the summer?"

She and Lily hadn't made any plans for anything the past two days, beyond how to keep out of each other's way. "No, we don't have any plans."

"Good. Why don't you two come over to my house and I'll barbecue up some chicken?"

"You know how to barbecue chicken?" She knew she sounded like an idiot but her brain staunchly refused to work at the moment.

"I've been on my own for nearly ten years. Of course, I know how to barbecue chicken. Do you?"

Caroline chuckled. "You've eaten my barbecued chicken. Several times."

"Oh right. So, do you want to come over Wednesday night for a cookout?"

"Sure. We'd love to. Maybe with other people there, Lily will actually speak to me."

"Why? What's the matter?"

"It's complicated," she hedged. "We'll talk about it then. What can I bring?"

"Some kind of salad?"

"Salad is fine. How about cole slaw? Cole slaw is good with grilled chicken."

"Great. See you about six?"

"That's fine. See you then." When she hung up, she realized she felt better. She always felt better after talking to Matt. When she talked to David there was tension and so much emotional baggage to deal with that she often ended up feeling worse.

But Matt was uncomplicated. It didn't take as many

emotional reserves to have a conversation with him. The question that begged to be answered: was that good or bad?

Caroline looked up as Mary came into her office. She could tell immediately something was wrong. "What is it?"

"It's happening. We just got a letter. They're laying off four hundred employees today."

"Letter? I didn't get any letter."

"It's probably on its way."

Just then, the department secretary stuck her head into Caroline's office and handed her an envelope. Caroline dropped it onto her desk and stared at it as if she expected it to explode or something. "I don't want to open it. What does it say?"

"It says they regret to inform us, yada, yada, yada. Then it says managers will begin calling in employees to notify them of their termination, starting at ten. Employees are asked to go with their managers to Human Resources where special stations have been set up to explain severance packages and a training and job center put together for helping former employees find other work."

Caroline's forehead sank onto her palm. "Oh my God."

"How do you think it really looks for you?" Mary took the chair opposite Caroline.

"I don't know. I've given them reams of material, including some tests last week that look promising to solve that solution stability problem, but I think it could go either way. What about you?"

"I'm not sure either, but I also think it looks promising."

"Lucky for you." She raised her head and stared at her friend incredulously. "We're supposed to simply sit here and wait for the Grim Reaper to just show up and tell us we're now unemployed?"

One of Caroline's technicians put her head in the door and announced. "I just got a call from my friend in production. Twenty-five coating employees have been called down to be laid off. They're going from three shifts to two in there."

"Thanks for letting me know, Connie. Keep me posted. You guys have the inside track."

"Will do."

"And so it begins," Caroline mumbled.

"Want me to stick around?"

"No," she protested. "You've got your own people to worry about. I'll be fine. I'm a big girl."

Mary left, and Caroline considered her chances. Of all the projects in R&D, hers had the most chance of being canceled. It wasn't anyone's fault. Sometimes these things just happened. A design might look terrific in R&D but all hell broke loose when you scaled it up to full production. In Caroline's project, it had been one thing after another.

Currently, they were having trouble keeping the solution kettles filled with coating emulsion stabilizer. The usual stabilizers weren't working and she'd just begun looking at some more exotic ones. She prayed she got a chance to finish her project.

Caroline left her office to roam around the pilot coating facility and stop in some of her cohorts' offices. Everyone was tense and many had already made panicked calls home in anticipation of the worst. R&D would most likely get hit hard. Research was always the first to go. It annoyed her that management stubbornly remained so shortsighted, that they'd cut off chances for future products to slice costs for the present. Didn't they realize they were slitting their own throats with cuts in R&D?

After giving her techs as much reassurance as she could, in good conscience, give them, Caroline returned to her office to sweat it out. Every employee waited in his own office as he'd been instructed. Many peeped out to try to get news whenever there was something. The phones rang constantly. At eleven, she got news that fifteen percent of the employees of the pilot coating facility were being let go. Shortly after that she saw the assistant supervisor of the eight millimeter coater go by on his way to HR with his manager.

It was bizarre. It was surreal. It was awful. The man looked as if he was being led to his execution. In a way, he was. Employees sat in frozen silence in their offices and watched him go by, relieved it wasn't them even as they felt badly for those who'd already left. There seemed to be almost a cannibalistic aura to it all. After he left, each employee went back to chewing his fingernails and wondering if he would be next.

She saw other members of the coating staff—techs mostly—go by on their way to their exit interview. A short time later, she watched each leave with wheeled carts carrying boxes of personal belongings, followed by an armed guard.

That shocked Caroline. They were escorting employees out by armed guard? Employees that had, hours before, been accessing computers and cleaning coating machines were now such persona non gratis that they had to be escorted out under guard? How dehumanizing. How humiliating. Couldn't they be more humane about all this?

Lunchtime came and everyone either opened up a bag lunch to eat nervously at their desks or scurried down to the cafeteria to get something to bring back. Caroline opened her lunch and looked at it in disgust. Her stomach roiled. How could anyone eat in circumstances like this? She threw it back into her drawer.

Mary called after noon. "Heard anything yet?"

"Nothing myself. They let about twenty people go here in the pilot facility. Jim's gone. And Pam, Erica, Rafique and Tommy. And many others."

"Yeah, I know," Mary said. "I heard from my secretary the count is now around two hundred and fifty."

"I wish they'd hurry up. Putting people through this agony of waiting is cruel."

"Yeah, well. . ."

"And did you see the armed guards escorting them out? I couldn't believe it."

"Pretty harsh," Mary agreed. "What do they think will happen? Do they think someone brought a pistol to work this morning, figuring they might get laid off and decide to shoot up the place?"

"I guess with the news stories you hear these days, they can't be too careful." Caroline wrinkled her nose, shaking her head at the ridiculousness of it all.

"Well, I would think—" Mary began.

"Oh, God." Caroline dropped the phone. Her manager stood in the doorway, looking ill at ease.

"Caroline? Are you there? What is it? Caroline?" Mary cried.

Caroline picked up the phone in a daze. "Bill Hawser's here. I've got to go."

"Oh Caroline, I'm very sorry. I'll call you later at home."

"Yeah."

Caroline hung up the phone, her stomach roiling, and faced a somber Bill. "They're axing my project, aren't they?"

He nodded. "You'll have to come with me."

She followed him leadenly out the door and past the other offices in the hallway. She tried not to look but couldn't help but notice the pitying glances she got as she followed Bill to his corner office.

Bill sat behind his mahogany desk and faced her. "Caroline, I hope you know how deeply I regret having to do something like this. It is the very worst part of my job and I hate it. You have been a loyal employee and have guided a number of projects through this department that have resulted in several very profitable products that have made a lot of money for this company."

"But all that doesn't matter now, does it? It all comes

down to, 'what have you done for me lately.'" Caroline was surprised she wasn't more upset. It probably hadn't sunk in yet. She sighed.

"It matters to me and to others who have worked with you. We will remember you fondly and will always be grateful for what you have contributed during your stay here."

Caroline nodded as if it mattered. "What about my staff? They're the ones I'm most concerned about. Are they all going to be laid off, too?"

"I'm afraid so. Your staff here and the staff in design that worked on the project. Everybody. I called you in first."

"What about the other projects? Which others are going to be terminated?"

Bill fiddled with his leather desk blotter. He didn't even raise his gaze to her as he answered, "I'm afraid I'm not at liberty to divulge that information."

Caroline nodded again. "I'll find out tomorrow when the dust settles."

"Probably. I have to take you over to HR. You have an appointment with their outplacement people and with the benefits people to discuss the terms of your layoff with regard to severance and insurance, et cetera."

In a fog, she followed Bill out of the building and could see, in peripheral vision, eyes boring into her back as she did so. The news of her dismissal would go out to the techs on her staff and she wished she could be with them when they heard. She owed it to them, but her hands were tied. She must follow this man to her own grave and she couldn't take a detour to help them dig theirs.

The interviews in HR took over an hour. A guard was assigned to go with her while she packed up. He was in his early twenties and looked very uncomfortable, but she was in no mood to make his job easier.

She found two cardboard boxes on her desk when she got back. “How thoughtful of them,” she murmured.

The guard stood inside her door while she loaded the boxes with her personal effects; pictures of her and David and Lily, her make-up from the top drawer, her mirror, a couple of books she'd read during her lunch hour, a crossword puzzle book, a half-eaten bar of candy she had bought because someone’s kid sold it, a picture off the wall. She put it all into the box in slow motion. It seemed unreal that the little world she'd made for herself in this office had, with no warning, been systematically dismantled.

She reached for some personal files from her file cabinet, and the guard stepped forward. “Ma’am, I’m afraid I can’t let you take company files.”

“These are my own files,” she said, shocked he had actually come forward and led her away from her own filing cabinet.

“They’re the company’s files now, Ma’am.”

“No, you don’t understand. These are not company files. These are my appraisals. They’re mine. I should be allowed to take them.”

He looked uncertain and then asked to see them. After he'd inspected them, he allowed her two of them but stressed she would have to leave the third one there.

Bill returned to her office while she added the files to her box. “Caroline, I have to take your lab notebooks. They’re legal documents and they contain proprietary information.”

“I wasn’t going to take them, Bill,” she said wearily.

“I didn’t think you would, Caroline, but. . .well, I need them now, before I let you leave the building.”

Caroline fetched the stack of brown, bound lab notebooks from her bookshelf and handed them to Bill. She stood silently while he checked all the numbers from the back binding of the notebooks and checked them off on a master list he carried with him.

"Thanks," he said and carried the stack out of her office.

Since her personal possessions filled both of the boxes, the guard found a cart she could roll out to the car. On their way to the parking lot, several of her former colleagues stopped her and told her they would miss her. They told her to call and that they would keep in touch. Caroline said all the right words but she knew none of these people would actually follow through and contact her. They'd probably be embarrassed if she called them.

She'd suddenly become an exile and an outcast in their world. It wasn't fair that the situation had been forced on her, but as she knew all too well lately, life wasn't fair.

Mary waited beside her car when she finally got that far. She enveloped Caroline in a bear hug. "You okay?" she asked.

"I'll be okay. How about you? Have you heard anything?"

"I think I'm set. They axed the inkjet project and your fax paper project but I think that's about it."

"That's good. I'm happy for you," Caroline said sincerely. She glanced at the guard waiting patiently nearby, and told her friend she'd better go.

"I'll call you," Mary vowed, hugging her again. "Really."

"I know you will."

Caroline loaded her boxes into the back seat and got into the car. Her entire body hurt and she felt as if it had been physically pummeled. Her head throbbed, her eyes smarted, and her limbs felt heavy from trembling for so long. Looking at the R&D building, her eyes filled with more tears. This building and the people in it had been an important part of her life for ten years. She had loved her job, loved the research atmosphere and the give and take of information. Caroline hadn't even minded the meetings, they stimulated her. Those conference table discussions of research results and problems were stimulating. Discussions about options for proceeding with the projects often got intense.

Now it was as if someone had died and she had the horrible feeling it had been her.

Chapter 12

It was after four when she finally dragged herself home. She called to Lily as soon as she walked in the door. When Lily strode into the den, Caroline looked at her and sighed. She hated being the bearer of yet more bad news, but it couldn't be helped. She rubbed her forehead. "I'm afraid I have some bad news."

"More bad news?" Lily drawled insolently. "How much worse can it get than Dad moving out on us?"

"Oh, it can. There was a big layoff at my company today. My project was canceled and I've been let go."

"Let go? You got laid off?" Lily asked incredulously.

"Yes, I've been laid off, down-sized in the popular jargon."

"How can they do that to you? You were a big cheese around there—"

"Not that big." Caroline gave the ghost of a smile. "The layoffs went all the way up through middle management."

"What are you going to do? What are *we* going to do?"

"I got a generous severance. And then I qualify for unemployment for six months. We won't starve for a while."

"You're going to have to collect unemployment from the government?"

"I've put in my time with the company and paid my dues. They owe me unemployment payments, at the very least."

"Mo-om."

"Don't panic, Lily. It may not even come to that. Maybe I'll get another job before my severance runs out. And thank you for asking. I'm doing fine after one of the worst days of my life." she yelled, the sarcasm dripping in her voice.

Lily's lips tightened but she didn't look contrite enough as far as Caroline was concerned. "Oh, and there's something else, Lily."

"What now?" Lily asked, throwing her arms out to the sides.

Caroline sighed. "It isn't anything bad. This is good. Matt called this afternoon and invited us to a cookout Wednesday night after your last day of school. Would you like to go?"

"Sure," she shrugged. "Why not?" And she turned back around to head for the stairs.

"I thought I'd make spaghetti for supper. That okay?"

"Oh, I forgot. Mandy asked me to come over for dinner. She's picking me up in a few minutes. I didn't think you'd mind."

"Ah, no, I guess I don't mind." So much for hoping her daughter would feel any compassion for her and wish to keep her company after her horrendous day. Things must have really deteriorated between them. Lily would never have left her alone if this had happened a month ago.

Lily paused in the doorway impatiently. "Can I go now? I want to change my clothes."

"For dinner with Mandy?"

"Why not?" she asked defensively.

"Never mind. Go change." Lily ran out as if pursued by the devil as Caroline headed to the kitchen to decide what to do for supper. She was hungry. She hadn't eaten her lunch and she didn't really feel up to making spaghetti for one. She spent five minutes going through the cupboards and the refrigerator but nothing looked even remotely interesting to her.

The front door slammed and she looked out the kitchen window to watch Lily run to a car at the curb. Caroline expected Amanda's mother to be at the wheel, but instead, the driver was a teenage boy. Perhaps he was Amanda's brother. She worried about Lily riding with a teenager, but it was probably okay. They seemed like a nice family.

Her stomach growled and she returned to the kitchen. Maybe she would go out for a burger. It was easier than trying to figure out what to fix for one person and it might take her mind off what she'd been through.

Her purse still hung over the back of a kitchen chair and she grabbed it on the way out. She drove to the closest burger joint and parked the car. A silver SUV pulled in next to her car and she saw it was David. He looked surprised when he recognized her.

"Slumming?" he asked with a raised eyebrow.

"Yeah, I know. I don't usually come to these places unless held at gunpoint, but Lily went to a friend's house for dinner and I really, really couldn't face the thought of eating alone tonight."

He looked intently at her. "I heard about the layoffs on the radio. You were okay, though, right?"

"Nope. I was laid off."

"You're joking."

"I wish I was."

"What about your project?"

"Axed, too."

"Caroline, I'm sorry." He slipped his arms around her. "I know how much that job meant to you."

Caroline wasn't sure how she should react to David holding her right now, but mostly she didn't care. It felt too good. She needed him, needed his comfort. After a minute, he let her go and stepped back, awkwardly.

"It was more than a job, David. It was my career. It meant so very much to me." Tears were gathering in her eyes again and she wiped at them with her fingers, trying not to make a scene in a public parking lot.

“Tell you what,” he said, gazing closely at her. “Let’s go inside and talk.”

“I’m not sure I want fast food anymore,” she said, searching for a wadded-up tissue in her purse.

He grimaced. “I know the feeling.”

She regarded the glass and plastic edifice of the restaurant with disdain. “I'd planned to make spaghetti for Lily and me, but she’s at Mandy’s for dinner.” Her voice reflected bitterness, that Lily had deserted her when she’d needed her.

“Sounds good. You make great spaghetti,” he smiled. “Want to go to Tony’s for some spaghetti instead of getting a hamburger here?”

“That’d be nice. I haven’t been there in a while.”

“Great.” He looked at her car and then his. “Shall we take my car?”

“Uh, maybe I should take my own. Then we can each head our own separate ways afterward.”

“Okay, sure,” he said. He sounded somewhat disappointed she wanted to be free to flee afterwards. “See you there in a few.”

He climbed into his SUV and backed out of the lot, and she followed. It was odd. They had done this before, probably hundreds of times when they had to drop one car off for servicing or something, but that felt different than it did now. Back then he had always made funny faces at her in the rearview mirror. It was one of their “things,” and even though it sounded silly she’d felt a bond, that she was his and part of a team even across distances. Now, he felt. . .separate.

She waited for him in front of the door and they went inside the warmly lit room, just as they had done many times before.

In the familiar restaurant, a waitress seated them in a booth where they’d often sat, and they ordered their favorite spaghetti and meatballs and a bottle of Merlot without bothering to read the menu. She didn't want to talk about herself and what she had been through that day. She needed some time alone to process it. Mainly tonight, she just wanted some company so she wouldn't have to think.

After the waitress brought their wine, Caroline leaned back in the booth. David appeared gaunt, as if he wasn't sleeping. Little wonder. Who could eat and sleep properly with all the stress they were under? She probably had a few ragged edges herself, but she didn't dare ask.

"If you don't mind, I'd rather not talk about the layoffs. I feel as if I've been living and breathing it all day and I just need to get away from the whole thing for a few hours."

"Okay. If that's what you want." David lifted one shoulder in what she had named, 'the David shrug.'

"How have you been?" she asked.

"I've been better."

"I bet."

His brows lowered as his eyes caught hers across the table. "I hoped we could have a nice dinner together."

"We can. I didn't mean it that way. I only meant I imagine it's been difficult for you. It's been difficult for all of us."

"More for you than for anyone."

"Perhaps."

"I want you to know how truly sorry I am and how much I wish I could turn the clock back."

"I know. Let's not get into all that. It'll ruin our appetite." She twirled her glass by the stem. "Where are you staying?"

He named a small, cheap motel north of town and she was surprised. "Why there?" she asked.

"I dunno. I think I felt like I should be punished. It didn't seem kosher somehow to register at the Hilton after leaving my family in the lurch," he replied, with a sad half-smile.

"Why don't you move, David? There must be room at one of the residence-type inns near the water. They have kitchenettes and are set up for longer stays."

He smiled that melancholy smile again. "I'm surprised you care what happens to me."

"Of course I care. You're my husband." The words were out of her mouth before she even realized what she was saying.

"Am I?"

"Why are you talking like this?" Did he want a divorce? She hoped he never asked her for a divorce. She didn't want to divorce him.

"Sorry. I've had a hell of a day, too. I had a visit from your friend and my *former* friend, Matt Deming, this morning."

She groaned. "You two didn't get into it, did you?" David didn't say anything, suddenly occupied with the Parmesan cheese container, twisting the lid on and off. That was answer enough for her.

"I feel really bad you guys have jeopardized a long-term friendship over me." Caroline set her glass down on the table, carefully aligning the ring of condensation so it matched, and then moving it sideways a centimeter to make a new one. She glanced at him as he fiddled with the grated cheese, then down at the row of circles she'd made and shook her head in disgust.

Maybe they were both coming unglued. "I should just stay away from both of you, and let you two mend your fences," she mumbled.

"That's not going to happen, Caro. Besides, you might need him. . ."

Her eyes widening, Caroline stared at him. "What do you mean?"

"Nothing. I just meant Matt can be a good friend and I want you to have someone like that in your life if I can't be there right now." She watched his lips press together, a slight tremor to them.

She stared at his bowed head, choked up at the thought he'd be that unselfish as to wish his rival on her just because he thought she might need someone. She remembered all over again why she loved this man so much and she reached over to cover his hand with hers.

He gazed into her eyes and she swore his heart was in them as they filled. Maybe. . .

But just then the waitress brought their plates of spaghetti and the moment was lost. He pulled his hand away and avoided her eyes as he screwed the top back on the grated cheese and held it out to her.

She didn't want to let the subject drop entirely. It worried her to think of what their situation had done to him and his friendship with Matt. "If you feel this way, David, why did you and Matt have a blow-up this morning?"

"Because I was angry and couldn't stand the thought of him taking my place."

"What changed between then and now?"

"I looked into your eyes."

Caroline felt as if she wanted to cry.

"Don't get me wrong, Caro," he said, his voice hardening. "The thought of you kissing him, or any man, makes me want to vomit. I get physically, honest-to-God, ill. But if it turns out I can't have you, then—"

She trembled, her dinner forgotten. "Then what?"

"Nothing," he muttered. "Forget it."

"Forget it? How can I forget it?"

He speared her with a look of such anger, such pain and remorse, it took her breath away. She swallowed what she had been going to say next and folded her hands in her lap to stop them from shaking. She kept her eyes on the plate in front of her even though she had no appetite left. She couldn't bring herself to look at David's face. For a long time, they sat there silently.

When she dared a swift glance upward, she saw him sitting with his elbows on the table and his forehead on his clenched fists. Out of her peripheral vision, she noticed their waitress start toward their table to check on their progress, hesitate and turn away.

Finally, he raised his eyes, held her wine glass out to her, urging her to take it. "Here. Have a sip. Maybe it'll make you feel better."

She took the glass and sipped the wine slowly as he did the same with his own. "David," she said shakily, looking back down at her lap, "I don't want to be with someone else."

"Shh," he whispered. "Don't get upset over all this. Nothing has to be decided right now. You don't have to make me any promises of undying love. I know what I've done and I know what my betrayal has cost us. I'm willing to pay the price if need be. That's all I wanted to say."

"But why? Don't you want to fight for what we had? Don't you love me anymore?"

He caught both her hands and brought them to his lips across the table. "Of course I still love you. Now, more than ever, I see what I lost through my stupidity. But this is an issue of accountability. Responsibility for one's actions doesn't seem to be high on anyone's list of priorities these days, but I can't live like that. And I have to be able to live with myself. If I can't, I won't be much good to you."

She studied his eyes for a long time, the eyes she knew so well, and finally she nodded. "I understand. At last, I understand. And I respect you for what you feel." She sat back in the booth and a faint smile flitted across her face. He smiled back in kind and their eyes held for a long time before he broke the contact.

"Eat your spaghetti," he urged.

"It's cold."

He glanced around and spotted their waitress, who approached their table. “We got kind of caught up in a conversation and our spaghetti got cold. Would it be possible to get it reheated?”

“Sure.” Their waitress smiled. “I’ll be back in a few minutes.”

When she came back, the plates of spaghetti looked suspiciously like fresh, steaming plates of pasta. “Enjoy.”

Caroline set to her meal with enthusiasm, suddenly famished. David ate all of his, too, and she teased him about mopping up every trace of sauce with his bread.

After David paid the bill, he walked her back to her car. They had been inside long enough, it was nearly dark outside. Caroline leaned back against her Maxima and looked up at him, standing with his hands shoved in his pockets. She hated to go and put off turning around to open her driver’s door.

He seemed to understand because he gave her a verbal nudge. “You’d better go.”

She nodded, but still didn’t turn around.

He leaned forward, hesitated an instant, then ran his fingers under her long hair. His mouth came down hard on hers, his tongue dipping into her mouth to tangle frantically with hers. His kiss was more than a little desperate, and she could taste the emotion in it, but it was over too quickly. He pulled back, and then turned to go without another word.

She watched him walk to his car, her lips still tingling from his kiss. Over the years, their kisses had settled into comfortable, affectionate affairs that rarely went beyond mild passion. He hadn’t kissed her like that in years. No, he had *never* kissed her like that. Even though it had been short, there was a wealth of feeling, passion and need, in it.

Caroline drove home in a daze and pulled into her driveway. The house was dark, and she felt actually relieved Lily wasn’t home yet. She needed to be alone for a while.

Chapter 13

Caroline rose at her usual time and saw Lily off for her last day of school, and then puttered in the kitchen, cleaning up the breakfast dishes. She finished loading the dishwasher and tried to decide what to do with herself all day. If it had been a normal day off, she would have had a million things planned or a million things that needed doing.

She looked around the room but couldn't muster the ambition to do any of those odd jobs she knew she could be doing, like cleaning out the fridge. She needed to make a bowl of cole slaw for tonight's cook-out with Matt but couldn't seem to make herself move to the refrigerator. With a sigh, she wandered through the house looking for something that piqued her interest. Nothing did.

In the den, she grabbed the remote, turned on the TV, and collapsed into the nearest chair. It was David's favorite recliner, and sitting in it took her aback.

I'm being silly. She settled back into the cushiony softness of the leather. She flipped through a bunch of channels, finding mostly morning talk shows and infomercials. *Mickey Mouse* and *Sponge Bob Square Pants*, were hardly even remotely interesting. She found a rerun of *Happy Days*. She watched that and then *Mork and Mindy* and a black and white episode of *I Love Lucy*.

Mid-morning, she got disgusted with herself and old TV shows and clicked off the set. She needed to get out of the house. She considered heading to the marina, but the thought of going out there on a weekday seemed weird. It made suffer her loss even more acutely. No, she needed to go somewhere neutral, somewhere impersonal.

On a whim, Caroline drove toward D.C. Within the hour, she sat in the grass gazing at the Washington Monument. Its size, huge and majestic, made her problems seem smaller, at least for a little while. Then, inevitably, they came rushing back to overwhelm her and she flopped backward, staring up at the clear blue sky.

She thought about the last month. In that short space of time, she'd lost her husband, her job, and, quite possibly, her daughter. She felt completely alone in the world, as if everyone and everything she knew deserted her.

David, the center of her world for sixteen years, betrayed her and her faith in him. Her job at the paper plant made her vibrant and alive and worthy for most of her adult life. Now it was gone. Her daughter was the most important person in her life next to David and they were barely on speaking terms.

Restlessly, she rose and got in line for the elevator ride to the top of the monument. She briefly considered walking to the top as she had when she'd been a teenager, but then dismissed the idea. She'd never make it now. The elevator doors opened and she stepped in alone. An older couple and a family with two small children entered after her.

Everybody has somebody.

At the top, the city of Washington humbled her with its nobility of purpose, its dignified government buildings and national monuments. It was a breathtaking sight, and she appreciated it even in her melancholy state. She hadn't been to Washington in years, probably not since she and David were first married. Lily went a few times with class trips and David spent half the winter here but, as a family, they hadn't visited in years.

She stood there gazing out at the city from different vantage points while several elevator loads came and went.

The elderly couple and the small family had long gone. She couldn't stop circling the observation deck, as if hoping to find an answer written on the water of the Reflecting Pool or the lawn in front of the Lincoln Memorial.

After receiving a number of strange looks from the elevator operator, Caroline finally descended again and sat on one of the benches at the edge of the grass. Whatever was she going to do? She couldn't very well become a professional tourist in the nation's capital. She couldn't spend her days making gourmet meals for her husband because she didn't have one anymore. She couldn't plan getaways with Lily because her daughter didn't seem to want her company.

Maybe I should take up quilting or knit afghans for charity.

She checked her watch. If she didn't hurry home, she wouldn't have time to make the salad for tonight's cookout.

There it is.

She dreaded the cookout with Matt after what happened with David last night. But she'd said she'd go and at least it was something to do. Besides, Lily was probably looking forward to it.

Well, Caroline assumed Lily was looking forward to it; she'd hardly seen her daughter all week. Lily left before supper last night to spend the evening with Mandy again. She hadn't been seeing nearly as much of Debbie as she used to. Mandy went to the same school Lily did, so maybe Lily had more in common with her than with Debbie, although she and Debbie connected with their interest in science. But more existed in this world than science to a teenage life and she was glad Lily had finally discovered it.

She rose and made her way back to her car, thankful she'd at least miss rush hour in the Capital, a harrowing ordeal on a good day.

Once home, she set to work on the slaw, and it felt good to have something to accomplish. She glanced at the clock.

She told Lily they needed to leave for Matt's no later than six and it was nearly that now. She threw the top on the plastic container of cole slaw and settled at the kitchen table to wait for her.

When she hadn't turned up by six-fifteen, Caroline called Matt and told him they were going to be late. He said not to worry about it, that everything would hold and he wouldn't start the grill until they got there.

It was six-thirty when she saw the same rattletrap car from last night pull up to the curb. Lily climbed out and waved at the same boy Caroline noticed the night before, a radiant smile wreathing her face, before she turned toward the house and her expression became shuttered again. She dropped her backpack by the door.

"Lily, where have you been? I told you we were supposed to be at Debbie's at six."

"What time is it?"

Caroline glanced up at the clock again. "It's past six-thirty."

She didn't look very penitent. "Sorry. I didn't notice the time."

"Who is that boy who drove you home?"

"Oh, he's Mandy's brother, Christopher."

"He drives you instead of Mandy's mother?"

"He's over sixteen. He has his license."

"I'm not sure I like the idea of a teenage boy ferrying you all over instead of Mandy's mother." Caroline frowned.

"He's an excellent driver. He took driver's ed."

Caroline made a noncommittal sound. At least he'd had some formal training, which was good, but she didn't believe it was much better. More existed than just the issue of Mandy's brother driving her home, too. Lily's entire attitude completely changed. She and Lily used to be best friends, and now there seemed to be a wall between them. The wall had been in place since the since the awful scene between her and David that she'd eavesdropped on.

Maybe Lily just needed time. Caroline briefly contemplated telling Lily things were a little improved between her and her father, but she didn't want to raise her hopes in case things didn't work out.

"Matt is waiting for us. We'd better get going."

"I have to run upstairs and clean up. Why don't you go over and I'll be there in a few."

"Okay, fine. I'll see you there." Caroline grabbed the bowl of salad off the counter and headed out the kitchen door. She heard Lily bound up the stairs. She walked the block to Matt's house and rounded the back of the house where she knew Debbie and Matt would be.

He had a gorgeous deck with an enormous gas grill, an outdoor kitchen, and benches built into the railing of the deck. Caroline often wished her house had been constructed more like his. They couldn't even get to their deck through the house, they had to barbecue in front of the garage. They only used the deck when they swam in the above-ground pool in their back yard. It was too much trouble to carry everything through the garage and out to the back to eat outside. Over the years they'd spent more time on Matt's deck than their own. Caroline often prepared the meat dish for Matt to grill.

Matt called a greeting from his position in front of the grill. "Saw you coming down the street, and I went ahead and started the grill. I didn't want to take a chance on you lighting it," he said, chuckling. "We're not as young as we used to be, and frankly, I don't move as fast anymore. You'd probably kill us all."

"Very funny," she said, setting her bowl and spoon on the picnic table. "Lily will be along in a few minutes. She has to clean up." She stopped short when she got a better look at him. His face was swollen on one side and a tinge of black underlined his eye. "What happened to your face?"

"David happened to it," He replied tersely.

"That's from your argument yesterday? He actually hit you?"

"Oh yeah—took me completely by surprise or I might have been ready for him and gotten one in myself." He tried to smile, but Caroline wasn't buying it.

"Oh Matt, I'm sorry. I feel awful that this is putting a strain on your friendship."

"I don't think there's any friendship left to worry about, Caroline." He sighed and fiddled with the grill, not meeting her gaze.

Suddenly overcome by everything, she turned her back to him and swiped at tears. "This has all been awful. I'm sorry," she mumbled.

She felt him come closer. He laid his hand on the middle of her back and gently rubbed, speaking softly. "It's not your fault, Caro. We're both grown men and can take responsibility for our actions. Besides, you didn't do anything. David and I made our own mess. You've been more of a victim than anything else. 'Collateral damage' is the term they use in the legal world."

Caroline snorted, shuddering, and straightened. Collateral damage, indeed. "I'm tired of feeling like a victim," she told him. "Look, you invited us over to have some fun. I think we should start on that before we get too maudlin. Besides, the girls will be out here soon and I don't want Lily to see me crying again."

"Sure, of course." Matt checked to make sure the grill was ready, then curled his arm around her, dropping a quick kiss on her forehead and then her lips. She stiffened and all but pulled away and he leaned back to look at her face, his brow furrowed. "Is something else the matter?"

"I—uh, don't think we should get into it right now," she hedged, as Debbie exited the house with another salad and a pitcher of lemonade.

He gave Caroline a long look, his eyes narrowed. "Okay. For now. But later. . ."

She nodded. "Hi, Debbie," she said as the girl came up to them.

"Hi. Where's Lily? I have a cool new game for my computer I want her to see."

"She'll be right along." Caroline caught a glimpse of Lily coming through the gate dressed in a clean pair of shorts and a new top she'd gotten at the mall the other day. "There she is now."

Caroline tilted her head and studied her daughter. She'd been wearing a new top earlier when she came home too, Caroline was almost sure of it. She wondered how much money Lily had spent the other day. David had given her some, she knew–guilt money—and it appeared Lily hadn't waited long to put it to immediate use.

The two girls went to check out Debbie's new game. As soon as their voices died away, Matt looked pointedly at her, but she swept past him and lifted the lid of the grill, choosing to ignore him. She wasn't ready to have this chat now. "I think it's hot enough to put the chicken on."

He let her get away with her evasion and added the chicken breasts to the grill, brushing each one with barbecue sauce from a bowl, probably homemade. He stood sentry at the grill, watching the chicken cook, and she sat at the picnic table, pouring herself a glass of lemonade to have something to do with her hands.

He came over to the table and picked up the bottle of beer he'd left there, taking a long draw. "I heard on the news about the layoffs at the paper company. I hope none of your friends got the boot."

Caroline stiffened. News traveled fast, but she'd been hoping to be spared all the explanations and pity. "Actually, several of my friends were laid off. As was I." She watched his face as she dropped the bomb and it was almost comical the way it changed from mildly interested to shocked. Strange, how people thought it would never happen to them, their loved one or their friend and, when it did, they were dumbfounded.

"Caroline." he cried, plunking his beer onto the table and nearly shattering the bottle. He slid closer to her and touched her hand gently. "Are you okay?"

"No. No, I'm not okay. In fact, I'm terrible."

"How can I help?"

"You can't. Nobody can." She pulled her hand from his and jumped up, pacing in front of him. "And I *really* don't want to talk about it."

"Are you sure? Maybe it would help to talk about it."

"Would it get me my job back?" she yelled at him. When he flinched, she was mortified. She screamed at someone who only tried to make her feel better. She couldn't believe she'd gotten strung out that badly. "I'm sorry. I shouldn't take it out on you. It's just that I've thought of little else besides the layoff in the past twenty-four hours and I don't think I can stand much more today. All right?" Her eyes pleaded with him to back off.

Matt nodded. "Well, sure. If that's the way you feel, of course I'll respect that. But I want you to know you can talk to me about it any time, day or night. I'm here for you, Caroline."

"Yeah, I know," she admitted. Maybe someday she could talk about it with him, but at the moment she couldn't imagine calling him. It would just make her more miserable thinking she was a loser than she already did. They made small talk while the chicken finished cooking. Taking it off the grill, he carried it over to the picnic table. He went to the screened sliding door and called, "Debbie. Lily. Supper's ready."

"Matt, are you sure the chicken is cooked? It wasn't on the grill very long," Caroline asked in surprise.

"I nuked it first so it wouldn't overcook and burn on the outside. I hate it when the barbecue sauce is all black and charred." His look appeared puzzled as he studied her. Uncomfortable with his scrutiny, she turned away and sat at the table. "You know, you're the one who told me I should do that last time you were here and we ate scorched chicken."

"Oh, right. I forgot. My mind is going, I think. Too much stress."

The girls came out and plopped down at the picnic table opposite her, and Matt sat beside her. The chicken tasted delicious. The entire meal was good, and they ate with relish until there was nothing left but bones. Caroline took seconds of almost everything. She noted Lily almost completely ignored her and Matt, choosing to talk to Debbie while she ate. Matt seemed to notice and made light-hearted conversation. If anyone noticed that Caroline seemed quiet, no one mentioned it.

The girls cleared the table and went back inside to play Debbie's computer game.

"So what's up with Lily?" Matt asked. "She hardly talked to either of us."

"We haven't been getting along very well the last couple of days. There was ah, a kind of scene with David over the weekend."

"What happened?" Matt's face betrayed his intense curiosity.

"David and I were in the den talking about our situation and she eavesdropped outside the door. What she heard upset her pretty badly and she lashed out at both of us afterwards."

He nodded. "It's got to be very hard on her. She's at an extremely vulnerable age."

"I know. That's why I've been giving her some latitude. Ordinarily, I wouldn't let her get away with the kind of things she's been saying to me, when she's talking to me at all."

"Lily? Wow, really?" Caroline could hear the disbelief in his voice, and wished again she and Lily could iron out their differences.

"It's hard to explain," she answered. "It's not what she actually says. It's more her attitude when she says it. You know, that insolent teenage rebellious stuff? I never thought I would hear it from her."

"No. She's always been obedient," Matt agreed. "You two have been more like buddies than mother and daughter. It must be hard to deal with her like this since you guys were always close."

"Exactly." Caroline sighed. Her hands clasped under her chin, she looked out over Matt's backyard and avoided his gaze. She knew he watched her expression, looking for an opening to bring up the other subject he itched to talk about.

Evening couldn't come fast enough for her. He wouldn't be able to see her face and read the doubts on it. She didn't want to hurt him–he'd been such a good friend to her. Nature, of course did not oblige, seeing as it was nearly the longest day of the year.

"All right," he said at last. "Spill it."

"I—um—I had dinner with David Monday night."

That caught his attention. He swung around until he straddled the bench facing her and sat up straighter. He looked carefully at her and then, apparently searching for some clue about what went on inside her mind, cocked his head. "And?"

"And we had a good talk."

"So, is he back home?"

Caroline hated to admit it to him. "No," she said flatly.

"I didn't think so. Did he say why?"

"He said he needed to work some things out. He feels a sense of responsibility for what happened and has to reconcile that within himself."

"Bullshit." Matt snorted.

Caroline jumped, her head snapping around so fast, she felt light-headed. "What?"

"You heard what I said."

His reaction astounded her. He was always calm, in control, and gave everyone the benefit of the doubt, but now he seemed really angry. "What do you mean?"

"David is stringing you along."

She bristled. "How do you figure that?"

"Look. It's been over a month and he's never once mentioned coming back home, has he?"

"Once, when Lily heard us talking, but it was just because of Lily," she admitted reluctantly.

Then she remembered their conversation about David moving into a residence-type inn and how he'd agreed to her suggestion so quickly. She wondered if there was any truth to Matt's words. She hated all these violent, emotional swings. It made her wonder if she'd lost her mind.

"He's afraid, Caro. Afraid, plain and simple."

"Afraid of what?" she asked, incredulous.

"Afraid it's going to happen again and again. It happened once and it could very well happen again." His words came out in a rush, as if he feared she'd stop him before he could finish.

"No." she nearly screamed. "You can't be serious."

Matt blanched, but continued doggedly. "Look at the statistics about men who wander. Then look at his behavior."

Caroline felt shaken. She'd had such confidence after the dinner with David and now she didn't know what to think. What if Matt was right?

Or, conversely, what if he wasn't and she let herself believe him, anyway? Matt had an ulterior motive for wanting her to believe the worst of David. He'd told her he loved her. Didn't that make his perspective anything but objective?

David had been sincere last night. On the other hand, he'd seemed sincere all those months he'd been seeing another woman behind her back. She didn't know what to think.

She closed her eyes, willing the day to end, hoping this had all been a bad dream and she'd wake up in her bed, with David next to her snoring away as he always did. She knew it was pure fantasy, but it felt nice for a minute not to have to deal with all the hurt, the pain and anger.

She felt Matt gently turn her so she faced away from him. His arms closed around her shoulders, pulling her back against him. "I'm sorry, Caroline. I'm sorry I upset you. I just can't stand to see you build up false hopes. I want to protect you."

She let him hold her. When he turned her, she rested her head against his warm chest and relaxed a little. God, it was nice to be held. She missed it, more than she'd ever thought she would. "I know that, Matt. And I appreciate it."

He started to lean in to kiss her but she held him off. "The girls."

He looked over her head. "They're on the phone. They don't look like they'll be off soon."

Caroline glanced inside and, sure enough, Lily lay on her back on the sofa with the phone cradled between her shoulder and her ear. Debbie sat on the floor with her elbows on the couch cushion, kibitzing in whatever conversation Lily was having.

She swung back to Matt. "I guess I just lost my excuse."

"Do you need one with me?" he asked, retreating a little, his eyes betraying a heady combination of lust and love. She couldn't help but smile.

"No, no. I'm sorry. It's just that, well, I guess I'm having a little trouble with all this."

"Ah, you mean how I've morphed from smiling Uncle Matt, the friend who's always cheerful and ready to be everything for everybody, to a man who's crazy about you and wants to make passionate love to you?" He buried his face in the crook of her neck, nuzzling gently at the sensitive skin.

Laughing nervously, Caroline ran her hands up his arms. "I wouldn't have put it quite like that, but yes, I guess that's the gist of it."

"Maybe you just need a little practice making the transition," he said, his eyes narrowing as he swooped down to capture her lips. He pressed his mouth against hers and his fingers grasped her hips, pulling her body flush with his.

Her arms automatically wound around his neck and her fingers tangled in his soft hair as he angled his head to increase the pressure on her mouth even more. His hands slipped beneath her top to explore her bare skin.

Feeling his fingers make contact, she started, gently pulling away from him. She couldn't afford to get caught up in his lovemaking. It was impossible to forget her earlier doubts.

Even so, she regretted she couldn't let him continue. He felt really good, and they'd been close friends forever, but she wasn't into teasing or deception. She didn't want to use him for comfort or to assuage her loneliness. It wouldn't be fair to him, especially knowing how he felt about her.

"Matt, I can't do this. I don't think we should let this go any further."

"Why not?" he whispered, nuzzling her neck again.

"Things are just too uncertain right now. I'm too confused about what I want and what I need. I don't want to lead you on."

"Go ahead. Lead me on. I don't care." His tongue came out to lick at the lobe of her ear.

"I care." She pushed him back a few inches.

His eyes hardened and he thrust his hands into the pockets of his shorts, clearly angry and frustrated. "If I don't care, why should you? I'm a big boy, Caroline. I can take care of myself and I'm willing to take the risk."

Caroline shook her head. "I'm not built that way, Matt. I can't just run pell-mell through someone's feelings like a runaway bull."

"Not even with permission?"

He tried to cajole her into saying yes, but she refused to let him change her mind. "Not even then. Look, Matt. I know you and David argued badly yesterday," she said, fingering his bruised face lightly. "But I'm hoping your friendship can be restored after this is all over." She held her hands out in supplication for him to understand. "I don't want to see the relationship you guys have had for that long go down the drain just because of this stupid situation."

"I suspect it's already too late for that," Matt told her, his voice betraying his regret. "If he manages to get you to forgive him and wins you back again, I don't know if *I* can forgive him. And if I win you over, I doubt he will ever forgive me. No doubt he'll blame me for his marriage ending rather than his cheating on you."

"Don't say that. God, Matt, I don't want to lose you as a friend. I don't know what I would do. You've always been there for me. For us. Don't say it could be the end."

"Okay, I won't, but don't get your hopes up." Matt reached over to tuck a lock of her hair behind her ear, and gently stroked his fingers down her face to her mouth. His index finger brushed lightly over her bottom lip. He raised his eyes to hers. "You know, you responded to me a few minutes ago. I felt it. Don't try to tell me you didn't."

Embarrassed, she didn't want to admit she enjoyed his kisses.

Matt held her gaze, finally turning his head to stare out into the increasing dark. "No sense in tearing yourself up over it, Caro. We've been close friends for a long time. You shouldn't worry because you felt something when I kissed you."

Caroline started to object, but he held up his hand, still refusing to turn back to her. "No, that's okay. I know you don't feel anything more than affection for me. But it's enough right now. If I take care of you and hold you in my arms now and then, maybe, when everything comes down, you'll turn to me. That's all I expect."

Caroline reached up to nudge his face back, forcing him to look at her. "You're wonderful. You know that?" She kissed him, a very brief and intentionally friendly kiss. He kissed her back but it was not friendly. His mouth grew more urgent on hers for a few seconds; then he put her at arm's length away.

"Better make your escape before I decide I'm not going to let you go. I'm not that honorable a guy."

"Yes, you are. You're a great guy and I'm very lucky I have you to help me over this thing with David."

"Aw shucks, Ma'am. Tweren't nothin'." She knew he was trying to lighten the mood, and she appreciated that he wasn't pushing her.

Lily giggled over the phone when Caroline went in to get her a few minutes later. She only agreed to leave when Caroline promised to let her call her friend back after she got home.

Caroline spent the next two weeks trying to adjust to being home all day. She wasted an inordinate amount of time watching daytime television and going on field trips to everywhere she could think of. The house got dirtier and dirtier and she couldn't seem to make herself care.

One day Caroline almost called a housekeeper to come in and clean, then remembered they couldn't squander money on such luxuries anymore. The next day, unable to stand the dirt anymore, Caroline made herself wash the kitchen and the bathrooms. As the scrubbing continued, her resolution to never become one of those stay-at-home moms got stronger and stronger. Sewing new curtains for the kitchen or painting watercolors for the living room wouldn't suit her. Besides, she didn't know how to paint.

Every day Caroline looked through the want ads, but there wasn't anything for which she seemed qualified. Would Caroline ever have the heart to try for a job, if something did turn up? Her skills were so specialized, it was not a sure thing she'd never find another job as good as her old one. The outplacement office at the plant would help, but it was devastating to face being back in the office when she wasn't part of it anymore. It would hurt too much.

Lily seemed content to spend her time with Mandy and her friends. Other than the picnic on the last day of school, she didn't think Lily had seen Debbie at all. When Caroline questioned her about what she did with her new friends, Lily said they played tennis and video games, listened to music and went to the mall. As Lily was going to be fifteen next month, perhaps it was time she spread her wings a little and hung out with friends her own age instead of Debbie.

One morning, Mary called and invited Caroline out to a long lunch. She accepted the invitation gratefully, needing to get out of the house and tired of taking solitary day trips.

They met out in the parking lot of a downtown bank, and Mary drove to a nearby restaurant on the water. They got a table on the veranda and watched the boats go by from the marinas down the quay. She knew Mary was anxious to ask her what was going on, but Caroline refused to bring up the subject herself.

"So, how's it been going?" Mary asked finally, her tone too casual to fool Caroline.

"Don't ask." Caroline answered, rolling her eyes.

"That bad?"

"Where do I start? Do I start with my husband, whom I have seen just twice in the last two weeks? Once when I accidentally ran into him in a fast food joint and the other time when he came to the house to pick up Lily for a movie? Or do you want to know how many showcases have been won on *The Price is Right?* Or should I tell you about Lily and how we never talk anymore and how she's spending every free moment with her new friend, Mandy, but never wants to bring her home to our place because she's apparently ashamed of me? Or, should I go straight to Matt, who says he wants to be my friend but doesn't act very friend-like? It seems he thinks kissing me may help me recover. Oh, and should I mention he's thrown his hat into the ring to become my next spouse? And should I add I'm so starved for affection and attention, I almost like it?"

Mary's eyes grew rounder and rounder as Caroline spoke and now she sat back with a low whistle. "Wow. As Caroline's World Turns."

"Tell me about it."

"I don't know what to say, Caroline."

"Me neither," Caroline shrugged, taking a quick sip of her water. "All I feel right now is confused. For a while I thought David and I were making progress and then Matt says all this stuff that made me wonder if I'm fooling myself. And I try to tell Matt to back off, but I always end up letting him kiss me and I always like it too much."

"Don't beat yourself up, Caro. If you're feeling rejected by your husband, it's not surprising you're flattered by another man's attention, especially one like Matt whom you've been close to for many years. And is, I might add, some pretty fine eye candy. But I must admit I can't quite imagine you kissing him. You've been too much like buddies for too long."

"Do you want a demo?" Caroline grinned.

"No, thanks. I think I'll wait for the beta version to be tested and check out the final product. But let me know when you're done with him." She winked at Caroline.

They watched a couple of sailboats go by in front of the restaurant. "This summer was supposed to be the summer of the sailboat." Caroline sighed. "After I finally learned how to sail it, this year we were going to relax and spend lots of time on it together, and really enjoy it."

"You miss the boat?"

"Oh sure, but it's more than that. I miss *us* on the boat. Last summer I felt incredibly close to David while he finally taught me to sail *Windswept*. I miss it this year." Her eyes were drawn back to the water, to a boat much like theirs motoring by, on its way to the bay. "You know something?"

"What?"

"I *do* miss the boat itself. I've been beating myself up over that too. But why should I? I can't be absolutely sure David and I will work out our problems. Why shouldn't I keep doing something I love? I went to the marina with Matt and motored around in the boat a few weeks ago but I felt guilty the whole time, like I should have been there with David. But life has to go on." Caroline paused. "Maybe without David."

Mary looked surprised to hear Caroline actually admit she might have to go on without her husband. "I didn't realize things had gone that far. But, if it's that bad, you're right to want to go on. And even if nothing else happens the rest of the summer, if things drag on without being resolved, you have to get on with your life and not let everything fester in your head."

"Yes," Caroline said slowly, nodding. She'd watched the sailboat getting smaller and smaller as it motored slowly down the channel, out to sea. That would be her, she decided, very, very soon.

David called last night to ask if she and Lily would go to his law firm's annual July Fourth picnic with him, and she'd reluctantly agreed. She'd known she should go, for his sake, because it seemed to be a politically-correct thing to at least appear to have a happy, loving family. But she also knew Matt would be there and she couldn't help but remember what it had been like the last time the three of them tried get along together at Lily's science fair. After the picnic on Thursday, she would probably need to set sail on the water and unwind.

Yes, that's what I'll do. She nodded resolutely.

"Caro?" nudged Mary. "Are you in there?" She waved her hand in front of Caroline's face.

Caroline started, realizing she'd been caught up in her own thoughts and that their lunch arrived while she'd been occupied. "Sorry. Yum, this looks good." And, indeed it was. The restaurant was well-known for its seafood and the crabmeat salad croissant Caroline had ordered tasted great.

After they'd finished their lunch, Caroline asked the question she'd been dreading ever since she'd seen Mary drive up. "So, how's work?"

"Awful," Mary admitted, clearly not comfortable talking about work. "Things are not the same. Morale is way down since the layoff because everyone wonders how long it will be until the next one and if they'll go next. I suspect the company is sinking. You're lucky you got out now."

"Right. I feel lucky," Caroline replied, a rueful grin on her face.

"No, I'm serious. The company is mired in technology of the past and there aren't enough new state-of-the-art products coming out to keep them afloat."

"So, of course it made sense to cut R&D."

"You and I know it's suicide to cut R&D," Mary said

soothingly. "But management is short-sighted. That's why I don't think the company will last. I give them two or three years."

"I could have used two or three years," Caroline grumbled. Even hearing how bad things were didn't make her anything better. She wouldn't wish her situation on anyone.

"No. It'll get ugly. I've been thinking of applying to some places. Getting out while the getting is good."

"At least you can do that while still working and drawing a full salary."

"I know. I'm not making light of what you're going through. I just want you to know it isn't a bed of roses back at work, either. Have you got any prospects yet for another job?"

"No." Caroline's eyes slid sideways so Mary couldn't look at them and see the truth. But it didn't work; her friend knew her too well.

"You haven't even looked yet, have you?"

"I've checked the want ads."

"Phht. The jobs for you and me are not in the want ads and you know it. They're found through networking and sending out scads of resumes. Why don't you come down to the outplacement center at the plant?"

"I—I can't. Not yet. I need some time."

Mary patted her hand. "I understand. Of course, you need time to get used to what happened. You have to grieve, just as if you'd lost a person you loved. You've lost something very important to you and you have to go through all of the grieving processes, from denial to acceptance."

"I think I'm still in the denial stage, although lately I've been getting so disgusted with myself, maybe I'm ready to move on."

"Don't be too hard on yourself and don't push things. You need to work through it gradually."

"I will." Caroline looked at her watch. "Hadn't you better get back while you still have a job?"

"I suppose. Everyone's been pretty lax for the last few weeks. I think they realize what a blow the layoff was to the employees still there and how low morale is at the moment. Management is more or less looking the other way in regards to our hours worked. But still, you're right. I'd better get going."

Mary insisted on taking care of the bill. She drove Caroline back to her car, hopping out to envelop Caroline in a quick hug. "It'll all work out, you'll see."

Caroline could only nod. She wasn't sure everything would ever be all right again, but she didn't want to weigh Mary down any more. She drove home, still thinking about that sailboat motoring out to the bay.

As she pulled into the garage, she could see something on the front porch that looked like a manila envelope. *Must be something the mailman couldn't put into the box*. She walked around to the front to retrieve it, noting the lack of an address on it. The front was blank.

"Now that's weird," she mumbled to herself. She tore off the top and peered in, dumping the contents into her hand. "Wha—my sailing gloves."

They were easily recognizable: butter-soft green and white leather, worn across the palm from years of pulling lines in strong winds.

She looked into the envelope again to see if there was anything else in there, but that was it. Had David. . . No, he wouldn't have any reason.

"Omigod," she whispered. "Alicia. Alicia snatched them off the boat when she'd been there and then left them on my porch for me to find. She knew it would freak me out to find them here."

And it did. It totally blew her mind the crazy woman

would do something like that. It was sick. It wasn't exactly a dead horse's head in her bed but it was still sick.

She started to rush into the house and call David, but she stopped herself. That was exactly what Alicia wanted—for her to run to David and get into an argument over the incident. No, she wouldn't play into that woman's hands. She'd pretend nothing happened and leave Alicia stewing over why there hadn't been any fallout from her stunt.

Caroline sat fuming. David was ten minutes late for their first marriage counselor session. Actually, it was their second as he'd completely missed the first. He'd claimed his secretary failed to give him the message. She didn't know if he'd been lying last time or not but she hoped he wasn't going to pull another disappearing act. She looked up as the outer door opened and David came bursting in huffing and puffing and with sweat pouring down his face.

"Sorry. Court ran over." He got out a handkerchief and mopped up the sweat. "Geez, it's hotter than heck out there. I had to take a cab because some idiot boxed in my car in the court parking lot."

He didn't have time to expand upon the horrible parking situation during tourist season in Annapolis. They'd already eaten into their time and Dr. Copeland motioned them into her conference room. David gave her a quick quirk of his eyebrow when he realized their doctor was a woman.

"Sit down, please." She indicated a small seating area in the corner. David and Caroline took the couch and the doctor took the chair. Caroline had a feeling it had been designed that way to force couples to at least sit together. "Please, call me Sylvia."

They both nodded, and Caroline tried to quell her awkwardness.

Sylvia, dressed in a stunning light blue flowered

sundress, waited for one of them to say something, then took things into her own hands. "Tell me why you've come to me."

Caroline and David stared at each other. His face worked and he repeatedly shifted to try to get comfortable, which he apparently was not able to do. Looking completely embarrassed and unlikely to say anything, Caroline turned to the doctor. "My husband engaged in an affair last winter when he was out of town for a case." She could hear the breathlessness in her own voice as she rushed through the explanation. "He worked in D.C. for three months and met her there." Next to her, David uttered a soft gasp that might have been dismay.

"I see." Sylvia jotted something down in a folder on her lap. "David, I assume it's true. What do you have to say about it?"

David turned bright red and looked guiltily at Sylvia. "Yes, it's true."

"Why do you suppose it happened?"

David squared his shoulders and glanced briefly at Caroline before he answered. "I was in D.C. and, after a while, began to feel separated from my wife and family, as if they were part of another life. Everyone up there messed around. I started seeing a woman from our team just to have someone to talk to and we began having, uh, sex."

"Why do you think this sex started? Was something going on back home that made you feel alienated? Or are you just the kind of guy that sleeps around?"

"No, I don't sleep around." He looked beseechingly at Caroline, who spoke up.

"Nothing like this has ever happened before."

Sylvia looked kindly at the two of them, as if she understood their situation. Then, she looked back to David again. "Anything more to add?"

He took a deep breath as if to brace himself. "I love

Caroline, but the last few years I've been feeling increasingly left out of things at home. Lily and Caroline are extremely close and have this little mutual admiration society going on."

Caroline opened her mouth to refute him but Sylvia held up her hand and then motioned David to continue. "I can understand it, I guess. Lily looks up to her mother's prowess in the sciences and wants to be like her when she grows up. Caro is naturally proud of her and dotes on her, but it sort of leaves me out. I feel like neither one knows or cares if I'm around."

"That's not true, David. We care about you."

"When you and Lily are nose to nose over some science thing, like her science fair, I cease to exist. You two would go at it for hours on the computer."

"What about when we're sailing *Windswept* together?" At Sylvia's raised eyebrows, Caroline quickly explained all about the sailboat and what it meant to their family.

Then David cut in. "When we're sailing has been the only time I've felt close to you and Lily for years. And it seems lately that even our sail dates have been fraught with difficulties. I get called at the last minute to bail some skuzzball out of jail, the storm last summer when water got into the cabin and ruined half the cushions. We missed the last third of the season. Repairing the leaks and replacing cushions took a long time. Nothing has gone right, lately."

Sylvia looked at her watch. "Unfortunately, we're out of time. We'll talk again next week. At that time I'll give you two some homework to complete in between sessions. The only thing I want you to do between now and then is to spend at least eight hours together, once a week. I don't care what you do, but we have to start bridging the gap that's grown since you two separated. Have Alice make you an appointment for about two weeks out."

Chapter 14

David came to pick them up for the July Fourth picnic about noon on Thursday. Lily protested about wanting to spend the day with her friends, but Caroline issued an ultimatum and she stomped upstairs to get dressed. There wasn't anything Caroline needed to pack except sunscreen and a sweatshirt for herself and Lily. The firm provided all the eats and drinks. It was usually a festive affair with snacks and hors d'oeuvres all afternoon and steaks for dinner.

Caroline wore white pants and a blue and white striped top. David also wore white pants and a navy and white print shirt. They looked as if they planned to match. She smiled when she saw him step out of the car. In that outfit he looked as if he belonged on the bridge of a hundred-foot yacht.

David looked happy when he came into the kitchen, and she realized he'd been looking forward to the day. She would have been, too, if not for knowing Matt would be there.

David noticed what she wore and laughed. "I guess we couldn't have done it better if we'd planned it. You look great."

"Thank you." Caroline had taken extra time to get ready this morning and even somewhat tamed her curly hair. "So do you."

He smiled and came over to give her a quick peck on the lips. "You two almost ready for the big 'do' at the park?"

Caroline could only hope Lily's rebellious snit that morning wouldn't continue all afternoon, spoiling her father's hopes for a nice family outing. They needed something like this and it would make their marriage counselor happy. She crossed her fingers Lily would behave.

“Lily should be down in a minute. She was late getting started this morning.”

“We have time. People just wander in for the first few hours. How have you been?”

“Well, you know. I kind of rattle around the house. I’m trying to get up enough nerve to go over to the outplacement center at the plant. The papers don’t have anything in my skill area.”

He nodded as if he knew how lost she must feel. “I was at the marina last weekend. I slept over Saturday night.”

Caroline felt a stab of anguish. Last summer, they often arrived at the marina Friday night and stayed the weekend. She’d missed it. “How’s the boat?”

“Fine. I went out alone Saturday and then Kathy and Bob invited me out for a ride Sunday.” He hesitated. “I had to tell them about us.”

She frowned. “I guess it was time.”

“Yeah.”

“I'd thought about going tomorrow.”

“Tomorrow I thought I should come here and mow the lawn and do some chores. Maybe get Lily to help me.”

“Then perhaps I should stay and help.”

“No. Don’t stay here on my account. I’ll be fine. It’ll give Lily and me a chance to bond again. We need to do more of that.”

“Okay, then maybe I will go.”

“Yes, do.” He started to open his mouth but apparently changed his mind.

"You were going to tell me to put the sails up, weren't you?"

"Guilty. But I didn’t want to put pressure on you. When you're ready, you'll do it."

Caroline stared at him. He regretted they hadn't been able to have the closeness they'd had all those years when they were sailing. She could see it in his eyes.

Maybe after Lily's fifteenth birthday party, she could ask him to go out with her. Just a friendly afternoon sail, no pressure, no strings.

Lily came in at that moment wearing a ragged pair of cut-offs and a Bruce Springsteen tee shirt which seen better days. "Lily." Caroline cried. "What are you thinking? You know what kind of thing you should be wearing to this picnic and that outfit certainly is not it. Now go back up and change into something nice."

Lily snickered and left the kitchen sullenly and with a definite attitude. "You have five minutes." Caroline called to her retreating back.

David watched his daughter's behavior in amazement. He swiveled to face her. "What was that attitude all about?"

"She said earlier she didn't want to go to the picnic. She wanted to spend the day with her friends. I thought I convinced her she didn't have a choice."

"That wasn't what I meant. A blind person could see this attitude thing is a regular pattern with you two. When did it start?"

"It's been this way ever since she caught us arguing that night."

"You mean all this time you've been putting up with her lip and you haven't called me?" David looked disturbed and annoyed she'd clearly left him out of something that important.

"You had enough on your mind and I thought she just needed a little time. She's been through a lot."

"True, but it's no excuse for her being rude to her mother."

"I didn't want to make things even worse with her."

"I think she needs to know she can't get away with insolent behavior. I'll be right back." He spun on his heel and strode up the stairs.

Caroline started to follow him, then paused. He needed to do this on his own. Sure enough, when he came back down the stairs, Lily followed meekly in his wake. She wore one of her new outfits with her head bowed. But she looked less sullen. David stood aside to let her approach.

"Mom?" Lily said, in a tiny voice.

"You have something you want to say to me?"

"Yeah, I'm sorry. Dad told me I shouldn't take out my hurt feelings on you because you were hurting, too." She avoided looking at Caroline's face. "I never thought about it that way."

Caroline stepped forward and pulled her daughter into a warm hug. "It's okay, sweetie. I've understood why you were being argumentative."

Lily hugged her back. Not as uninhibitedly as she might have a few months ago, but more than Caroline would have expected.

"Can I have a hug, too?" David asked, a hopeful look on his face.

Lily let Caroline go and turned around to put her head on her father's chest. He held her close for a long time and she didn't seem to want to leave. Caroline's eyes filled up at the touching scene.

He patted her back once more and said, cheerfully, "We have a picnic to go to. Let's get a move on."

Most of the firm and their families were already there when they arrived. It was a large firm with about twenty lawyers. With spouses and kids, quite a crowd gathered under the big pavilion. Fortunately, it turned out to be a nice day, and people were able to sit in the sun on lawn chairs.

David pulled three chairs out of his car. There was a game of softball going on beside the pavilion and several family games were planned for the afternoon, complete with nice prizes.

Debbie sat on the grass with a couple of other teenage girls and Lily meandered over to join the club. Matt stood under the pavilion with a beer in his hand, talking to some of the men.

"Why don't we sit over here in the sun and talk to the Harolds and the Petersons?" David suggested.

They set their chairs down and ambled over for appetizers. Settling in their chairs with plates on their laps and their beers precariously resting in the high grass, they munched and gossiped about the goings on in the firm and how everyone's children were doing. Someone mentioned Lily's science fair win and Caroline explained her project to them.

After a while, one of David's friends came over and asked them to join the softball game. Caroline begged off but he dragged Lily and Debbie into it. Because he was a lefty with an innate athletic ability, he'd played first base every year for years, and his team cheered when they saw he'd joined the game. Debbie and Lily were relegated to the outfield with the other kids.

The team wasn't sexist, though. Their pitcher turned out to be a twenty-something young woman who worked as a law clerk for one of the partners and apparently had played softball in school. She had a wicked arm and worked her way through one after another of the opposing team. Eventually, she showed them some mercy and retreated to the outfield to help Lily pick daisies.

David's team had been losing when he joined the game, but they finally won a defensive duel by mid-afternoon. Then it was time for the father-daughter three-legged race and the mother-son three-legged race. With no one to race with, Caroline relaxed and enjoyed watching David and Lily struggle across the field and laugh as they got their legs entangled and hit the turf in a heap. They lost. They did, however, win the wheelbarrow race by a mile. Debbie and Matt lost both.

The egg-toss was an adult event and Caroline lined up opposite David with an egg in her hand. She tossed it up and down in one hand and grinned at David. He looked askance at her, as if not sure he should trust her with his dignity. She caught Matt watching them, a frown darkening his face.

The starter bell sounded and the contestants tossed their eggs across a modest six feet. Everyone survived the first throw, but the women were the recipients of the upcoming throws, and some of the husbands were taunting their wives. There had occasionally been some shenanigans and egg-citement in previous years.

The men stepped back two feet and they threw the eggs again. Caroline caught the egg by palming it and swinging it backwards to absorb the impact. She was an old pro at this game. One couple got eliminated in the first round of the game when one of the husbands tossed his egg at his wife's head and egg yolk dripped off her nose.

The husbands stepped back another two feet. Caroline's throw went wild but David leaped sideways and with a low swoop managed to catch it in one hand. Three couples fell with the throw, one of the husbands literally with egg on his face.

Three rounds later, only David and Caroline and the Petersons remained. They were forty feet away and it was the women's turn to throw to the men. Caroline had seen Katie Peterson play softball the last inning of the game and knew she could throw. Caroline herself wasn't sure she could even make it that distance without throwing it wildly.

David shouted encouragement to her and she decided she might as well go for it. She tossed it as far as she could but it went way up in the air and came down far short. David dived for it and landed in the grass on his stomach with the egg clenched in his hand but with broken, raw egg yolk dripping through his fingers.

He sat up and looked in dismay at the mess all over his hands, but Caroline couldn't stop laughing at the spectacle he'd made, leaping for the egg like a ten-year-old at a Little League game. The Petersons were celebrating their victory and, when Caroline's laughter eased, she ran over to help David up.

"Oh, David, you have grass stains all over your white pants."

He looked ruefully down at the smear on both knees and shrugged.

"Men," she huffed.

Lily ran over and knelt in the grass, giggling at her father. "Dad, you looked so funny trying to catch the egg."

"I'm glad I provided some amusement for you two," he groused. One of the wives handed out paper towels to those who needed a fast clean-up, and he grabbed one.

"More than just the two of us appreciated the show," Caroline added, looking around at the couples who stood grinning at the spectacle they made. Several of them had egg all over themselves too but they were not above getting satisfaction from others' misfortune.

He groaned. "There goes my reputation."

"I think you'd better go to the rest room and take advantage of soap and hot water. I'll ask around and see what I can find out about getting grass stains out of white cotton. If that doesn't work, I'll Google it later."

He looked at his hand and arm. The paper towel removed some of the worst of the egg, but the rest congealed in a mass of dried yolk and shells. "I think you're right." He levered himself up and headed across the park.

Caroline turned to realize Lily had watched their interaction. "Everything has been just like it used to be today, hasn't it?"

It felt as if someone had stabbed her in the heart. She couldn't answer Lily. She'd no idea what to say. In a daze, she walked over to some of the wives who were helping set places for the steak dinner. She glanced back to see if Lily followed her, but Lily was gone.

Matt came over and set his and Debbie's places opposite theirs. Caroline gave him a stern look but he ignored it. When David came back, he eyed the setup but he didn't say anything. They all sat down in a festive atmosphere.

The firm had ordered the picnic dinner catered from a steak house downtown, and the grilled T-bones were delicious. The potato salad and tossed salad were excellent, and cheesecake, hardly picnic fare but not about to be turned down by the diners, was served with fresh strawberries on top and a sinful heap of whipped cream.

After dinner, the picnic tables were cleared and pushed back to make room for dancing. A local band set up in one corner and warmed up to play oldies. David and Caroline listened and watched for a while, letting the younger couples have the floor for the fast dances. Darkness had fallen when the band played their first slow song, a ballad made popular by Nat King Cole.

David reached for her hand. "Dance?" he asked her.

She nodded and swallowed the lump in her throat as he led her onto the crowded dance floor. To the lovely strains of 'Moonlight Becomes You,' David pulled her into his arms. They weren't in the habit of dancing often, but always enjoyed themselves on those rare occasions. Tonight, it was heaven to be in his arms again, both familiar and yet new and exciting.

They fit together like a hand inside a glove and knew how to move together smoothly and effortlessly. An excitement burned in their touching, and she felt the tingle all the way to her toes. Maybe there was something to be said for fighting if it felt like this to make up.

She laid her head on his shoulder and he released her hand to press both of his against her back. They swayed slowly in a tight embrace, seeking that closeness the way kids do, lusting after their first crush.

"I've missed you, Caro," he whispered. "I ache for you."

The haunting tones of the King crooning his sweet melody lingered in her head. Her consciousness wrapped up in her husband as surely as her body was wrapped in his arms. A buzzing sounded in her ears and she felt fuzzy, light-headed.

She badly wanted him to kiss her, and she raised her head to seek his lips, but realized he'd stopped dancing and stood gazing at her. The music had ended and she hadn't even realized it. Still, he reached down to kiss her softly and with infinite tenderness. She would've let him go on forever but the dance floor was empty and she felt ill at ease.

She stepped away in embarrassment and he gazed into her eyes in understanding, making a silent promise to continue later what he'd started on the dance floor. He kissed her fingertips and led her back to the picnic table. The next few songs passed in a haze for Caroline as she sat and listened to the conversations go on around her. One of David's buddies from the office came up and sat next to him.

"David, Tom says he wants to buy a sailboat and I told him you were an expert. You gotta come over and talk to him, my man."

David turned to Caroline. "Will you be okay for a few minutes? I'll go give Tom the lowdown and be right back."

"I'm fine. Go talk boats." She watched him talk animatedly for several minutes, giving his expert advice. Matt approached the other side of the picnic bench and sat beside her.

"Deserted?"

"No. He'll be back in a minute."

"Sure. Get him talking about boats and he may never come back."

Caroline shot him an annoyed look and continued to sit restlessly, waiting for David's return. One song ended and the couples filed off the dance floor. Next came a jitterbug, 'Rock Around the Clock.'

"Hey." said Matt. "They're playing our song."

She grinned. "Yes, they are." She and Matt had danced a wicked jitterbug to 'Rock Around the Clock' at some of the other company picnics. Not being a fast-dance kind of guy, David hadn't minded.

She looked at the hand Matt held out. "I shouldn't."

"Caroline," he said impatiently. "We dance to this song every year. You know David hates to dance the jitterbug. Come on, he won't mind. It's a tradition."

She'd been jiggling her feet up and down to every fast tune all night and finally decided one little jitterbug couldn't hurt, especially since Matt was right and they'd done this every year.

"Okay." She jumped up and they made their way onto the dance floor. They jitterbugged wildly, grasping first one hand and then the other and then both, and doing spins every which way. Matt happened to be a great dancer and they made a spectacle of themselves when they jitterbugged, but she'd always enjoyed it.

In the middle of the dance, when they faced each other with both hands clasped, he began, much to her alarm, to sing along with the lyrics.

He sang loudly enough that all the other dancers stopped to watch and laugh. Caroline would have liked to sink into the floor, but she was laughing so hard she held her stomach to keep from getting sick. Finally, Matt grabbed her shoulders to lead her back to the picnic bench and she sank weakly onto the seat, trying to get control of her giggling.

David was there and he was not laughing.

Matt plopped down breathlessly on the other side of her and leaned back to catch his breath. "Caro, that was something."

"It seemed like a ridiculous exhibition, that's what it was," David said harshly.

"Oh, lighten up, buddy," Matt retorted.

"I don't think we're buddies anymore, Matt." He grabbed Caroline's shoulder roughly, his fingers bruising her skin. "Caroline, what were you thinking, dancing with him, after—" He didn't continue, but stared hotly at Matt sitting there, smirking at him and mocking him.

"David, it didn't mean anything." Caroline shook his fingers off her shoulder. "We dance it every year."

"I think this year it was inappropriate."

"You were across the pavilion, talking to your friends about boats," she said, annoyed. "What should I do? Sit and fold my hands and wait obediently on the bench until you decide to come back? I danced and had some fun. Why does that bother you?"

"If you don't know," he said cryptically, "then it probably wouldn't do me any good to tell you." He rose from the bench. "I need to get some air." And he walked off into the night.

Caroline snickered. They were sitting in an open air pavilion. What he really needed was to walk off his temper. She felt discouraged. What they'd experienced when they danced together was special and he'd ruined it with his jealousy. As far as she was concerned, he could get over it. Or not.

"Are you all right?" Matt asked.

"I'm fine," she replied. "I think I'm going to walk over to the rest room."

When she returned, David still wasn't back. She sat next to Matt but didn't say anything.

About twenty minutes later, she saw David talking again to the group requiring his expertise about sailboats. She ignored him and listened to the music. 'Moon River' started up and, in shock, she saw David lead his secretary out onto the dance floor. It was almost as if he were saying to her, "See? Two can play this game."

She turned to Matt. "Let's dance."

On the dance floor, he pulled her up against him, but she resisted. "Let's give him a show," he whispered in her ear. "He deserves it."

At first, she stiffened, because for her it went against the grain, but then she relented and molded herself to him. Her heart beat crazily and she hoped she wasn't making a mistake. Her motives were different from Matt's. She wanted to make David jealous. Maybe, between their close, passionate dance earlier, and the show Matt now wanted to put on, David would be aroused enough to make a move. She didn't care if it was anger that aroused him as long as he reacted. Maybe it would be enough to bring him back to her.

For once, she felt no response to Matt as he all but made love to her on the dance floor. Her mind stayed on her husband, staring angrily from a few feet away. Her heart sank. He looked furious. Turning away from his gaze, she put her head on Matt's shoulder. She felt miserable.

She leaned back to tell Matt this had been a mistake and they should stop, when hard fingers bit into her shoulder and jerked her away by force.

The look on David's face was thunderous as he pulled her further away from Matt and glared at him, obviously trying to decide whether to give him another black eye. Matt was visibly angry, too.

Fearing violence would break out, Caroline turned to David with her hands on his chest. "Please, David, don't. Everyone's watching."

David pushed past her and strode out into the dark again.

Shaken, she spared one glance for a white-faced Matt, and then took off after her husband. She passed by Lily, standing on the edge of the crowd looking stricken and pale. She would have to deal with her later.

She found him leaning against his SUV, his hand holding the back of his neck as his head sagged onto his chest. “Are you all right?” she asked hesitantly.

“No.” His voice was hoarse.

“Is there anything I can do?”

“I think you’ve done enough, Caroline.”

“David, you were dancing with another woman, you know.”

“She’s my secretary.” he yelled. “It was an obligation dance.” He was visibly trying to calm himself down as he lowered his voice. “I was on my way back to you to apologize when I saw her sitting by herself and I decided to do the socially correct thing and ask her to dance while I had a few extra minutes. And then, you—” He stopped, apparently speechless to describe the sight of her dancing with Matt.

Caroline bit her bottom lip and stood, wrapped her arms around herself both to warm herself in the cooling night air and to keep from shaking. David ran his fingers through his hair and straightened from the side of the car. He paced away, then came back to her side. She couldn’t move.

“My God, Caroline,” he said, finally coming to a stop in front of her. “What were you thinking? Or were you not thinking at all? Were you just feeling? Feeling another man’s arms around you and liking it?”

She started to contradict him but he cut her off with a vicious movement of his arm. “Never mind. There is no excuse. You can’t imagine what it felt like to stand there and watch him practically crawl into you.”

His fury made her angry. "Oh, can't I? Then again, maybe you're right. At least I didn't have to watch."

She stomped away and left him standing next to his car, staring bleakly into the black night.

When she returned to the pavilion, she noticed the festivities had started to break up. Those who left avoided looking at her, as if she had not been party to a huge scandal that could rock the firm and provide gossip fodder for weeks.

Lily stood alone in the corner of the pavilion, in the same position as earlier and with the same expression on her face. Her eyes flashed when Caroline tried to gather her in her arms.

She moved back to avoid Caroline's embrace. "Mom, what on earth were you doing out there on the dance floor?" she snapped.

"Lily. I'm sorry. It—well, it got out of hand."

Lily looked at her as if she were insane. "Out of hand? You were all over Debbie's dad."

"We were just trying to make your father jealous."

"You certainly managed that, I think."

"I didn't intend it to go that far," Caroline said, defensively.

"All I know is, you really messed it up this time." Lily tried to rush away, but Caroline stopped her.

"You don't know the whole story. You weren't here when your father started everything."

"What difference does it make who started it?" Lily said with youthful candor. "You just finished it."

Lily glared at Matt as he walked over to them. "Want me to take you two home?"

"I don't want to go anywhere with you," Lily said. A sneer curved her lips.

"I think we should go home with David. We came with him, and—"

"David's gone. I saw him leave a minute ago."

Caroline stood, stunned and dismayed that David actually drove off without them. He must have been truly devastated, to have left them for Matt to take care of.

She nodded and walked over to the lawn chairs David had abandoned. She folded them up and carried them to Matt's van. Debbie must have talked to Lily and convinced her to go with them because she sat in the back seat with Debbie's arm around her. Caroline climbed into the front seat and they silently drove home.

Caroline entertained a wild hope David's car would be in their driveway when she got back, and he would be eager to talk out their situation. But her hope was dashed when they turned into the driveway and it was empty, except for her car.

Lily clambered out of the back seat and ran into the house, murmuring something about having to call a friend. She went upstairs without another word. After collecting her lawn chairs from Matt and thanking him for the ride, Caroline headed inside.

She tried to relax in a hot, fragrant bath but her mind kept going in circles. Tonight she'd made a big mistake. In trying to force David's jealousy, his fury over what she'd done had driven him away from her.

Chapter 15

Caroline hardly slept at all. If there was ever a time she needed to relax, it was today. She dragged herself out of bed at seven and sat with a cup of coffee, staring at the kitchen clock for over an hour. After last night she thought Lily should go with her instead of staying at the house with her father, but she didn't dare go up too early and ask. A donut took up all of about ten minutes and then she fetched the paper from the front porch.

At nine she finally decided she didn't have the patience to wait any longer, and went up to Lily's room. Stretched out on her stomach, her arms and legs flung in abandon with the covers on the floor, Lily didn't appreciate being awakened that early during summer vacation.

"Let me sleep," she mumbled, flopping over onto her back.

Caroline shook her shoulder. "I'm headed to the marina to spend the day on the boat. Do you want to go with me?"

"No, stay here," Lily whined.

"Dad's coming to mow the lawn and do some chores. Are you sure you want to stay here with him?"

"Don't care."

"All right. Fine. But if you're not coming with me, I may stay over and spend the night on the boat. I'll call Matt. I want you to spend the night at Debbie's. I'll have my cell phone if you need me."

"Okay." Lily rolled back onto her stomach.

Shaking her head, Caroline called Matt and arranged for

Lily to spend the night with Debbie. She briefly considered asking him to accompany her on the boat, but knew she needed to be alone.

She'd packed the car trunk with her boat bag filled with food, plus a cooler for drinks and a small overnight bag, when David drove up and parked next to her. He looked like hell. If she hadn't slept much, she surmised from his haggard face that he hadn't at all.

He got out and stood watching her fuss with the cooler, his hands in the pockets of his cut-offs. "Hi," he said grimly.

She straightened. "Hi."

"Anything in particular you want done around here today?"

He didn't seem inclined to mention their blow-up. Just as well. Right now, she didn't think she could cope with talking about last night with him or anyone.

"You probably know better than I do what needs to be done."

"I haven't been here," he reminded her.

"Nothing's changed."

He nodded. "I'd like to start."

"Can you wait a minute? There's something I need to talk to you about. It's about Alicia. She's been harassing us and I'm getting really concerned.

"Harassing? Like how?"

"There have been several things and none of them is threatening or anything, but taken together it's a disturbing pattern.

"Caroline, what? Talk to me."

"Okay." She took a deep breath. "You know about the scarf she planted in the cupboard. Well, since then, she's dumped orange fingernail polish all over the vee berth and—"

"Wait. I haven't seen any nail polish."

"It's on one edge—quite a lot of it. I turned the cushion over so it was less visible. We'll have to get a new cushion cover."

"Is that it?"

"Oh no. There's more. She also stole my sailing gloves and put them in an envelope and left them on our porch. It felt really sick and I ended up throwing my gloves away. I couldn't stand to use them. I bought new ones but I loved those old soft gloves, David."

"I had it out with her, Caroline, and I thought she understood and was going to go away. She's been calling me at work too and my secretary has instructions to tell her I didn't want to talk to her."

"She's not going away, David."

"Then I'll have to make her. I'm going to call the police Monday morning and have an order of protection taken out for her to keep her away from you and Lily. And I'll call her and tell her that if she keeps calling me, I'll extend that order to include myself. I'll stop her. Don't worry."

"I'll try to stop worrying, but I'm still going to keep an eye out for her."

"If you see her, call the cops. Period."

"I will. Thank you, David. Now, you'd better get going.

"Yeah, it's going to heat up later and I want to get this yard work out of the way before it gets too scorching." He turned and opened the garage to drag out the mower. "Have fun at the marina."

"You know where I'll be if you need me," she called after him.

"Have fun," he replied, only a bit sarcastically.

She intended to.

It took her two trips from the parking lot to the boat when she got there. Her top stuck to her back and sweat dripped down between her breasts by the time she stowed everything. To alleviate the stuffy air, she opened every porthole and hatch on the boat.

Kathy sat in the cockpit of her boat reading a magazine and she called a greeting. Caroline waved back but didn't try to engage her in conversation. She wasn't up to dealing with anyone's questions.

Standing on a seat in the cockpit, she looked out over the marina and drank in the atmosphere. A lot of the boats were already out on the water. A light breeze wafted its way across the air, carrying with it the scent of the sea. It would be a perfect day to try her wings at single-handling the boat if the weather report agreed with her observations and if the breeze out on the bay wasn't much stiffer than in the marina.

She stepped into the cabin and turned on the battery to listen to the weather report on the VHF radio. Reports from the Washington, metro area came first and then she heard what she'd been waiting for.

And now for the marine forecast for the upper Chesapeake Bay area including Annapolis, Baltimore, St. Michaels, Cambridge, and Easton. Today's weather will be dominated by a high pressure system centered over central New England. High temperatures expected later in the high eighties with wind out of the west-northwest, light and variable, less than five miles an hour. Waves less than two feet.

Bingo. It sounded perfect. She set channel sixteen to monitor, and tossed the items she would need out onto the deck. Her new red sailing gloves she stuffed into the equipment locker since she wouldn't need them today. As she shoved them in, she shivered slightly and thought about her old beloved gloves. They'd gone right into the trash in the kitchen. It would be impossible to use them again without thinking about Alicia.

Slathered in sunscreen, she headed topside to get the

boat ready to sail. Then she started the engine, nervous yet excited.

"Caroline?" Kathy called. "Are you going out?"

"Yes. Do you think you could give me a hand casting off?"

"Exactly what I was going to suggest."

"Thanks."

Kathy tossed the dock lines onto the deck just as the boat started to slide soundlessly backward. She waved and Caroline drove the boat slowly out of the marina.

The inlet was busy since it was a holiday weekend and a sunny day, but she motored along in line and cut away from the others when she got to the bay. The last thing she needed was to worry about another boat being too close when she attempted to get the sails up. The breeze was slightly more out on the bay, as usual, but a glance at the meter told her it only measured five miles per hour and there was barely a ripple on the water. Perfect. Even a wimp like her could do it under these conditions.

Well away from the other boats, she stepped out from behind the wheel. She stood for a moment in the middle of the cockpit to make sure everything seemed copasetic and under control.

I can do this.

Her fingers fumbled as she put up the huge mainsail. That done, she viewed the sail with pride. It was up. Useless and flapping lightly, but up. With a deep breath, she slowly let out the jib. Fastening the control line, she stepped back behind the wheel.

Her breath whooshed out. This was the moment of truth. Still under engine power, she turned the boat to port and waited for the jib and mainsail to fill.

Both sails were now taut and raring to go. Caroline closed her eyes with a quick prayer, then turned off the engine.

She waited for the moment of complete silence before she heard the quiet whisper of the wind in the sails and the soothing sound of water moving softly along the length of the hull. Caroline gasped in wonder at the magical moment. *Windswept* was sailing.

Nervous at first without the engine on, Caroline soon found her groove and sailing once again became a natural thing. She actually felt at ease behind the wheel.

I did it. I can't believe it. I really did it.

She looked up at the sails, nicely taut but not straining, and then out at the water, a pleasant ripple running by the boat. The knot meter showed she was only going a little over three knots, but it was enough for her.

Inevitably, there came the time when she needed to make her first tack. She got more and more nervous as the shore got closer and she knew she would have to do it.

You can do this. You've done it before, lots of times with David and there's hardly any wind. In fact, the wind had dropped a little and she now slid through the water at less than three knots.

She prepared for the tack, then let the sails come around before she ran back to the helm and stabilized the boat to head in the new direction.

Whew. I did it.

That turned out to be nerve-wracking business. She hadn't thought about her problems once since starting the motor in her slip. That was one of the best things about sailing. It put you into another world where cares and anxieties didn't exist.

Caroline took the boat on several more long tacks. The breeze grew less and less and she managed to run down to grab a sandwich she'd made earlier, and a can of soda, and bring them up to eat while she steered with her toe. Afterwards, she turned the boat around and headed back.

With the bare whisper of wind that now blew, returning would take longer.

The small amount of wind that blew an hour earlier disappeared completely by around mid-afternoon and she waited in the hot sun, the sails hanging uselessly. By then, she felt as if she might die of the heat with the sun beating down on her relentlessly and reflecting off the water. She looked around. Many of the boats were anchored and children and adults were swimming in the cool water around their boats.

Now there's an idea.

She was excited about swimming off the boat. She and David had done so several times last summer in similar conditions, but she knew she couldn't manage the heavy anchor by herself. The air was still and calm, though, and she should be able to just jump in. The boat shouldn't go anywhere.

Figuring she wouldn't have use of the sails any longer after she finished swimming, she took them down before she went to change into her swimsuit. It was hot work with the sun beating down on her, and by the time she got the sail ties on, she was exhausted and sweat freely ran off her body.

She shed her clothes eagerly and put on her suit, and slipped a life jacket over it, for safety. Whenever swimming, they wore jackets.

She grabbed one of the extra lines from the storage compartment and tied it around a loop on the jacket, then lowered the swim ladder at the back of the boat. Checking one more time to make sure *Windswept* wasn't anywhere near any other boats, she climbed over the rail and down the ladder.

Cautiously, she eased one foot into the water and then the other foot. Just standing with the water up to her ankles made her cooler. It was five minutes before she managed to get her overheated body into the icy water but, when she did.

It felt like heaven. She quickly cooled down to a comfortable level.

Cautiously, she swam a foot or two away. From her vantage point the boat looked huge. Every time a wake came by, the boat rose and fell. To avoid a possible bonk on the head, she stayed away from the back of the boat where it rose highest. No sense risking injury when she had no one there to help her. Mostly she just floated and enjoyed the cool water.

After a while, staying in the shadow of the boat chilled her skin. Moving around to the sunny side gave her a different view of other boats off in the distance, each time a swell brought her up in the air.

When sufficiently cooled, the heat would be easier to tolerate for some time to come, so Caroline climbed back on board and stood dripping in the cockpit, not bothering to towel off. The evaporating water felt good on her skin and kept her fresh. The swim ladder came up with several gallons of water, and the engine started without a hitch. Sitting in the puddle of her wet suit, she motored back to her slip in the inlet.

All she needed to do now was manage to dock the boat alone without crashing into anything. Fortunately, this was her strong suit since she always brought the boat in, although of course she'd never done it alone. She hoped fervently Kathy or someone else she knew still hung around at the marina.

Luck was with her because Kathy sat in her boat crocheting when Caroline came into view, and she ran over to *Windswept*'s slip to help Caroline tie up. Little help was needed after all, except for Kathy to grab the dock lines Caroline threw and secure them onto the cleats until she could jump off the boat and take them.

"Thanks," she said in a heartfelt manner.

"Any time," Kathy replied.

Caroline tied up the boat and made little Flemish coils for David out of the excess. He would smile when he saw them. When she went back into the boat to finish up, Kathy called across the space between the boats.

"I wish I could invite you for dinner, but I didn't know you were coming and I only have enough hot dogs for two. Sorry."

"That's okay. I have some hamburger I hoped to try grilling."

"Next time e-mail me when you're going to be up here and I'll bring enough for all of us."

"All right. I didn't decide until last night whether I was coming today, or I might have." Which wasn't exactly true. She just hadn't been in any mood to talk to anyone, even Kathy, when she'd come earlier.

After the boat looked shipshape again, she got out the gas grill and struggled to fasten it to the back railing. It took her awhile since she'd never done it before, and she didn't want to drop it overboard into the seven feet of water the boat sat in at the marina. She'd dropped David's favorite flashlight last year, and it had been bye-bye flashlight.

She lit the burner, fortunately without incident, since a conflagration in the middle of the marina would attract a lot of spectators.

Standing on the seat of the cockpit with a spatula in her hand, Caroline looked wryly at the lone hamburger sitting in the center of the grill. It looked pretty pathetic. This single life was the pits. When the patty tested done, she sat in the cockpit against the bulkhead and ate her burger and potato chips as she watched the boats come back in after a day on the water. There were reddened arms and shoulders and youngsters in swim suits and runabouts dragging stringers of fish.

She sat for a long time watching the people and the

boats, until dusk. Finally, the ducks that had set up residence in the marina started swooping across the mast tops and landing with long graceful descents onto the water between the boats. Before long there were dozens of them, quacking and swimming around, grouping and regrouping, looking for handouts. Whenever a couple of kids from one of the boats decided to feed them bits of broken-off bread, ducks from every corner of the marina heard the racket and came swimming swiftly over to join in the quest for crusts. They fought like children for each tiny morsel and some even got mean, chasing away competitors for the free food. When it was dark and she couldn't see anything more than the silhouettes of the ducks settling in for the night, Caroline went below.

She got out her book and tried to read it but felt restless. It seemed too silent and solitary down here. She was used to having David here to share the day's adventures with, and that was half the fun of coming to a place like this. She missed him, especially here.

She looked up at the Vee berth they always slept in together, and it made her even sadder. Many boating couples she knew slept in separate berths because they tended to be small. But she and David always enjoyed sleeping close together in the Vee berth. With the smoky glass hatch close above their heads, they could see the stars. The thought of sleeping there alone tonight was depressing when her sadness seemed especially acute.

Restlessly, Caroline set her book aside and made herself a cup of coffee in the small galley. Sitting on the settee with the cup on her lap, she continued to listen to the sound of silence in the small space. She sipped her coffee and opened her book again.

I can't concentrate. Might as well go to bed.

She climbed out of the closed up boat. A final trip to the bath house, and she was ready for sleep.

Back in the boat, she started to undress, then looked again at the Vee berth with its orange nail polish stain. The thought of spending the night there seemed suddenly intolerable. She always loved spending the night on the boat but, without David, it didn't feel the same. The joy was gone from it.

"I'm going home," she muttered to herself. "I can't stand this."

Chapter 16

On the way home, Caroline beat herself up over her decision not to stick it out for the night. After she'd been so brave going out on the water, she had wimped out at the thought of sleeping on the boat by herself. It was easier to be courageous about something like sailing than dealing with what was happening between her and David. It was a strange dichotomy. She was a fledgling, sailing the boat. She never knew what to say to David these days. At work she had been strong and in charge, but the rug had been pulled out from under her when she'd gotten laid off. So now she felt rudderless and without purpose, and she hated it.

Her strength and courage had never been tested until David's infidelity. Everything in her life had come so easily—she'd met David while in college and had fallen in love instantly. They'd married right after graduation, and since chemical engineers were in high demand she'd landed a great job. Lily, who had been born a year and a half after they got married, had been an easy child, bright, obedient, and outgoing. Maybe life had simply been too easy and she'd grown complacent, believing naively her future would be comfortable and stress-free. She had taken her marriage, her husband and her wonderful life for granted.

Then, when disaster struck, she'd had no skills to cope with any of it. All she'd known for certain, during all of this, was David's absence. Hopefully, not forever. Still, his leaving had pulled the pins from the foundation of her life, and she felt as if she was spinning in circles. Her elusive thoughts had rendered her unable to latch onto anything long enough to figure out what she was feeling or thinking or even what she wanted.

She hadn't done anything proactive, she'd only reacted, to David's self-doubts, first with angst and then anger and limited understanding. She had reacted to Matt's friendship and later pursuit, first with naive acceptance and then flattered interest. She was sick of having everyone else make decisions for her, of having others run her life. It was time to take control. Maybe today had been a baby step.

Lily had been the most tragic victim of her vacillation, and Caroline felt horrible about her ineptitude in dealing with her daughter. When David first left, Lily had reacted with distress and confusion and then, when the days and weeks went by and her father hadn't returned home, with anger and rebellion.

After the horrid scene at the firm picnic yesterday, Lily had been beside herself. Caroline hoped David had spent some time with their daughter today to at least try explaining what happened last night. She should have mentioned it to him this morning before she left, but things were already tense between them.

She was done with just waiting for things to happen to her. Her first order of business was to take advantage of the outplacement and look for a new job. Then she had to regain Lily's trust. Matt also had to be dealt with. Anything more than friendship between them was simply not going to happen, until or unless she was ready.

And David. . .if he wasn't ready to come home now, she was going to get on with her life.

At their lunch, she and Mary talked about Caroline moving ahead with her life, and it was about time she did it. She had to get out of this holding pattern, whether or not David was going to be a part of it.

Her relationship with David caused her the most confusion. Moments when she'd have taken him back at all costs, conflicted with her anger at what he did and confusion over her own wants. She still loved him, of that she was sure. But she wasn't certain she could make a life with him again.

Lily's fifteenth birthday was next weekend. She would invite Mary and Shelly, and Doug and their families, as well as Matt and Debbie and, if he wanted to come, David. She would put on a party for Lily and it would be the start of their new lives together.

As she pulled into the driveway, the house was dark. Lily was most likely already at Matt's. She considered going to get her, but it might be better for Lily to spend the night with her friend. Furthermore, she wasn't up to confronting Matt right now. She would have to think about what to say to him to keep from hurting him any more than necessary.

As she entered the house through the kitchen she thought she heard music. She put down her first load of stuff from the car so she could listen. Yes, it was music. It sounded as if it was coming from the den. Caroline shivered for a moment.

It's silly to be frightened. Lily must have left something on the CD player.

She crept down the dark hallway and saw a faint glow coming from the den. Puzzled, Caroline stood with her hand resting lightly on the doorjamb and peeked in. The dimmer was down almost all the way, giving the room the illusion of twilight. Then she saw a movement out of the corner of her eye.

Caroline jumped a foot off the floor when a scream sounded from the sofa. Twisting fast, she slapped the light on full-blast and saw a sight she never thought she would see. Lily, on her back on the sofa and a boy Caroline had never met, stretched out on top of her with his hands under her tee shirt. They had been kissing passionately. Both were panting and their clothing was awry.

Lily frantically pushed the boy off her and leapt from

the couch. Caroline was rooted to the spot, her mouth open in horror and her hand still on the dimmer switch. The boy, about six feet tall, with brown hair and a guilty expression, sidled to the corner, trying to unobtrusively tuck his shirt back in and slick his long hair back.

Shaking off her shock, Caroline's rage surged. "What the *hell* is going on here, Lily?"

"Uh," Lily said, obviously trying to stall, "What are you doing home, Mom?"

Wrong thing to say.

"It's my home. I can come here any time I want—announced or unannounced. Looks like unannounced was the best way tonight. I repeat, what's going on here?"

"This is Chris, Mandy's brother." Lily replied. He tried to grin but when he saw the look on Caroline's face, the grin died a quick death.

Caroline nodded. It was all starting to make some sense now. The dinners at Mandy's house, the days she wanted to spend all her time with Mandy, the evasions when the boy had picked her up. It wasn't Mandy who was the attraction at Mandy's house, it was her older brother. She turned to face him.

"You're, what, sixteen, right?"

He nodded.

"When are you going to be seventeen?"

"Uh, September."

Caroline sighed. "You just finished eleventh grade and are going into twelfth?"

"Yes, Ma'am." He looked more and more nervous.

"And you're aware Lily just finished eighth grade and is going into ninth?"

Chris shot Lily a supplicating look. "Mom," she pleaded, "I'm going to be fifteen next weekend."

Not sparing a glance in her daughter's direction,

Caroline told her, "I'll talk to you in a minute." She turned to Chris. "Don't you think you're a little old for her?"

"I—I love her," he stammered.

Caroline's stomach fell like a stone and she felt sick. "What—what did you say?"

Lily stepped over to Chris and grabbed onto his hand. "We love each other." Her voice was defiant and her stance aggressive.

"You're both practically children—"

"We're old enough to be in love." Lily turned to gaze into Chris's eyes.

Caroline put her hand to her head to massage her aching temples. "I don't believe this is happening." She glared at Lily. "Besides the age issue, which, believe me, is not resolved by a long shot, why have you been going out with this boy behind my back?"

Lily had the grace to look guilty. "I knew you'd be upset."

"Of course I'm upset."

"See, I knew you would be."

"Did you think I wouldn't find out?"

Lily didn't say anything, but Caroline could tell by the look on her face that was exactly what she had been hoping. "Parents always find out, Lily."

"Apparently."

"And you thought it would be better for me to walk in on the two of you like this than to sit down and talk it out?"

"I didn't think something like this would happen. I thought you were spending the night on the boat."

"Lily, even if I had not come home and found you tonight, I would have found out sometime. Why aren't you at Matt's house?"

Lily looked guilty again. "I called him and said I was spending the evening with Mandy and I would have her drop me off at ten."

Caroline glanced at her watch. It was almost ten. "More lies."

"I guess."

"And was it worth it, all the lies?"

"Yes. We love each other," she defended.

"Love doesn't justify lies," Caroline replied.

"Daddy said he loved us and still lied."

Caroline blanched. She and David had not given their daughter much of an example the past few months. It was no wonder she had gotten into trouble and thought it was okay to sneak around behind their backs.

She chose to take another tack. "What about you, Chris?"

Chris jumped and his eyes shot to Caroline's. He had probably thought he was out of the firing line for the time being and had been lulled into a sort of stunned stupor. "Ma'am?"

"What do your parents say about all of this?" Caroline stood with her fists on her hips. "Do they approve of you going out with such a young girl?"

He looked uncomfortable for a moment. "My mom wasn't too thrilled." Then he brightened. "But she likes Lily."

"And how does she feel about you two not informing Lily's parents of your relationship?"

"They—ah—they don't know we haven't told you and Mr. Hartford." He gripped Lily's hand harder.

"I see. So the two of you told Chris's parents about your relationship but chose to keep it from us and go around behind our backs? Is that about the gist of it, Lily?"

The two teens glanced at each other, then Lily stepped in front of Chris, reaching behind her to keep hold of his hand. "Are you going to make us stop seeing each other? You can't do that."

"I think you know what I'm capable of doing, Lily."

"Mom. . ."

"I'm not sure what I'm going to do. This is all very new to me and I have to admit, I wasn't expecting to deal with something like this at your age. It's hit me pretty hard."

"Don't make us stop going out," Lily pleaded, moving forward and dragging him with her. "We won't do it." Her voice got more demanding as her level of distress increased. "We won't stop seeing each other."

She turned to clutch at Chris's sleeves and laid her head on his chest. He closed his arms around her and his cheek lowered to the top of her head in a gesture of comfort.

Caroline stared at them in astonishment. They really did seem to care for each other.

It was obvious from that moment, however badly she had botched the last several months of her life, she could not afford to botch this with Lily. She made a decision.

"No one is going to make you stop seeing each other," she said gently.

Lily, tears streaming down her face, ran to Caroline, grabbing her around the waist. "Thank you."

Caroline snuggled her daughter for a few minutes while Chris looked uncomfortable, then she held Lily at arm's length and wiped the tears from her cheeks. "But there will have to be rules. You are still very young and I think it would be best if we limited your time with Chris to when you can be chaperoned. I'll call Chris's mother and make sure she understands I think you're too young to be alone together like you were here tonight."

"She doesn't let us spend time all alone at my house either, Mrs. Hartford," Chris chimed in. "We can't go up to my room unless someone else is up there."

So at least the couple had had some sort of supervision, and Chris's mother sounded conscientious. "Good. You can go on dates as long as they're multiple dates with other couples or group parties. I intend to keep track of what is going on between you two from now on and I expect you both to be honest with me about your relationship. If this kind of thing happens again, the relationship *will* be over."

The two nodded eagerly, their relief evident. Caroline hoped they considered themselves lucky after the compromising position they'd been found in tonight.

"And now I think it's time for you to be getting home, Chris. Lily and I still have some talking to do and we have to call Lily's father." Lily's eyes flitted to hers in distress, but she didn't object.

"Okay," said Chris, sidling toward the door and raising a hand slightly to Lily.

"Wait a minute, Chris." Caroline stopped him. "Where do you live? I didn't see your car."

His eyes flew to Lily's in guilt once again. "It's—ah—in your garage. We hid it so Mr. Deming wouldn't see it." He chewed his lip.

"I see." Caroline pursed her lips. "You two were quite clever, weren't you?"

They both stood uncomfortably, and then Chris stared longingly out into the hall. "Uh, may I go?"

"Of course." Caroline shook her head. Never in a million years did she think she'd be in this situation with Lily. Her little girl was growing up. "I'm sure I'll be seeing you again soon."

Chris fled without another word and Lily sank onto the sofa with her face in her hands.

"Lily, you understand I have to call your father." Lily didn't raise her head but she nodded slightly.

"Okay, then. We'll resume this conversation after your dad gets here."

Caroline picked up the cordless phone and took it into the dining room. She sat on one of the stiff chairs and cradled her forehead as she waited for the call to ring through.

"Hartford."

"David, it's me."

"You sound odd. What's the matter?"

She hesitated, not sure how to bring up the fact that she had walked in on their almost-fifteen year old daughter necking on the sofa. "Did you see much of Lily today?"

"She was there for a couple of hours and we talked a little, but then she said she wanted to go visit her friend Mandy and I think Mandy's brother came and picked her up."

"Well, I have news for you. Mandy's brother is more than her brother. He's also Lily's boyfriend."

"Boyfriend? I didn't know she had a boyfriend."

"Neither did I."

"Isn't she a little young? She's only fifteen."

"Yes, I think so, too. And that's probably why they hid it from us."

"How did you find out? Did something happen? Your voice is shaking."

"Oh yes, I'm upset, although not as much as I was when I walked in on the two of them a little while ago and found her stretched out on the couch with him on top of her, kissing her."

"Oh, my God. That's what happened? You walked in on them? Were they. . .uh. . .both dressed?"

"Yes, thank goodness. But his hands were underneath her shirt. It was quite a scene."

There was silence on the other end of the phone.

"David? Are you still there?"

"Sorry. I was just trying to wrap my brain around that image. I'm not sure I can. Are you okay? Is she okay?"

"We got through the initial onslaught of accusations and recriminations, but I think you should come over so we can talk this out with her."

"Yes, I think so, too," he said. "I'll be there in a few minutes."

Caroline set the phone on the dining room table and tried to relax while she waited, but the phone rang again right away. "Hello?"

"Caroline." Matt sounded relieved. "Why are you there? I thought you were going to stay over on the boat. Is Lily with you? I've been trying to find her, but your line's been busy. She's fifteen minutes overdue and when I called Mandy's house, Mandy's mother said Lily left there a couple hours ago. Have you seen her?"

Matt. She had forgotten about him. "I'm sorry, Matt. I just got home. Lily is here with me. We got to, er, talking and I forgot the time and that you were waiting for her."

"So why aren't you at the marina?"

"I decided to come home."

"You came home instead of staying over? And Lily was there? Alone?"

Something in his voice tipped her off. "Matt, did you know about this Chris kid?"

There was a telling silence on the other end of the phone. "How long have you known?"

"Only a few days. I've been trying to get Debbie to convince Lily to let you know she's been seeing the kid. I take it he was there tonight. He seems like a nice boy."

"Yeah, he does." Geez, was she the last one in the world to figure out everything? Was she that tuned out? That clueless? David had carried on an affair under her very nose for months and Lily had been seeing this boy behind her back.

"Look, Matt, thanks for agreeing to let Lily stay there tonight. I'm home now."

"No problem. Glad I could help. I'll always be there for you. You know that, Caroline."

Caroline had a feeling they weren't talking about sleepovers with teenagers anymore. "I know. Thank you."

Caroline heard David's car in the driveway. "Look, I have to get going. I'll talk to you soon. And thanks again."

"Anytime."

Caroline left the phone on the dining room table and reached the kitchen just as David walked in. "Where's Lily?" David asked.

"I think she's still in the den. I just got off the phone with Matt."

He stiffened.

"It's not like that," she said, annoyed at his reaction. "Lily was supposed to stay with him tonight and he called because he was worried when she didn't show up as expected."

He nodded but didn't comment as he went into the den. Lily sat on the couch with her feet tucked beneath her, looking contrite.

"Your mother called me and told me what happened here tonight, Lily," David said. Lily's head drooped even more. "What do you have to say about it?"

"I'm sorry," she mumbled.

"What did you say? I didn't hear you."

"I said I was sorry," Lily flared, coming to life.

"What made you think you could get away with this?" He quizzed her.

Lily shrugged her shoulders. "You guys didn't seem to be paying much attention lately and I didn't think you would notice. Or care."

"We haven't been paying enough attention to you and we're sorry we've been so preoccupied." He sat with his hands clasped between his knees. "But you're wrong if you think we don't care. Maybe we have to be hit over the head with things these days, but it doesn't mean we don't love you. We love you very much."

"It didn't seem like it," Lily said in a small voice. "You guys don't notice me at all lately."

"We notice you," Caroline refuted. "I knew something was going on, but I assumed you were seeing a lot of Mandy because you needed a friend. It never occurred to me you were seeing a boy. You're so young the possibility never even entered my mind."

David didn't say anything, and Caroline was grateful for that. They needed to present a united front on this, and on everything else with Lily from now on. His eyes met Caroline's over Lily's head. "What did you decide to do about Lily and this boy?"

"His name is Christopher, Dad. He's not just 'this boy.' I love him," Lily retorted.

David raised his eyebrow at Caroline and she shrugged.

"I told Lily we wouldn't ask her to stop seeing Chris," Caroline said. "But I told her there would be some rules."

"Sounds fair."

"I would like to discuss with you in private what I told her. If you have anything to add, I want to make sure your wishes are part of our decision about how we'll proceed with this boyfriend-girlfriend thing between Lily and Chris."

"Thank you. I appreciate it. Is that all right with you, Lily?"

Lily looked at him, tilting her head as if trying to judge which of them would be harsher. She nodded. "I think I'll go to bed if it's okay."

"Sure. We can talk more about this tomorrow," David assured her.

"Good night, Mom."

"Good night, sweetie."

"'Night Dad." Lily kissed them both and then plodded up the stairs. They both watched her go and then turned to each other.

"I think she'll be all right," David said.

"I hope so. But you didn't see her with that guy."

"No, I'm glad I didn't." He sat back in the chair and put one ankle up on the opposite knee. "I'm pleased you want to include me in the decision about how to handle Lily and Chris, but I think you've done a fine job with the situation already. Anything you decide is really okay with me. I'm sorry I wasn't here, though. I'm sorry you had to deal with this alone."

Caroline sighed and pushed off her sneakers, pulling her feet up under her on the sofa. "It wouldn't have made much difference, you or me. And if you had been living here, we probably would have spent the night on the boat and she would've gotten away with it."

"But you've borne the brunt of Lily's anger over our separation. I can't even imagine what it's been like for you, handling her and all the problems she's had as a result of my stupidity."

"David, it doesn't do any good to keep berating yourself over all this. What we have to do now is deal with Lily and her rebellion."

"I agree. I was thinking while I was on my way over here, we need to make an effort to behave in a polite, considerate manner toward each other when Lily is nearby. Regardless of what we're going through personally, Lily's home life shouldn't suffer any more than it already has." He gazed into her eyes. "And I was thinking maybe I should move back into the house."

The statement caught Caroline's attention, but strangely, didn't make her as ecstatic as she would have thought. She knew he made the decision at least partially for Lily's sake. "I don't think that's a good idea right now, David." She stared at her clenched hands in her lap.

"I was hoping you would agree to it," David admitted. "I thought we made some progress when we talked about things last week at Tony's, and when we were dancing at the picnic last night, you seemed to want me."

"I do want you, David. I always have." Her eyes sought his again. "I'm just not sure we can live together yet."

"We can give it a try."

"For Lily," Caroline replied. She needed to know if there was more to his suggestion than just wanting to provide a more stable environment for Lily.

"Yes, for Lily, and for us." His gaze was earnest, but did not hold the emotion she needed to see. She wanted to see love and desire and longing. They couldn't base their relationship on obligation and duty. There had to be more, or it wouldn't be worth salvaging.

Sadly, she broke eye contact and shook her head. "I'm not angry at you anymore, David. I'm long past that. And I would love more than anything to make our family whole once again. But I know you. You're ready to come back to Lily, but not to me. And I won't settle for anything but your total commitment. I can't afford to."

"Caroline, don't say that. Maybe we could give it a try."

"'Maybe' isn't good enough, David. I've learned a lot being by myself these last few months. I can be an independent woman without you if I need to be. I don't want to be alone, but I can do it if you find you're never ready to return to me."

He rose from the chair and sat next to her, taking her hands in his. "Caroline, our daughter needs us. We can make this work if we want it to."

Caroline leaned forward, her tear-filled eyes only a few inches from his. She briefly squeezed his fingers and then gently drew her hands away. "David, you don't know how much I want to say yes to what you are asking. But I can't bear to have this happen again, to lose you again. I have to be absolutely certain you love me so much you can't live without me. We can't do this for anyone but ourselves, not even for Lily."

"Caro, we love each other."

"I know, but we loved each other when you were unfaithful and look what happened."

"I know. I regret it more than you could possibly ever know. I miss you like hell and want to be close to you again."

She gazed into his hot eyes and wondered if she dared answer the question evident in them.

"Caroline, please let me make love to you." He cradled her head in both hands, pulled her toward him, his mouth coming down hard on hers. She could feel desperation in his kiss and couldn't stop herself from responding. He was her husband, the love of her life. Her mouth opened, their tongues seeking, rekindling.

David pushed her down onto the chintz cushions of the sofa. Before Caroline could process what was happening, he was on top of her. His erection pressed into her belly. He slipped one arm around her back to pull her tight against him, tilting his head for a deeper kiss, as if he were trying to be a part of her.

She said a quick prayer of thanks she could still elicit this reaction from him, and ran her fingers lightly over the muscles of his back, renewing her tactile taste and knowledge of every part of him. She gasped for breath as the kiss went on and on.

It felt so good to kiss him like this again, but finally the passion-fueled cloud in her mind lifted. She couldn't let the fervor she felt for him at the moment obscure her judgment. She was adamant about needing a total commitment from him.

Although she wanted nothing more than to keep kissing him and feeling his body press against hers, she somehow gathered the strength to push him away.

"I love you Caroline," he rasped, clutching her harder despite his trembling fingers. "I want to make love to you again. I've missed you. I've missed our closeness, how we used to lay together after making love. The way our bodies melted into each other as we fell asleep."

He was seducing her with his words. She wanted him so much, wanted to believe it would make everything better if they made love.

As he tried to lean in for another kiss, she forced herself to resist. "No, David. We can't. It wouldn't be right."

"Making love would bring us closer again," he pleaded. "I need you."

"I don't think so. If we made love right now it would confuse everything. We might make a decision in the heat of passion that we'd regret later. If we get back together, I don't want there to be any regrets."

His shoulders sagged and he leaned his forehead against hers, unmoving. He was breathing hard and obviously trying to get himself under control. Caroline gripped his shoulders, savoring his closeness and hoping to hell she'd made the right decision about turning him away. She prayed this wouldn't be the last time he held her, wanted her.

He leaned back on his heels, his palms on his thighs. When he finally looked at her, she knew he'd come to the same conclusion she had. His expression held regret, mixed with hope.

"I know you're right. I didn't want to admit it. I think I was trying to convince myself as much as you. I want you back, but I think, at this point, it's just not right yet. I have to need you more than life itself. As God is my witness, though, Caroline, it will happen. I swear it."

His words sent a stab of hope through her heart. But he wasn't ready to come back to her, in spite of his vow. It still hurt too much. Love shouldn't hurt.

But will we ever stop hurting each other?

He chewed his lower lip between his teeth briefly. Finally, he sighed and pushed to his feet, turning away from her as if trying to distance himself emotionally. Caroline knew how he felt. Her emotions were so close to the surface, she felt rubbed raw.

Gently, she said, "I think the best thing we can do is keep going to see Sylvia and work on the exercises she's going to give us. Do our best to get our lives back on an even keel."

Unsure if she should share what was on her mind, she paused, hesitant. "David?"

"Hmm?" He didn't turn.

"You were right about Lily." When he faced her, she said, "We need to give her a more stability. I'm going to try to build a life for just the two of us." He winced. "I would like to include you in it as much as possible, but we need to be independent."

"Thank you. I'd appreciate being part of your lives when I can."

Caroline knew he was trying to pull himself together, but his self-preserving, polite, distant demeanor felt so horrible, so cold after what had just happened between the two of them.

She wrapped her arms around her stomach. "Whenever we're together with Lily, I want it understood our personal feelings do not matter. We need to present a friendly, united front for her, no matter what the two of us are going through."

"I agree."

"We can start with her birthday next weekend. I'm planning a big celebration with a lot of our friends and relatives here at the house, and I would like you to come."

He looked annoyed for a moment. "Of course. I wouldn't be anywhere else."

"I'm sure you wouldn't. But there's something else. Matt is going to be here, too, and I want to make sure there aren't any scenes. He's been a friend for a long time, and I don't want to shut him out."

His mouth tightened. “There won’t be any scenes, although I still can’t tolerate the thought of you two being together.”

Caroline refused to say anything about her plans to put some distance between her and Matt. She hadn’t talked to Matt yet and had no idea what he would say about her decision. It probably wasn’t a good idea to mention it to David until things were settled. It might give him false hope.

“Thank you. Her birthday is Saturday. I’ll give you a call when I know the specifics of the party,” she promised.

“I’ll be here early. Then if you need me to help with anything, I’ll be nearby.”

Caroline opened her mouth to object, but thought better of it. “Fine.”

Chapter 17

The next morning, Caroline dressed in a skirt and blouse, took a deep breath, and headed for the plant. As she drove past the R&D buildings, her heart thumped rapidly and tears filled her eyes. She recognized many of the cars. The knowledge that all her friends were inside the building, continuing on with their work, hurt more than she'd expected. The ugly old building looked divine to her. She was familiar with every room, every lab bench. Until last month, she had walked the halls intent upon her job, suffering failures and celebrating triumphs with her co-workers. She didn't have much in common with them any longer.

She would never forget the first time one of her products rolled off the production line in the big coating facility, a block away. She would never forget her first raise, or her first promotion. She would never forget her friends, or her accomplishments. No one could take those things away from her. Despite what had happened, she had a right to feel pride. Even if she never walked those halls again, she had a right to be proud of what she had done there.

Her fingers gripped the steering wheel hard as she maneuvered past the R&D buildings and pulled into the visitors' lot in front of the main entrance of the company. In the lobby, her eyes were drawn to a mural on the back wall. Several of the company's key products were artfully arranged with some model-types standing by, wearing immaculate lab coats that had never seen the inside of a lab. Two of her products were in the display, and she felt a surge of self-satisfaction coupled with the pain.

She had tons of skills and a lot of knowledge to bring to another company. The economy was not great and it might take her a while to find a new job, but she would find one, somehow. If not, she would start her own business, maybe doing consulting work. She would survive.

It took the entire morning to complete all the tasks the staff had lined up for her. She took aptitude tests, hammered out her resume with the resident resume guru, poured through the Maryland State Job Center listings on their website, and attended a session on interviewing skills. When she left, she held a fistful of handouts from the interviewing skills class and a sheet listing the three jobs she had electronically submitted her resume to. Things had certainly changed since the last time she'd looked for a job.

She was surprised at how nervous she felt about sending her resume to the three chemical firms in the area. What if they had PhDs lined up around the corner for the positions? What if they didn't like her?

No, she wouldn't let herself think like that. She couldn't. She thought she'd gotten past those initial negative thoughts, but it was easy to slide back and let the fear take over. She refused to be a victim again. It was hard. Darn hard.

Caroline spent the next week perusing the various job search sites on the Internet. It was incredible how many there were. There were general job websites, as well as some devoted specifically to chemists. By Friday, she had greatly improved her skills for navigating around the web. She found many websites filled with fascinating articles and abstracts. Exploring them helped her catch up with what was going on with the internet.

Caroline had met with success when she invited people to Lily's birthday party. Caroline's mother lived in Florida and couldn't make it, but her brother Tim, along with his wife and their two children, were attending. Her other brother lived in San Diego, so he was obviously out. Mary said she could come for the afternoon but had another engagement later on, and Michelle and Doug and the kids would arrive around noon and stay over for the night.

Now she had to call Matt. She'd been avoiding it, but she was running out of time. She paused at her desk with her hand poised over the phone, not sure how best to strike the proper balance with him. She wanted to be friendly, but didn't want to give him the wrong idea.

His secretary put Caroline through right away and he answered with a short, "Deming."

"Matt? It's Caroline."

"Caroline. How wonderful to hear your voice. I've been thinking about you a lot. We ought to get together for dinner sometime this week. Is that why you called? To invite me over?" He sounded happy and hopeful, and Caroline cringed.

"No, Matt, I didn't call to invite you to dinner. I'm kind of tied up this week."

"Too bad. Maybe over the weekend?"

"The weekend is why I called, actually."

Damn, he's getting the impression I was calling to arrange a date.

Now inviting him to the party might seem like a date, even though her invitation included both him and Debbie. "I'm having a party for Lily next Saturday," she said, stressing the 'I.' "She's turning fifteen and I'm having a big cookout and pool party for her. I'd like you and Debbie to come."

"Absolutely. Couldn't keep me away. I'll have to get Debbie to go shopping with me to find Lily something special."

Caroline had the distinct impression 'something special' meant he wanted to get something for Lily above and beyond the normal Uncle Matt-type of present. He would probably buy something totally out of whack with what she'd be getting from others.

"Matt," she said cautiously, gripping the receiver tightly, "David is going to be there on Saturday, too, and we have decided we need to keep personal things under control when we're with Lily. She needs stability. So I'm asking you to cool it on Saturday and not make a scene."

Especially not on Lily's birthday. Don't pick a fight with David or with me.

"No problem. I think you're right. She can get used to me gradually so we don't get her upset again. Last weekend was hard for her."

Caroline wished he was not being quite so presuming about their relationship. But she couldn't say anything over the phone about her decision. It wouldn't be fair to him. "And, Matt?"

"Yes?"

"I think it would be a good idea if you kept the gift thing casual. I'm sure she would like some school clothes for next year. You know how teenage girls are, they can never have too many clothes. Debbie knows what she likes."

"Okay, sure, I understand. We don't want to rush things."

Caroline swore under her breath. "I'll see you on Saturday at one. Bring your swimsuits."

"Great. Can I bring anything else?"

"Just yourselves," she said brightly. "I have everything under control."

Sure I do. Everything's perfectly under control.

She hung up the phone and laid her head on her folded arms atop the desk. How on earth was she going to manage all this? Everything had gotten so complicated. She had to carve out a life for herself and Lily. But how was she going to do it without misunderstandings over her intentions, causing people to get hurt and friendships ruined?

At home that night, she broached the topic of a party to Lily, as they sat at the kitchen table eating grilled cheese and ham sandwiches. Some meal.

"Lily, your birthday is on Saturday. . ."

"I know. I can't wait."

"I was thinking about having a party."

"Oh yeah? That would be cool. Can we have all my friends over and get some pizza and stuff?"

"I was thinking about something more like a pool party, and a cookout."

She frowned. "I kinda wanted to have a thing with my friends for my birthday. I want Chris to be there and I don't know if you'll let us be together."

"Of course we can invite Chris. I want to get to know him and this is just the sort of family get-together I would like to have him over for. We can invite Mandy, too, and some of your other friends. And we can invite the rest of the gang, too."

"Wow, a lot of people."

"I can manage. Your father said he would come over for the day to help out. And we could still have pizza, along with the usual hot dogs and hamburgers. Would you like that?"

"Yeah, it'll be fun as long as Chris can be there. After Saturday, there'll only be one year between us."

"Until he turns seventeen."

"All right. Sure."

"Do you have any requests for side dishes?"

"Can you make the jello-chiffon stuff with fruit cocktail in it? I love that."

"Sure. Anything else?"

"Can I have a chocolate cake?"

"Is there any other kind?"

"Oh, and Mom," Lily fluttered her eyelashes. *Chris had better watch out*. "Can you make it from scratch instead of getting one from the bakery? I love your cake."

“I guess I could manage.”

“Great,” she said, gulping down the last piece of sandwich and grabbing a cookie from the package on the table. “Can I take this into the den and call Chris and tell him about the party? He’s baby-sitting for the Smiths.”

“Sure. Go.” Caroline shooed her out of the room and got up to do the dishes.

Chapter 18

Caroline was a nervous wreck Saturday morning. She had no idea how she was going to pull off this happy family routine. Standing in front of the counter with her big mix-master going full-tilt, she didn't hear David come into the kitchen.

As she lifted the beaters to check her cake batter's consistency, she caught a movement from the corner of her eye that startled her. With a squeal, she jumped and the heavy head of the mixer fell backwards, beaters still spinning, splattering chocolate batter all over the counter, the floor, and the front of Caroline's tee shirt.

She yanked on the power cord. "Oh no," she moaned. There was chocolate everywhere. She looked up to see what had startled her and found David leaning against the counter, immaculately clean and grinning with an evil glint in his eye.

"Sorry. Didn't mean to startle you." He watched her brush at the batter dotting her shirt. "A little jumpy, are we?"

"*We* may not be but I certainly am." She indicated the mess on the counter and floor. Her shoulders hunched and trembled and she like crying. "And this doesn't help matters at all."

He grabbed her by the shoulders and pushed her toward the hallway. "Since this appears to be my fault, why don't you go on upstairs and change your shirt?" He looked down. "And maybe your shorts. And your socks. And sneakers. I'll clean up the mess down here."

She bit her bottom lip to keep it from trembling and fled up the stairs without an argument.

David used wet paper towels to wipe up the sticky batter on the floor. Then he wiped up everything else. He'd filled the cake pans and was putting them in the oven when Lily walked in.

"Daddy. You're here."

He closed the oven and she ran into his arms. "Happy birthday, sweetheart."

"Thanks." She searched his eyes. "It's early. Did you sleep here last night?"

He drew her into his arms again. "No, sweetie. I didn't." He felt her sag against him. "But I'm here now."

Lily escaped from his grip and flitted across the kitchen, a little too nonchalantly. "Okay." She looked out the window. "Looks like a nice day for my party. It's gonna be hot, so we'll probably spend most of the day in the pool."

"I'm looking forward to meeting Chris. Your mother has told me a little bit about him."

She turned around and grinned. "He's cool."

"Your mom said he seemed nice. And smart."

"Of course he is," she said pertly. "He likes me, doesn't he?"

David laughed. "Of course. How could I have doubted it?"

She sauntered over to the counter to open the door and peer at the assortment of cereal inside. Obviously his little girl was very, very excited about her birthday party and trying to hide it with her newfound teenage cool.

With her head deep inside the cupboard, she asked, "Where's Mom?"

"She went upstairs to change her clothes. We had a little accident with the cake batter."

As Lily ate her cereal and gave David a running discourse on the marvelous attributes of her new boyfriend, Caroline came back into the kitchen.

"I took an extra ten minutes to do some relaxation exercises," she told him.

David nodded approvingly. "You do look a little more in control."

She eyed the countertop. "Where's my cake batter?"

Grinning, he pointed to the oven.

With her baking well underway and her potato salad already made, Caroline could start on the Jello salad. David leaned against the counter with his arms crossed and watched her assemble the ingredients.

"What time is Shelly and her family supposed to get here?"

Caroline looked at the clock. "Any time now."

"Is there anything I can do?"

"Actually, you could take care of the pizza. Call Tony's and order two sheet pizzas. Ask Lily what kinds she wants. Have them delivered, okay?"

"Sure thing." He levered himself off the counter and headed for the phone. The number was on a menu tacked to the bulletin board over the telephone.

"Lily, you'd better get dressed. You don't want to be sitting there with just a tee shirt on when your cousins get here."

"Okay."

By one-thirty, everyone had arrived and Caroline had the cake decorated. A constant stream of people had gone through the kitchen toward the garage after changing into their swimsuits. The extra traffic made her more determined than ever to remodel the kitchen and add that new door.

David came in from the garage, wearing only his suit and a towel around his neck. She had to stop herself from staring at him in admiration. He had always looked good in swim trunks.

"Anything I can do?" he asked.

"Not right now. The pizza is out there and people are munching on that for now. We'll do the hamburgers in an hour or so."

"Okay, I'll bring the grill around. I'd just as soon you didn't go near it." He laughed.

"Ha, ha, ha." He turned to go.

A wet washcloth hit him in the back of the head. He laughed harder.

"David? If you can stop laughing for a second?"

"I can manage." But there was still a twitch in his lips. He looked back at her.

"I've been watching everyone traipse through the kitchen and the garage to get out back, and I was thinking. Would it be possible to put a door through there right onto the deck?" She pointed to the back wall of the kitchen.

"You know, I was wondering the same thing. I didn't want to mention it because it's, well, it's not exactly my house anymore."

"Of course, it's still your house."

He walked over to the wall and looked through the window at the back yard. He gauged the distances between. "I think we could put one right here where the window is, if you don't mind losing it."

"Wouldn't be a problem. We could buy a door with a window insert, have it match the other one."

He stood back and eyed the wall again. "I think there might even be room for a sliding glass door or French doors. I'd have to measure it, of course."

"French doors? I'd love that. Would it cost a lot?"

"Not if I did the work."

"I hate to bother you to come over and take on all that work. We can have it contracted."

He placed his hands on his hips. "It's not a problem. I'd enjoy it."

"If you're sure. . ."

Just then, Matt came in, dripping water on the floor. She had a pile of old towels on the table for just the eventuality and handed him one. He didn't look pleased at the family-like atmosphere between her and David.

But he smiled widely, as if trying to break through the intimate ambiance. "Hey. What's going on in here? You two gotta come out and jump in the pool. Water's great."

"I know," said Caroline quickly. "It's getting hot in here and I was just going to put my suit on. I'll be back in a jiffy." She ran out of the room, hoping the two men would not come to blows in her absence.

David pointedly ignored Matt's presence and took a measuring tape out of the kitchen drawer to make some preliminary measurements. He ran it into the corner and noted the distance, then over to the counter along the back.

"Planning some remodeling?" Matt asked.

"Yes."

"I'm sure there are plenty of qualified carpenters in the area."

David refused to rise to the bait and give Matt something to fight about. He was determined to keep this day peaceful for Lily and Caroline. "I'm sure there are," he replied, measuring the distance between the ceiling and the top of the window. He jotted the figures down on a napkin from the table.

"Excuse me," David said. "I'm going to go out to the pool now and enjoy the afternoon with my daughter." He gazed purposefully at Matt. "It's her birthday." And he left Matt standing in the kitchen, fuming.

Matt was still standing in the kitchen, obviously waiting for her, when Caroline came through on her way outside.

She didn't like the angry look on his face, and wondered what the two men had said to each other. She hadn't heard any shouting.

"Caroline, are you really going to let him come in here and work on a remodeling job in your house?"

She held up her hand. "Don't, Matt. Don't even start."

"But Caroline. . ."

She shook her head and strode toward the door with her beach towel under her arm. She was already tense enough, and wanted to try to enjoy this day with all of her friends. She wasn't going to let Matt or anyone spoil it for her.

Out on the deck, she surveyed the scene before her. Most of the pizza was gone, and the kids and a few of the men were in the pool playing Monkey-in-the-Middle. The game worked very well in their six-foot circular above-ground pool. David was currently in the middle, surrounded by screaming children. It was a good thing they had invited their neighbors so no one would call the police. Everyone who would call was already there.

The kids threw the ball wildly and he leaped again and again, once tipping it so it flew out of the pool. One of the mothers fetched it and threw it back in. Evidently it flew out quite often, because she appeared to be stationed there, ready to go for it whenever it landed on the lawn.

Finally, David caught the ball and Kristi ended up in the middle. She didn't stay there for very long; she could leap like a gazelle and soon caught it. Her brother, Jimmy, was next, and his smaller frame kept him in the middle for a long time. Lily took pity on him, threw the ball right to him and went into the middle herself. It was a mistake. Since she was the birthday girl, all participants doubled their efforts to keep the ball away from her. She laughed and squealed and dove and bounced but no one took pity on her.

Finally, Chris fell over on his back as he grabbed the

ball and Lily leapt on him to yank the ball away. It wasn't fair, but it worked.

Out of the corner of her eye, Caroline saw Matt come back out on the deck, but she ignored him and went over to talk to Michelle.

"Nice party," Michelle remarked, as Caroline sank into the lawn chair next to her.

"Thanks. I think Lily's having a good time."

"If the level of her screams is any indication, she is. Who's the dude?"

Caroline looked at her friend. "Oh, I forgot to tell you about Chris. He's the boyfriend."

Michelle lifted her eyebrow. "Lily has a boyfriend? She doesn't waste any time. You approve?"

"It's a long story." Caroline wiped at some splashes on her thigh from a particularly exuberant chase in the pool. "She'd been seeing him behind our backs for some time and we were not pleased about it. But, now we know what's going on and have gotten to know him some. He seems like a nice boy."

"Yeah, I've been watching them. He does appear to be a nice kid."

Caroline nodded. The two were on opposite sides of the pool now but they managed to throw the ball to each other whenever possible.

"Lily and Chris are not the only ones watching the goings-on today. My brother's doing a lot of watching. Only he's just watching you."

Caroline reddened and tried to cover it by mopping the sweat from her forehead.

"What's going on, Caro?"

"Matt has been very good to Lily and me while David and I have been going through this rough patch," she answered evasively.

"I know my brother, Caro. Last time he looked at you like that was when you two were in college."

"Oh, Shelly." Caroline leaned back in her chair to gaze at the cloudless sky. "Do you know how he feels about me?"

"I know how he used to feel about you. It *is* past tense, isn't it?"

"Apparently not."

Michelle sat up in her chair and leaned over to whisper fiercely in her ear. "He's not still in love with you, is he?"

"Yes, he is. Shelly," Caroline gripped her friend's arm, "I had no idea how he felt at first. He was there for me when I needed him and I relied on him. Then he told me one night how he felt and he was so dear and so fervent and so familiar. I let myself be lulled into a relationship with him because I was too needy and he was so attentive and affectionate."

"But you look like you're avoiding him today."

"Yes," Caroline sighed. "I need some space. I don't think we should see each other anymore and I haven't had a chance to talk to him yet."

"Then things are getting better between you and David?"

"Somewhat, enough that I don't want anything else to go wrong. To interfere with our chances of getting back together again."

"And Matt would definitely interfere."

"Oh yes." She sought her friend's eyes. "Shelly, there have been some terrible scenes. Matt and David used to be best friends and now they're enemies because of me. I feel awful."

Michelle put her hand on Caroline's knee. "It'll work out. You'll see. Listen, it's getting hot out here. It looks like the game is breaking up. Why don't we go in the pool?"

"I have to start the hamburgers pretty soon, but I'd love to cool off in the pool first."

"Great, let's go." They waited for some of the kids to clamber off the pool deck and then climbed the stairs and slipped into the water. It felt cool and wonderful. Caroline dipped her shoulders under and swam using a breaststroke through a clear lane of water. Once on the other side, she pulled up and braced her elbows on the side to watch Lily and Chris cavort on the lawn. They acted like children one minute and like lovers the next.

She'd noticed he rarely let Lily out of his sight all day. It was odd, watching them. She had never pictured her daughter behaving like a typical teenager in love, until this had been thrust upon her so suddenly.

David appeared at her elbow and he joined her watching their daughter. "Quite a sight, huh?"

"Yes. I don't think I'm quite ready for it."

"Me neither."

"She certainly caught us by surprise with that one."

"She's never been slow."

"I hope she takes her time with this boy," Caroline said. "I've been worried ever since they both proclaimed they were in love with each other."

"It's just puppy love."

"I know, but puppy love can hurt sometimes and it can cause you to make highly emotional decisions you regret later."

"She's going to be hurt now and then, Caro." He slid his arm around her shoulders and squeezed them affectionately. "It's part of life. And if she makes an unwise decision, it will teach her to think more carefully next time."

"I understand it's part of growing up, but I keep wanting to shield her from any hurt. She's been hurt enough this summer."

He turned her in his arms. "We'll watch her as much as possible and try to stave off any disaster we can foresee. But that's all we can do. We can't protect her forever."

"I know you're right," she said, laying her hands on his wet chest. "It's just so hard."

"Nobody ever said being a parent was going to be easy."

"She should have come with an instruction manual," Caroline said, laughing.

"Indeed. Hey, the troops look like they're getting hungry. Should I start the grill?"

"I think you'd better before they revolt. The patties are all made up and are on a cookie sheet in the fridge. There are a couple pounds of hot dogs in there, too. You handle the cooking and I'll do the rest."

Chapter 19

For the better part of an hour, David kept busy, cooking and serving the hungry crowd. With everything laid out on the picnic table, the party guests could help themselves. Caroline had to smile at the sight of Chris sharing a chaise with Lily, while she fed him potato chips. Nobody complained about the typical summer fare, of hamburgers and hot dogs. Everyone offered compliments as they stuffed themselves.

It made Caroline happy to see everyone having a bang-up time, and she allowed herself to relax as she visited with Michelle. Matt, sitting next to her, plowed through two big hamburgers and generous helpings of both salads.

"Great job on the salads, Caro," he said.

"It's a talent." She flicked her fingers teasingly.

"I cook, but I never seem to be able to get anything that tastes like this," he admitted.

"I'm surprised you do any cooking," his sister added. "The deli menu on your refrigerator looks pretty dog-eared."

He threw her a dirty look. "Check out Lily and Chris. They look cute, don't they?" It was an obvious ploy to divert their attention away from his poor cooking skills.

"Yes." Caroline nodded. "I'm not quite used to it yet, though."

"I don't blame you. I can't even imagine Debbie acting all mushy in a year or two. But you'll survive." He reached over and gave her arm an affectionate squeeze, trapping her hand on the arm of the chair.

As Caroline tried to figure out how to extract her hand

without making a scene, Lily leapt off her chaise and ran over to confront Matt.

"Take your hand off my mom. You can't do that. My Dad's here."

Matt pulled his hand away in shock and Caroline's heart fell like a stone. So much for not making a scene.

"Lily, you have no right to talk to Mr. Deming so rudely."

"Yes, I do!" She stomped her foot like a child. "Don't tell me I can't say anything. I have to."

Chris came up behind her and slipped his arms around her. "Come on, Lily. Let's go back in the pool," he said soothingly. She still protested but she left with him.

David took Lily's place in front of Matt. "Nice move there, hotshot. Way to ruin my daughter's birthday party." He spun on his heel and followed Lily and Chris.

Humiliated, Caroline wished the earth would open up and swallow her. She didn't look at Matt but she knew he, too, was upset about what had happened.

Mary knelt in front of Caroline's chair. "Caro, everyone here is your friend. Your friends know you've all been having a difficult time this summer. They understand."

Michelle reached for Caroline's hand and patted it. "Mary's right, Caroline. This'll pass. It'll all be forgotten in a few minutes."

"Thanks. But we seem to have made a habit of public spectacles lately, and I think I've had about all of them I can take." She jumped up and ran into the house, passed by David and the kids, sitting at the kitchen table drinking sodas, and ran up to the bedroom.

She lay down on the bed, damp suit and all, with her arm over her eyes. Eventually she'd have to talk to Lily. But she needed a couple of minutes for herself, to calm down. Lily probably needed a couple as well.

"Caroline?"

She lifted her arm to see David leaning against the door jamb, a soda can still in his hand. "I'm really not feeling up to another fight if it's all the same to you, David."

"I came up to find out if you're all right."

"No, I'm not all right. Satisfied?"

"Of course not." He stepped into the room. "I didn't want a scene. I did everything I could to prevent it."

"I know," Caroline sighed. She plucked the spread with her fingers. "I didn't do anything to invite Matt to hold my hand, either. He didn't even mean anything by it. We were just talking about Debbie and Lily and we felt a sense of camaraderie. It was just a 'friends' thing."

"I believe you."

"Good." Caroline levered herself off the bed. "I have to go talk to Lily. I can't leave things the way they are." She left him staring at the sweat dripping down the side of his can.

Everyone seemed mightily interested in what they were doing when she walked through the grouping on the deck and headed for the pool. Lily floated on an air mattress, watching the water run through her fingers.

Caroline moved through the water and reached her side. "Lily?" she asked gently, but Lily refused to look at her. Caroline swung the mattress around. "Lily, are you all right?"

"Yeah, I'm okay."

"I want you to know that you misinterpreted what went on with me and Mr. Deming. Nothing happened that shouldn't have, between friends."

Lily eyed her uncertainly. "Really? Are you sure?"

"I'm certain. We were just talking about Debbie. He was imagining what it would be like when Debbie had her first boyfriend. I think you overreacted a teeny bit."

"Maybe just a teeny, teeny bit," she admitted guiltily. "I'm sorry, Mom."

"I'm sorry, too, honey. Sorry there was anything for you to misinterpret."

"Will you tell Mr. Deming I'm sorry?"

"I think he already knows," Caroline said with a small smile, "but I'll make sure. Now, there's a big pile of presents over there you have to open up."

Lily groaned. "Everybody's gonna be staring at me 'cause I made a fool of myself."

"You didn't make a fool of yourself. You were upset and you spoke out. Everyone understands. And they've probably already forgotten."

"Yeah, right."

"You've got to face them sometime. They came here to help you celebrate your birthday and I'm sure they still want to do that."

"Okay. I'll be right there."

Caroline swam to the ladder and climbed out as Chris joined Lily. He curled his arm around her and whispered in her ear.

Maybe he's kind of handy to have around, after all.

David had been standing next to the pool, watching their conversation, and he stopped her as she went by. "She okay?"

"I think so, now. She's going to open her presents. That'll take everyone's mind off what happened and get the party back into a festive mood, I think."

"Good idea. Want me to take all the presents out to the picnic table?"

"Please. I'll bring out the cake and plates. We can serve it after she's through with her presents."

After the boxes were stacked in a pile and the guests had gathered around, Lily wrapped a towel around her waist and took her place at the table. She sat with her hands folded between her knees and gazed at all her friends and family.

"I want to apologize to everyone for the stupid scene a while ago. I guess I overreacted." She placed her hands on either side of her mouth to compress it into a comical clown-face. "I can be such a dork." She grinned. "Now I'm going to open up your lovely presents before any of you decide to take yours away because I've been a dope."

"If you decide to give any of them away," Debbie piped up, "I want mine back 'cause it's a CD *I've* been wanting, too." Lily stuck her tongue out at Debbie, who returned the favor.

Their goofiness helped break the tension, and Caroline felt her eyes mist. She felt proud of her daughter. Her eyes met David's across the space of the deck and she could see his eyes looked a bit shiny, too.

Caroline caught the expression on Matt's face when he intercepted the exchange between her and David and it was clear he was upset about it. He'd been watching them furtively all day and must have noticed how she avoided him. It frayed her nerves to keep having to duck him. She knew he would be cornering her at some point. She could feel it coming.

Lily opened Debbie's CD first and told her she would burn a copy for her if she wanted. David had given her the high tech tennis racket she'd wanted badly.

"Yea," she yelled. "Junior varsity tennis team, here I come."

Caroline gave her some pierced earrings and a bracelet. From her friends she got more CDs and some nail polish and lipstick. Matt's gift was a fancy organizer for school and her Uncle Tim gave her a "Save the Bay" sweatshirt.

Finally, she had opened all the presents on the table and hadn't gotten one from Chris yet. He pulled a small package out of his pocket and gave it to her. She opened it shyly, clearly not knowing what to expect from a boyfriend for her birthday since this boyfriend deal was so new to her.

She pulled out a fine gold chain with a small heart hanging from it that boasted a miniscule diamond chip in the center. "Ooooooh," she whispered.

All the other girls oooh'd and aaah'd, and all the boys snickered. She held it up to Chris and he fastened it around her neck.

While Lily fingered the gold heart and admired it, Caroline cleared away the gift wrap debris and set the cake on the table. David brought out a gallon of ice cream and an ice cream scoop.

After blowing out all fifteen candles and sitting, embarrassed, through a tuneless rendition of 'Happy Birthday,' Lily cut up the cake while David scooped ice cream and Caroline handed out the plates. The kids fell on the ice cream and cake as if they had not eaten a ton of picnic food, a scant hour before.

Barely a crumb remained on the cake plate when Caroline pushed all the dishes aside. Mary and some of Lily's friends left. Tim came over and chatted briefly, but the party slowly broke up.

"Okay, everyone's pretty much gone. Want to try out your new racket?" David turned to Lily.

"Sure."

"Anyone else want to come along?"

Doug spoke up. "What the heck, we'll go. Michelle, you coming?"

She shook her head. "I think I'll stay and help Caro clean up."

"You don't have to, Shelly," Caroline assured her. "Everything is disposable. All I have to wash is a cake plate, two salad bowls, and a few spoons. You go play with your kids. There're extra rackets in the garage. Maybe I'll join you in about fifteen minutes."

"Well, if you're sure." Michelle relented and left with the others.

Caroline filled the kitchen sink with soapy water and started on the dirty dishes.

"Caroline?"

Startled, she dropped the slippery cake pan. Matt stood in her kitchen. *How did he sneak in without me hearing him?*

"What are you doing here? I thought you left with Debbie some time ago."

"David stopped at the house. Debbie took her racket and went with Lily. I knew you were alone here and I came back."

"I'm just going to finish up these dishes and then head over to the courts myself," she said, hoping to stave off whatever conversation he obviously wanted to have. "I wanted to watch Lily try out her present."

"I need to talk to you."

Matt seemed determined to find out what was going on with her and David. With resignation, she left the dishes soaking and dried her hands on a dishtowel before taking a seat at the table. *Damn, I wish I'd changed out of this skimpy swimsuit.* She hated feeling vulnerable in front of Matt.

He regarded her in disbelief. "We're going to sit here across the table and talk like this is some sort of business conference?"

Caroline gave him a surprised glance. "I didn't intend it to feel like a meeting. Do you want to go into the den where we can relax?"

"I'd rather."

"Okay." He seemed really wound up and she didn't want to challenge him on such a small issue when she felt sure he had bigger ones he planned to bring up. She led the way into the den and sat on one end of the couch. He crowded next to her and kept clenching and unclenching his fists as if agitated.

Better find out what's bothering him before I hit him

with my decision. She knew he wouldn't take kindly to cooling their relationship.

"What is it you wanted to talk to me about?"

He swung around to confront her, his face taut and tense. "David has moved back in, hasn't he?"

Taken off guard, she answered him without thinking. "No."

He leaned back in relief and his fists unclenched. "Thank God." Then he looked askance at her. "But you two looked so lovey-dovey today. I thought for sure he'd come back."

"We weren't acting lovey-dovey."

"Could've fooled me. You certainly seemed to be getting along well. At the very least."

"It's true we've been getting along better."

"But he isn't planning on moving back?" he asked, grabbing her hand fiercely.

Caroline tried to pull her hand away but he held it tighter. "No, he is not planning on moving in again. At least, not at the moment."

"What does that mean?"

"Dammit, Matt, it doesn't mean anything. What's gotten into you?"

"I'm afraid I'm losing you," he said, his fingers so tight they hurt. She winced and he let up.

"Well, if you weren't before, you could very well lose me now, the way you're acting." Caroline's anger spiked as she yanked her fingers away.

"I'm sorry, Caroline. I'm really sorry. Please don't be angry with me. I love you."

He reached for the back of her head and pulled her toward him, his mouth coming down hard on hers. A few seconds passed before she could get her arms up to push him away.

"Matt," she pleaded, her hand pressing on his chest. "Please don't kiss me like that again."

"I love you, Caroline. I know you care a great deal for me."

"I do. Which is why I have to talk to you before I hurt you any more."

"Sounds ominous." He leaned back, his eyes wary.

"Oh, Matt, this is such a mess." Tears formed in her eyes. "I never wanted to hurt you. I really didn't. If I'd had my way, we'd have been just friends these past months and nobody would have gotten hurt."

He sat opposite her, stone-faced, but his eyes were bleak. *Apparently I don't have to spell it out for him*. Matt was a smart man, and very sensitive. It was why she had always liked him and why she had responded to him as more than a friend this summer.

He rose from the sofa and stood with his back to her, his hands shoved in the back pockets of his shorts. For a long time he stayed silent. "David hasn't asked you to let him come back home, but you'd let him in a New York minute if he did, wouldn't you?" he asked quietly, turning around to look at her sadly.

"It might surprise you to know he has already asked me if he could move back in."

"I don't understand. Why would you turn him down?"

"It's very complicated. What's happening with us is between him and me. I don't feel I can talk to anyone, especially you, about it."

"So, even though you turned David down when he offered to come home to you, you are still giving me the gate. Am I seeing this right?"

"I have to do this, Matt."

He wouldn't let the subject go, though. "You have to kick me out because, even if you won't let him back at the moment, you want to be free to work things out with him sometime later," he said astutely. "You don't want anyone else getting in the way. Like me."

"I told you, Matt, it's very complicated. I need some time. And I need to be alone for awhile. If and when David and I get back together, it needs to be because we decided it ourselves, not because there were outside influences on either of us. I made a mistake allowing anything more than friendship to develop between you and me. I think we're all paying for it."

"I don't regret what happened between us this summer," he said, kneeling in front of her and taking both of her hands in his.

"How can you say that? I've hurt you."

"These past few months with you have fulfilled a fantasy for me. I can never regret that."

"Oh Matt," she whispered, placing her hand on his cheek. "I wish I could have been what you needed. You deserve someone wonderful."

"I couldn't ask for someone more wonderful than you," he murmured, covering her fingers with his own.

"No, Matt." She shook her head sadly. "You need someone who can be yours forever. Someone who can love you as you deserve to be loved. That someone is not me. I thought differently for a while, but it's not going to happen. You have to face that."

Caroline leaned forward and curled her arms around him. "You'll meet someone. Don't give up. Find a new dream, Matt," she whispered.

"I can see why you couldn't find time to join Lily and me at the park." David spoke from the doorway. Matt and Caroline leaped back, guiltily.

Caroline's eyes swept the room swiftly, fearing Lily might also be witnessing the suspicious-looking scene, but she didn't see her daughter.

"Where's Lily?" she asked.

"Fortunately, she went with Chris and Debbie and some of their friends to Chris's house. But I think you two might want to cool it because Doug and Shelly and the kids are still here. They went out to the deck to watch the sunset."

"Nothing happened here, David. You're jumping to conclusions."

"Yeah, I could see that when I came in. Hey, look at the time," he said airily as he looked at his watch. "I have to get going, back to my solitary motel room to ponder yet another of the disasters that has made my life endlessly fascinating recently. You two kids spend a couple minutes letting the heavy breathing settle down and I'll go tell Shelly you'll be right out. Then I'm afraid I have to split, much as I'd like to stay."

David turned on his heel and headed for the door without a backward glance. Caroline jumped up to go after him, but Matt caught her elbow and stopped her.

"It won't do any good to talk to him right now. He's all steamed and convinced he saw something going on. Let him cool off."

"I can't let him leave angry." It distressed Caroline that David had misinterpreted what he'd seen. "I have to tell him we were saying good-bye."

"I doubt he'd believe you right now, especially after the scene with Lily earlier."

Caroline groaned. David would probably think she'd lied about this afternoon, too. She had to distance herself from Matt before things got any worse.

"Matt, I think you should go. And I don't think we should see each other for awhile."

"We can still be friends, though, can't we? I can bring Debbie over for a cookout once in a while?"

"I don't think so. I think we should just keep our distance. For now."

His eyes, hurt and pained, kept staring at hers as if hoping she would reconsider and tell him they could at least remain friends. At last he seemed to give up, and turned away. He stopped at the doorway and gazed back at her.

"Good-bye, Caroline." He pressed his lips together, and his eyes turned liquid. "I do love you. I'll always love you." And he turned to go.

Caroline sank onto the sofa cushion, dropped her head in her hands and cried. Her husband had hurt her and then she had hurt her dearest friend. In return, they'd both hurt her husband. When would the hurting stop?

What a mess they had all made of their lives.

Now she was truly alone. Maybe it was for the best. Maybe she didn't deserve either of them. An arm went around her shoulders. Michelle had come in and tried to comfort her. She turned her face into her friend's shoulder and cried harder.

"Shhh, it's okay, honey. Just cry it out and you'll feel better." Michelle rubbed her back in circles. Finally, Caroline regained control of herself and Michelle handed her a handful of tissues. "Dry your eyes now."

Caroline cleaned herself up and leaned back wearily. "Oh, Shelly, I've made such a mess of this."

"Caro, it's been a difficult situation for you and for everyone. You haven't made a mess of anything." She lifted Caroline's chin with a finger. "Don't forget, you did not start this. David did. And, ultimately, it's his responsibility for straightening all of it out."

"But I must have been doing something wrong for him to be unfaithful to me. If he had been having his needs met, he wouldn't have strayed."

"Some husbands have affairs through no fault of their wives."

"But David isn't like that."

"No, I wouldn't have thought—"

"He isn't," Caroline objected.

"Then have you given any thought to what might have been going wrong with your marriage?"

Caroline laughed humorously. "Have I thought about anything else?" She methodically started to shred the tissue in her fingers. "I think I let our marriage get stale. Maybe we both did. Anyway, I got busy with work and with Lily and I suspect David felt left out."

"A lot of marriages go stale and a lot of wives are tied up with careers and families. Not every husband in that situation strays."

"No, I know. It's hard to explain. But he suddenly found himself alone for months in a city where sex and drugs and power are the norm and he got pulled in because he was lonely. Also, as strange as it sounds, I think it has something to do with the boat."

"What on earth could the boat have to do with it?"

"Well, like I said, it's difficult to explain. David and I had been drifting for a long time. Each of us had our own separate little lives and we just co-existed at home. We talked around each other instead of talking to each other. It seemed like we were close only on the boat. Last summer was especially wonderful on it. Out on the water we were closer than ever. But it seemed like we led two separate lives—the one at home where we didn't even seem to connect and the one on the water when our personal lives came second to managing the sails and dealing with the wind and the waves. We ignored the fact that other parts of our lives were not going that well."

"This isn't making any sense. It sounds like the boat brought you together, not vice versa."

"It did. At least for the summer, it did. But then we put it away for the winter and David became really involved in this case in Washington. I think our closeness last summer, followed by our increased distance this winter, made the separateness seem much more pronounced to him."

"I still don't understand."

"It was like he wouldn't have noticed anything wrong if we hadn't had such a good summer. Then we were back the way we'd been before, only worse. Subconsciously, he knew something went wrong. We didn't learn from our experiences last summer, and we should have. We should have let it carry over to everything else in our lives, but we didn't. And suddenly it felt like a void to David."

"If he felt a void, why didn't he do something about it?"

"It's only in retrospect I can see what happened. He worked in a strange city and there were women who were willing and anxious to fill his needs. He drifted into a relationship with one of the women he met on the Washington case because he wasn't feeling any connection to me at home. Everything just felt empty, filled up with meaningless conversation neither of us ever really paid attention to.

"When boating season started up again, and we had that incredible first sail last April, I think he realized what 'we' meant to him. I think he started to think about what he was doing and that's when he started acting weird and I started noticing. And then everything fell apart. On the outside. It had fallen apart on the inside long before that, but I just didn't know it. I got all self-involved and too busy with Lily and with work. Our love of *Windswept* this spring blinded us to the changes in our relationship until the clues practically hit me in the face."

"When you explain it like that, it makes sense. Weird sense, but sense. Now what are you going to do?"

"I don't know. It's gotten much more complicated since the first deception."

"Because of my brother."

"That, and a hundred other things."

"I'll kill him."

"No, Shelly, don't lash out at Matt. This isn't his fault, either. He's gotten hurt just as much as the rest of us. I told him earlier I couldn't see him anymore. I think he might need you tonight."

"I suppose I could walk over and hold his hand for a while after we get done talking, but I still have a hard time justifying what he's done."

"He loves me, Shelly. He has for a long time, and I can't blame him for trying to take this opportunity to change things between us."

"Whatever you say. But if you told Matt you couldn't see him anymore, why did David look like thunder when he left?"

"He came in and saw me holding Matt and consoling him and he jumped to the wrong conclusion. I tried to talk to him but he left without waiting for an explanation. I wanted to go after him but Matt said he wouldn't listen to reason if I did, and I let him go."

"Matt's probably right. Give David a chance to cool off and then you can reason with him."

"I will. Now I think you should go to your brother. He's going to need you."

"If you're sure you're all right. I don't want two casualties to deal with."

"Don't worry about me. I'll be fine as soon as I can talk to David."

As it turned out, Caroline wasn't able to talk to David for several days. She spent most of the week stewing over their last incident. He had been called away to Philadelphia to consult on a case one of his partners handled, and he didn't get back to his office until Thursday. When Caroline called, his secretary took her messages that she wanted to talk to him, but he never called back.

Caroline went through a gamut of emotions, ranging from hope to despair to indifference to anger as the week wore on and she wasn't able to talk to him. Finally, by late Thursday afternoon she'd had enough. She gave up trying to reach him and decided to take the boat out the next day. David probably wouldn't need it on a Friday, especially since he had such a busy week.

The weather report said it would be hot and clear and sunny, except for a front going through late in the day. She'd be well off the water by then. Lily usually spent the day with Chris and his family, and she wouldn't miss her if Caroline played hooky.

Chapter 20

While Caroline readied herself for her day at the marina Friday morning, she listened to the weather report, and it sounded fine, except for the cold front later. It wasn't due until late afternoon and the day looked gorgeous and clear at the moment. Chesapeake Bay often got hot and flat in the middle of the summer and she would probably bake out on the bay, but she could always swim from the boat again. She didn't always need to sail. She just needed the water's soothing tranquility as a balm to her frazzled nerves.

She had told Lily the afternoon before that she planned to spend the day on the water and Lily could reach her on the cell phone if need be. Since it was such a hot day, Caroline stuffed lots of cold drinks and some sandwiches in the cooler. She packed the car up and, with a light heart, headed for a relaxing day on the boat.

In court until ten at night, dealing with a client's deposition, David ran late getting to the office the next day. He was impatient to tackle the paperwork piled up to the ceiling. It'd been a rough week and it hadn't been made any better by Caroline leaving him a string of messages he'd been trying to ignore. He'd wanted to return her call more than anything in the world, but he had been afraid of what she might to tell him. He'd seen her with her arms around Matt last Saturday and was petrified the real reason she had rejected his offer to move back home because of a desire to have Matt instead of him.

David didn't know what he would do if she told him she didn't love him anymore. The past week, when he contemplated the reality of actually being alone without her the rest of his life, he had realized what she meant to him. She meant everything. And now, it might be too late.

No.

He had to make her understand how much he loved her; that his life would not be worth living if he had to live apart from her.

Restlessly, he punched the button on the radio to his favorite oldies station and listened to Nat King Cole sing about love. Just what he needed.

After he suffered through the song, the weather report came on. An intense squall line with very severe thunderstorms had been spotted traveling in advance of the cold front, across western Virginia at the rate of thirty miles per hour and expected to be crossing Chesapeake Bay by early afternoon. Strong wind gusts of up to fifty miles per hour were expected in the vicinity of the thunderstorms and severe lightning were anticipated. Small craft warnings were posted across the entire bay.

David groaned. He had to go out for a court date after lunch and he would probably get caught in it. All he needed to do was get his best suit drenched in the rain.

He groaned again when he pulled into the parking lot and saw Matt heading for his van. The last thing he wanted to do was to have it out with Deming at the moment. But Matt had seen him pulling in and waited for him in front of the only spot left in the lot.

David got out of his car, set his briefcase on the roof, and leaned against it with his arms folded. "All right, let's have it," he said with resignation.

"We need to talk about Caroline." Matt's mouth grew tight and determined.

"Give me a break."

"I'm serious. There's something I need to tell you about her."

"I doubt there's anything you could tell me about *my wife* I don't already know," David retorted viciously.

"Oh, but there is, and you'd better listen to what I have to say."

"Get out of my life, Deming." David grabbed his briefcase and turned to leave.

"Caroline told me she didn't want to see me anymore, David."

That stopped him in his tracks. He spun around. "What?"

"You heard me. She gave me the gate, the old heave-ho, hasta la vista, baby."

"When did that happen?" David asked warily.

"Saturday night. What you walked in on was her giving me a last good-bye hug. She tried to tell you, but you wouldn't listen."

"So, this week she's been trying to contact me to tell me—"

"Most likely she's been trying to call you to tell you how much she misses your sorry butt. I know she's been really upset all week."

"I thought you said you hadn't seen her," David pointed out, suspicious to the last of his friend.

"Lily sees things. And Lily tells Debbie, and Debbie tells me. At least she's going to be able to relax out on the bay today. No thanks to you."

David's heart started to pound. "What?"

"I said it's no thanks—"

"No. Not that. You said she's going out on the bay? In the boat?"

"Yeah, Lily mentioned it to Debbie on the phone last night."

David grabbed one lapel of Matt's suit with his clenched fist. "Tell me she's not going to go alone out on the water. She's not going to put the sails up by herself this afternoon."

Matt looked astounded at his reaction. "Why, I suppose she might. Why not?"

Dropping his briefcase so he could grab Matt's other lapel, David shouted, "Because there are some intense thunderstorms coming. A bad squall line is headed our way. Caroline hasn't got enough experience sailing alone. If she's out in it—"

He let go of Matt's jacket and, his hands shaking, fumbled for his car keys and reached for the door handle. "I have to get to the marina. I have to stop her. She would never know how to deal with something like this on the water."

"Wait, she's got her cell phone. Call her."

"Good idea." He reached for his cell and punched in her number. It rang several times with no answer. He disconnected, then threw the phone on the seat. "Shit. I'm going down there."

"I'll go with you." Matt ran to the other side of the car.

"No. You go home and get Lily and keep her with you. That way I know she's safe and I can call her when. . .if. . .look, I gotta go. After you get home, call the Coast Guard."

David jumped into the car and spewed gravel leaving the parking lot. He drove like a demon toward the marina, hitting the redial button on his phone every two minutes, but still he got no response.

He made it to the entrance of the marina in eighteen minutes flat and screeched to a stop in the middle of the lot. He swore when he saw her car. At the same time he prayed the boat had not already gone. He had no idea what time she had gotten to the boat or how long she would putter once she got there.

Damn that deposition.

His heart leapt into his throat when he spotted *Windswept*'s mast down the pier and realized Caroline had not left yet.

Then it started to move backward and he yelled, "No!" at the top of his lungs. He raced down the pier as she turned to look behind her while she backed into the channel.

"No." he shouted again and she looked up in shock as he ran toward her. Startled, she jolted and the throttle jerked in her hand, making the boat rev in reverse. It shot quickly back at an angle. Throwing it into forward, she revved it again to stop the momentum and straightened the boat out.

"David, what on earth are you doing here?" she called across the water.

"Come back in," he shouted. "You can't go out. Come back into the slip."

"I'm on my way out for a ride. I'm not going to come back in just because you don't want me to go."

"There's a storm coming. It's too dangerous."

Caroline's heart thudded when she heard what he said, but she didn't know whether to believe him or not. "You're crazy. The sky is clear blue."

He glanced up. "The report on the radio said a bad squall line of intense thunderstorms is on its way. You can't go. You can't handle rough weather alone. Please, Caroline, come back in."

"I listened to the weather report and it didn't say anything about storms. I thought you wanted me to learn to sail alone."

"I do, but not today. Caroline, come back in and we can talk. I'm begging you. Don't go out on the bay."

David stood on the end of their slip pier, reaching out with his arm to try to send her a physical message in addition to his verbal message. "Please, Caroline."

Caroline looked around anxiously. She'd throttled down to an idle and the boat lost steerage. *Windswept* drifted too close to Bob and Kathy's boat. By increasing the forward speed, she inched along until she regained steerage.

Suddenly David saw the boat start to move forward again. Without thinking, he yanked off his jacket and wing tips and dove into the water, landing a couple of feet from the hull. Caroline gaped at him in shock. "What the hell do you think you're doing?"

"I'm coming on board," he yelled from the surface of the water as he treaded water next to the boat. "Idle the motor or the prop will chew me up." He started swimming toward the back of the boat.

In a panic, Caroline pushed the throttle into neutral before he swam pell-mell into the propeller. "You're insane," she shouted, hanging over the back of the cockpit as he gained the swim platform.

"Toss down the swim ladder."

She tossed it over. "I can see that you're determined to climb on board, so I'll argue with you later."

David climbed up the ladder and into the cockpit, dripping water from his suit pants and white dress shirt. His tie twisted in a mangled mess and his socks were half off.

He looked down at his clothes wryly. "Jeez, leaping into the channel, fully clothed. . .here I was, worried about getting caught in a shower downtown, and instead I end up in the channel."

Caroline slapped her hands on her hips and watched him drip. "You're crazy, David. Why did you do that?"

"I have to stop you from going out."

"If I want to go, you're not going to stop me."

"I'll wrestle the wheel from you if I have to. Someone

has to protect you from yourself. You can't go, Caroline. I told you—"

"I'm tired of listening to you tell me what to do." In a huff, she pushed past him to the wheel and put the gears into forward, throttling up slightly. The boat slid past their slip and out toward the entrance of the marina. "I came here to go sailing and I'm not going to let you spook me into staying. The radio said the cold front was coming through later than anticipated. I can leave you at the transient dock if you don't want to go. Or if you want to come, fine. I don't care either way."

"I'm not leaving. If you don't believe me about the storms and insist on going out anyway, I'm not going to let you go out alone. You're stuck with me."

"Whatever," she said caustically. "Just stay out of my way."

"Willingly. I'm going to go down below and change out of these wet clothes."

"Fine. I can handle the boat without you."

She felt him glare at her, and with a gesture of disgust, he took the steps into the cabin.

She felt a lot of anger at him. Her heart tripped furiously as she replayed his storm warning, but she'd already lost way too much self-confidence because of him. She couldn't afford to lose any more. She had to stand up to him.

But what if he's right about the squall line?

She tried desperately to remember what she'd learned about squall lines in the safe boating course she and David had taken. She recalled they sometimes developed, especially in the heat of summer, in advance of a cold front. That fit with what he had said, and she shivered. The winds in the squalls could be gusty and very strong. Sometimes, rarely, they spawned tornadoes. Maybe she should turn back.

No, she wouldn't let herself cower in fear. She had accomplished a lot with the boat this summer and she wasn't going to turn tail and run just because David wanted to play devil's advocate.

She glanced down into the dim light of the cabin and saw David walk naked from the head to the Vee berth and its small built-in dresser. He tossed aside the towel he'd been using and pulled a pair of sweats from the drawer, stepping into them as he leaned against the wall.

She had seen her husband nude countless times over the years and their familiarity with each other had reached a point where she hardly noticed his nudity. Today, though, he looked magnificent. She had forgotten what a splendid body he had, and she was suddenly, acutely aware how long it had been since she'd seen it. She shivered and felt warm all over, her hands gripping the wheel to steady herself.

David glanced up and caught her staring at him. He stilled, his fingers still gripping the cords he had just tied in a bow at his waist. They stood like that for the longest time, unwilling to look away from each other. Caroline felt the heat rise in her face and knew she looked flushed. He, on the other hand, looked perfectly composed.

Embarrassed, she broke the invisible contact and looked out across the water. They were leaving the little inlet and coming out into the bay. There weren't many boats out, and most of them were power boats. Determinedly, she throttled up and sped into the bay in order to put up the sails.

David returned to the cockpit wearing only the bottoms of the gray sweat suit. They hung low on his hips and she had to force herself to look away.

"Are you going to put up the sails?" he asked.

"I don't see why not. There's just a small breeze from the southeast. I can keep an eye on the horizon in case those phantom storms come up."

"They'll come. You might as well let me be useful, and help you hoist the sails."

She shivered again. He seemed sure. “I can put the sails up by myself.”

“I know you can. I’m not questioning your skills. But I’m here, whether you like it or not, and I may as well do something.”

“If you want.” She shrugged her shoulders and watched as he raised the mainsail partway, but then he wrapped the line around a cleat and started yanking on the reefing lines.

“What are you doing?”

“I’m putting a reef in the mainsail. I don’t want too much sail up there when those squalls hit.”

“David, there are only three knots of wind. We’ll have plenty of warning before anything hits. If it does.”

“Things can happen pretty fast out here on the bay. I’m not taking any chances,” he said, giving one last hard yank on the reefing line.

She pushed the button for the autopilot and went forward to grab his arm. “This is my sail today and I say full sail up.”

“Over my dead body.” He leapt, barefoot, onto the cabin top to tie the reefing lines around the boom.

Realizing she wasn’t going to shake his determination, she stomped back to take the boat off autopilot and gain control of the helm once again. She didn’t say anything else as he finished his work on the top of the cabin and jumped down to unfurl the jib. He only let out part of the sail they had available, and she bit her tongue but didn’t object. Automatically, she bore off the wind to let the sails fill, and then cut the engine.

The wind blew fluky and variable, changing direction every five minutes and gusting, then dropping to nothing. It all should have warned her, but she let her stubbornness rule. She tried to concentrate on the steering, while David stood with his hands on his hips, staring at her. His silent, intense attention made her nervous.

"Stop staring at me," she shouted.

"You've changed."

"I hope so. I don't intend to get stepped on again."

"Touché."

"I've learned a lot this summer."

"I can see that. More than just how to sail the boat, too."

"Damn straight."

"I've learned a lot too, Caroline." He sat on the cockpit seat with his back against the bulkhead, his arms crossed over his bare chest. "I've learned that, over the past few years, I'd begun to take many things in my life for granted, especially our marriage. I developed a sense of complacency. I felt invincible. When I started the affair with Alicia, it didn't even occur to me I might get caught."

Caroline shifted in her seat behind the wheel and swallowed a painful lump in her throat. It still hurt to hear him discuss the affair he'd had. They'd never really talked about why the affair had happened. Maybe that was one of their problems in trying to get their marriage back together.

She clenched her teeth as he continued. "It felt as if I had two lives and one didn't affect the other. I wasn't hurting you because it had nothing to do with you. Or at least it didn't in my warped mind at the time."

He leaned forward to make a point. "That's why I could let it go on as long as it did. You know, I think sometimes you go on and on doing something you know is wrong, hoping it will turn out in the end not to be so wrong. You just hang around, pretending, and being disappointed in yourself, but powerless to do anything about it. Because it doesn't seem real. It wasn't my real life. It seemed separated from our home life."

"We didn't have much of a home life at that point," Caroline pointed out.

"No, you're right. We didn't. We just kind of co-existed.

I think it was my fault, too. I got involved with the firm, and I let my personal life slide."

"Funny," she confessed. "I've been thinking it had to be my fault. I ended up too involved in my own career and with Lily."

He pursed his lips. "I guess we were both at fault. We both got too apathetic about our marriage."

"Yeah."

"I'm not apathetic any more, Caroline," he vowed. He looked into her eyes and slid down the bench toward her. "These past few months have made me realize what I lost when I foolishly disregarded my vows to you."

Caroline gripped the steering wheel, hard. "I—"

Then she screamed as a tremendous gust hit the sails from abeam and the boat lurched wildly as it fell over on her side.

Chapter 21

David and Caroline had been so absorbed in their conversation they hadn't seen the dark clouds streaking across the sky. One minute the sky was clear and blue, and the next it hung dark and threatening over their heads. In terror, Caroline watched the towering, sinister black clouds tinged ominously with ugly green. Shafts of blinding lightning shot from the clouds and struck something on shore, and the loudest clap of thunder she'd ever heard boomed in her ears. She screamed again, spinning the wheel hard to force the floundering boat into the wind. It took all her strength to fight the gusts blasting the boat on her starboard side. If the heavy wind and seas hit the boat straight from the starboard direction, she could broach to and roll over.

David had tumbled off the bench seat, landing on his back on the floor of the cockpit. He scrambled to his feet, bracing himself on the side of the boat as the bottom became the side and the side became the bottom. Caroline saw him grab hold of the mainsail line to help her gain command of the boat again. The boat heeled over at a terrifying angle, the lower side in the water, until the sail spilled enough wind to bring it back up. Caroline's heart pounded in the chaos.

"Start the motor," David yelled at her once the boat stood upright again. She couldn't move, frozen to the spot with fear, and David had to wave a hand in front of her face to pull her out of her stupor. "Caro."

Blinking to clear her head, Caroline's hands shook as she threw the gearshift into neutral and reached down to hit the start button, just as another huge gust rocked the boat.

This time it hit further forward because she had managed to get the boat around a little. *Windswept* heeled way over again, but not as badly as before. She could brace herself long enough to punch the button until the engine caught, and she shifted it into forward.

In the short time it took her to get the engine going enough to gain steerage, the sea became a tempest. A wave hit the starboard bow, flew up over the cabin and into the cockpit, instantly soaking them both. The rain came down in sheets, blown nearly horizontal to the water in the high wind. Within moments they couldn't even see the shore, much less where they were going.

"David! Take the wheel. Please. I can't handle this." Caroline screamed over the noise of the storm.

"I can't. I have to get more sail down before we get hit again. You'll have to do it," he yelled back.

"No. Please! I can do the sail," she begged him.

"Not in this wind, you wouldn't have the strength." He turned away to push through the rain toward the wildly flapping sail.

Caroline clenched her teeth in fear, fighting the wheel as another gust battered the boat. She knew they had to get the sail down fast or the boat would capsize. She had no choice but to keep steering as best as she could. "Okay," she reluctantly capitulated, grabbing the wheel again with fingers shaking from the potent combination of fear and cold.

David braced himself against the edge of the cockpit bench to hold the furling line with one hand and the jib line with the other so he could play them against each other to roll the jib up. He'd want a sliver of sail for stability, but no more. The muscles in his shoulders and arms bunched as he struggled to pull in the furling line as he let out the jib line. Too much wind caught in the sail, and it wouldn't give. Another strong gust hit the boat from a different direction, and the lines raced through his fingers as he lost control and the sail blew out again. He yelled as the rope cut into his hands.

"Dammit," he muttered. "My sailing gloves are below." There wasn't time to go for them. The angry red burns on his hands bled as he reached for the lines again, his mouth set in a grim line.

"Caroline!" he shouted. "Bring her into the wind more."

"I'm trying," she sobbed. In all their years sailing *Windswept* on the bay, she'd never seen it like this. The boat had been dear to her, but now it would become their salvation or demise.

Then, a wall of water shot *Windswept* along the trough of one huge, long wave, an eerie dark green tunnel that seemed surreal and unending. In an instant their world changed into blinding white, rearing up in a thundering spray that looked as high as the top of the mast.

Pulling so hard she grunted with the effort of it, she managed to work the boat along the slope of the wave to turn it into the wind. But that left them vulnerable to the vagaries of the wind again, and *Windswept* slewed broadside once more.

"I can't," she screamed back. "The wind is coming from everywhere at once. I can't control it." She noticed the state of his hands, and paled. "I'll try."

Caroline succeeded a bit and the immense pressure lessened for an instant. Wincing, David wrapped the furling line around his injured hand to keep it from slipping again and gave a vicious yank, while feeding out the jib line. It became a long battle. He continually lost part of what he had gained when the wind shifted, but he finally had the jib safely in, leaving only a tiny handkerchief of sail out.

He sat for a moment on the cockpit bench, sucking air

into his lungs with huge gasps. He turned his hands to the sky, hoping the rain would wash some of the blood away and cool the burning pain from the multiple rope burns he'd suffered.

"David. Your hands," Caroline cried.

He gazed briefly up at her, proud of how she'd held up. "I'll live." He gave a rueful grimace and then rose.

"They must hurt. Go get your gloves," she replied.

"Yeah they hurt, but I've got to get another reef in the mainsail. I don't have time to search for my gloves." He had to shout to be heard above the shriek of the wind and the roar of the waves.

He pointed to the mainsail. "There's still too much sail up. We should double-reef the main. I don't think we can control the boat enough if we don't. There's just too much wind and the waves are piling up one atop the other."

She had been battling the helm through the vicious wind coming from starboard for several minutes, yet still it kept pushing the boat over to horrible, deadly angles. They had to get down some more sail. The wind had lessened in the past few minutes and now would be the best time to do it. David knew he should have his life preserver on to climb up on the deck in this kind of weather, but he had to take the chance; they were pushing it already.

Caroline wrestled with the wheel while David struggled with the lines and the wildly flapping sail. He stood on top of the cabin, barefoot, wearing no life preserver. The rain came at him in sheets, making even the non-skid surface treacherous.

He followed the rule of keeping one hand on the boat and the other on what he tried to do, but continually slipped, barely saving himself over and over, as he tried to gain control of the hundreds of yards of heavy, whipping dacron. He had a horrifying vision of going over the side of the boat into the water, leaving Caroline alone to deal with the boat.

He managed to get the reefing line secured to tie the second row of reef points to the boom. He put one arm over the boom to steady himself, feeling the boat pitch to the left and then back to the right as it rocked. At last all the points were tied. He looked up just in time to see something he had hoped never to experience in person.

"Caroline. It's a waterspout. It's heading this way."

The volatile thunderstorm cells had spawned tornadoes, just as he'd heard. This one had picked up water as it passed over the bay. It seemed to be about fifty yards away and heading straight for them like a freight train. There wasn't any way the boat could survive a direct hit. If the boat capsized they'd both be thrown into the violent, churning waters without life preservers. They'd never survive.

Caroline kept an eye on the waterspout as she continued to fight with the wheel. "I think it's veering away a little," she shouted.

"It's going to be close. Hold on, as tight as you can. I love you!" He put his arms around the mast and held on tightly.

The incredible swirling winds from the waterspout sideswiped them viciously, spawning a killer wave that came at the sailboat in a huge wall of water. David clutched the reefing line, the sheer force of his will keeping him from going overboard.

I haven't come this far with Caroline just to die out here on the bay with her.

Caroline opened her mouth to say something but never got the words out. She screamed, grabbing hold of the steering wheel to keep from being swept overboard. Then her fingers gave way and her body flew toward the white foamy brine. David saw it all happen as if it was a dream and he stood outside the boat, looking in.

Regaining his senses, he frantically clutched at a

lifeline and managed to get hold of one as the force of the water swept her over the side.

She screamed, "David!" over and over again but the boat righted itself enough that he succeeded in getting one leg over the top lifeline to make a desperate reach for her as the water took her with it. He was not going to let her die.

An instant later he managed to grab hold of one sneaker. Feeling it sliding inexorably off her foot, he leapt again and got three fingers on her ankle. Feeling the boat hesitate instantaneously, he put every muscle in his body into yanking her into the boat. She flew across him and landed on the seat cushion, a whoosh coming from her lungs as she lay in a heap, unmoving. He glanced at her to see if she still breathed.

However, the split second of inattention cost him dearly, and another massive surge of water hit him face on and flung him backwards toward the bow.

When the wave blasted the boat, it wrenched him away from the boom, his wet feet slipping out from under him. He tightened his grip on a thin reefing line with one hand and clasped the boom with the other. The boat slid sideways wildly. His body slammed against the boom and he heard a sickening crunch in his arm, and then something broke in his back.

Screaming in agony, he lost his hold on the reefing line, sliding toward the dark, churning waters. Everything happened too fast–there was an incredible amount of water, he didn't even know which way pointed up. He hit something hard, and the silver mast against the roiling heavens became the last thing he saw before everything went black.

Caroline had awakened when David landed on her. He moaned as Caroline eased him off, enough to get purchase on the slick leather cushions. She knew they needed to slither down into the cockpit so they could stay lower in the boat and there'd be less danger of falling overboard. But how to get to it? David was only semi-conscious and he moaned and flinched every time she tried to move him.

She didn't want to hurt him more. Inching her way along the seat with one hand on the lifeline, she judged the distance down to the cockpit. David's dead weight on top of her slowed progress as she dragged them both along. Carefully, she rolled him to the left. Even in his semi-conscious state he screamed in pain when weight pressed on his injured arm.

She threw her body to one side, enough to get out from under him, then dropped into the cockpit, taking him with her. He moaned again as he landed, but at least now he was safer. She straddled his hips, pulling him away from the side of the cockpit so he wouldn't hit his injured arm as the boat continued to pitch with the wind.

The cockpit wasn't a safe place for him in his condition, not with the way the boat sluiced through every wave trough. There wasn't anything else she could do. At least the small area sheltered them somewhat from the storm and remained the most secure place she could haul him to.

She was afraid to move him any more than necessary. There could be ribs broken near his lungs or heart. He laid face up, sheets of rain pelting his face. Finally his eyes fluttered open. "Caroline," he groaned. "What happened?"

"The boat lurched. I felt myself start to go overboard but my ankle caught on something. I don't really remember what happened or how I got back into the boat."

"I grabbed your ankle and pulled you back in. The last thing I remember is you collapsed in a heap on the cushion." He felt a sharp stab of pain and looked down at his arm, bent at a strange angle, then back up at her. "I broke my arm. And something in my back, ribs or spine."

He put his good hand to his face and rubbed his eyes groggily. "I think I remember that you grabbed me."

"Yes," she said, pushing his dripping hair off his forehead. "We both landed on the gunwale."

His eyes were glazed with pain, but intense as he gazed into hers. "You saved my life."

"Only after you saved mine." She smiled into his green eyes.

"How?—" He winced as the boat rolled over another wave. "How?"

"If I had been out here alone, I couldn't have handled it. The boat would have capsized for sure. You got the sails shortened and we can ride it out."

"We make a good team." A small smile tugged at the corners of his mouth.

Caroline's heart pounded, but she didn't dare indulge in the luxury of responding to the message in his eyes. They were still in too much danger and she would have to get them back to the marina without David's assistance. She rose onto her knees, peeking out at the water. The boat did not lurch as badly as it had a moment ago. She started to push to her feet but he seized her hand.

"I love you," he whispered, kissing her fingertips. "I don't want another nanosecond to pass until I know you believe you mean the world to me." He laid a cold, shaky palm against her cheek.

"I love you too, David. I felt like part of me had gone missing when you left. It felt horrible and I don't ever want to feel that way again."

Caroline stood up, tears springing to her eyes. "I'd better find out what's going on out there." She'd hoped to find the storm was over, but when she looked toward what she thought faced east, she saw another black squall on the horizon.

"Oh no," she said, slapping a hand over her mouth.

"What is it?" David asked.

"It's another one. I can't do this again, David."

David tried to struggle up, but fell back. "I can't get up. You have to, Caroline. You can do it, I know you can."

"I guess I don't have any choice, do I?"

"You did it before and you can do it again."

"Last time I wasn't watching it come closer and closer. It was just there and I dealt with it. This is scary, David. I feel like we're sitting ducks."

"You'll do it the same way you did it before. I have faith in you. I trust you." His quiet voice calmed her. Staring down at the impassioned look in his eyes, she felt him reach into her soul in a way he never had before. He trusted her with his life.

With a shiver, she gaped at the blackness that would engulf them in moments. Wishing she were anywhere else in the world, Caroline made her way back to the wheel.

"Into the wind, Caroline," David said gently. "Take the waves about thirty degrees off the bow."

She nodded, turning off the autopilot and steering the boat as he'd instructed. She had no idea where they were on the bay. She couldn't see much and had lost her sense of orientation in the storm. She spared a glance at the depth finder. At least they were in deep water. The compass next to it showed the boat headed west toward shore and she hoped they weren't too close to it. She would have to keep her eye on the gauges to make sure they didn't go aground. There was too much to do. Caroline closed her eyes for just a moment and centered herself. She had to do this.

When the first turbulent gust hit *Windswept*, Caroline felt ready for it. The boat, now trimmed safely for the weather, plowed through the waves, sending greenish-white foam crashing up over the bow and into the cockpit, then through the drains in the floor. Caroline muscled the boat across the tops of the waves and down the other side through the eerie, bottle green troughs.

Whenever she came back out on top of a wave, the

wind would hit them with renewed force. It took all the strength she could muster to keep it in position for the next onslaught. Her shoulders ached with the strain of holding the wheel over to the right. David had managed to brace himself on the cockpit floor so he didn't roll when the boat did, but she could see sweat pouring down the sides of his face as he coped with the pain.

It seemed like forever before the storm started to recede, but probably only minutes passed. The wind and rain lessened to manageable proportions for Caroline. Like a beacon in the night, she saw a good-sized boat heading for them, a Coast Guard ship. She had never been so glad to see anything in her life.

The cutter angled in as close as it safely could. A white-uniformed guardsman shouted, "Are you folks okay?"

"We had some trouble, but I think we're okay now." Caroline yelled back.

"The Doppler doesn't show any more storms. I think things will start to calm down now."

"Thank God," she cried in a heartfelt voice.

"Are you alone? Do you need assistance?"

"My husband is here." Caroline pointed to the cockpit floor. "He's injured pretty badly."

"We have paramedics on board. Want them to take a look at him?"

"That would be fantastic. I think he has at least a broken arm."

The boats were close enough now that shouting wasn't necessary. "We have inflatable splints we can put on his arm to make him more comfortable until you can get back to your marina."

"Oh, thank you."

"We'll raft up to you port-to-port. Please put out some fenders if you can, Ma'am. I'd appreciate it."

The guardsman tossed her a stern line. She tied it off on

a cleat and ran forward to help with the bow. Within minutes, two paramedics were attaching the inflatable splint on David's arm and strapping the whole thing close to his chest to immobilize his shoulder. They laid him on a backboard to keep him from moving his spine. She breathed a sigh of relief.

It tore at her heart to see him in that much pain, but the splint and the board would help a little. One of the paramedics murmured to David, and he nodded, accepting a shot of painkiller.

"Ma'am?"

"Yes?" She turned back toward the guardsman aboard the Coast Guard cutter.

"With your husband injured, I suggest you let us transport him on the cutter and then to the hospital. Do you have any preference about getting your boat to shore?"

"Is he badly hurt?"

"Looks like two fractures of the ulna, one of them compound, and then the back injury. It's probably broken ribs but we won't know until he's X-rayed. The painkiller will kick in soon, and he'll feel more comfortable."

"Where are we now? Our home port is Annapolis."

"We're south of St. Michael's," he answered.

"Wow, the storms blew us way south. We could probably motor back, but it's been an exhausting afternoon. I think we'd be smart if both of us just go with you."

"That's no problem, Ma'am. We have a man who can deliver your boat back to its slip if you give us directions."

"Thank you. That would be lovely. Just out of curiosity, how did you find us out here? I wasn't able to get down to the cabin to send out a distress signal," Caroline explained.

"We got a call from a Mr. Deming. We've been searching for you for more than an hour."

Matt had called the Coast Guard and told them to look

for her and David. “Could you please call Mr. Deming back and let him know we’re all right?”

“Yes, Ma’am. I have his cell phone number.”

“Good. Thank you.” Caroline skirted past the paramedics working on David, and started to climb up on the cabin top to take the rest of the mainsail down. One of the guardsmen offered to finish the job, and she gladly let him do it.

Before long, the sail was tied down and David’s arm had been secured in a bright orange, inflated splint. They wrapped him in a blue blanket and hoisted him over the side of the cutter to be carried to their sick bay. She said a quick prayer of thanks that God had brought them through the ordeal, and crossed over onto the cutter behind David.

Her blood still pumped furiously through her veins. She and David were safe again. She sat down abruptly next to him on the hospital bed and pulled her blanket around her as she crossed her arms over her churning stomach. She began to tremble all over.

“Hey, don’t fall apart on me now. You already did the hard part.” He placed his good arm and the blanket around her shoulders and pulled her against him.

“I—I’m sorry I’m blubbering.”

“Don’t worry about it. Happens to everybody. You handle a crisis fine because you get a surge of adrenaline to act in an emergency, but when it’s over and the adrenaline is gone, everything hits you at once. Just relax. You’ll feel better in a minute. We aren’t going anywhere. We’ll let the Coast Guard take care of us and we don’t have to be heroes anymore.”

She leaned against him, seeking the warmth from the blanket and his body. She was still soaking wet. Not wanting to get him damp and cold again, she backed away.

“Hey, come here,” he said, pulling her back against him. “Don’t go away. Don’t ever go away.”

This time she let him hold her while she battled the release of the stress. As she sat there, it all came rushing back: the first realization of the storm, the horrible way the boat had heeled over and the way the gusts had pounded mercilessly at the sails.

Most of all though, she remembered the sickening moment when David's arm broke and he fell headlong toward the roiling ocean before he caught himself. She'd realized what was happening through a half-awake fog.

At that moment she knew she didn't want to live if he wasn't there to share life with her. They had a lot of work to do on their relationship, but it would be worth it.

David felt her shudder and knew intuitively the thoughts that were going through her head. They were most likely the same thoughts that raced through his mind when he saw her fall. In that instant, he had tried to clutch any part of her to save his chance at a life with her. Then something like an angel had come and given him the strength to grab onto her.

He squeezed her shoulder and turned her head into his chest. After a moment, he whispered, "Caroline. Look at me." He lifted her chin with one of his good fingers. "Caroline, what I told you before is true. I've loved you ever since I can remember. I never stopped. Even through everything, I never stopped loving you."

"And I love you, David," she whispered, cupping his cheek with her trembling fingers.

He pulled her to him at the same moment she leaned into him and they met halfway in a blaze of need. Their mouths opened and mingled desperately as each sought, once again, to lay claim to the other. David felt as if he'd come home. He dragged himself reluctantly away, and Caroline gazed at him expectantly, seemingly knowing he needed to say something else.

"But the difference now," he panted, "the difference now is I can't imagine living without you. I might as well have been swept overboard if I couldn't have you back."

She chuckled. "Exactly what I thought a minute ago."

He grinned. "We belong together." Then his smile faded, his eyes narrowed. "I mean it, Caroline. I want to come home and I want you to take me back so we can live out the rest of our lives as we were meant to, as we vowed, sixteen years ago. We'll continue therapy and work very, very hard on building a strong foundation for our relationship. And I promise to love you every moment of every day for the rest of our lives."

A sudden thought occurred to him. "I think we should renew our vows, do the whole shebang. Church, reception, everything. I want you to have complete faith in my promise to you today."

Caroline smiled at him. "I do have complete faith in you. I don't need all that stuff again."

"Maybe not. But you'll have it."

He kissed her again, endlessly, so she would know their future was boundless. Several minutes passed before they came up for air, but he would've hardly noticed if it weren't for the burning in his arm. Reluctantly, he pulled away from her. Caroline beamed at him. Life was going to be perfect again.

"Later on, after we get you taken care of, I need to run to the marina and make sure *Windswept* is all right," she said. We don't know if there's any damage from the storms."

"I don't think there's anything serious. She's built to last. Like us."

Lightning Source UK Ltd.
Milton Keynes UK
UKHW02f2338120618
324135UK00005B/396/P

9 781619 351837